MEADOWLANDS

MEADOWLANDS

Elizabeth Jeffrey

severn House

This first world edition published 2014
in Great Britain and 2015 in the USA by
SEVERN HOUSE PUBLISHERS LTD of
19 Cedar Road, Sutton, Surrey, England, SM2 5DA
Trade paperback edition first published 2015 in Great
Britain and the USA by SEVERN HOUSE PUBLISHERS LTD.

Jeffrey, Elizabeth author.
  Meadowlands.
  1. Aristocracy (Social class)–Fiction. 2. World War,
  1914-1918–Social aspects–Fiction.
  I. Title
  823.9'14-dc23

ISBN-13: 978-0-7278-8469-5 (cased)
ISBN-13: 978-1-84751-572-8 (trade paper)
ISBN-13: 978-1-78010-618-2 (e-book)

Typeset by Palimpsest Book Production Ltd.,
Falkirk, Stirlingshire, Scotland.

ACKNOWLEDGEMENTS

Acknowledgement is due to the book *The Home Front* by E. Sylvia Pankhurst, which provided many graphic details of the hardships suffered by women left at home when their husbands went to war.

The soup club is, of course, entirely my own invention.

One

It was Saturday, the first of August, 1914, the day of the silver wedding celebration. Lady Adelaide Barsham regarded herself approvingly in the mirror of her dressing table at Meadowlands as Polly, her maid, put the finishing touches to her hair, making sure that the curls that spilled forward from the top of her head to mask her rather high forehead were quite secure before adding a sweeping peacock-blue feather that exactly matched the trimming on her dress. The dress itself was a quite stunning creation in various shades of the same peacock blue and it hung in diaphanous folds from a rather daringly low-cut, tight-fitting bodice. Even her satin shoes were peacock blue. Lady Adelaide gave a sigh of satisfaction as she reached for her jewel box, confident that nobody would guess that she was only two years short of her fiftieth birthday.

The connecting door to her husband's dressing room opened after a brief knock and Sir George Barsham MP entered the room.

Lady Adelaide looked up in surprise. 'Thank you, Polly, I'll ring if I need anything more,' she said, dismissing her with a brief gesture. 'You can go and see if Miss Georgina and Miss Millicent need your assistance. I expect they're waiting for your attention.'

'Yes, m'lady. I believe they are.' *And have been for some time,* Polly added under her breath. With a sketchy bob she left the room and hurried along to the two daughters of the house.

As soon as the door had closed behind Polly, Sir George approached his wife with a velvet-covered box. 'I thought some kind of a trinket was in order to mark our twenty-five years of blissful union,' he said with only the faintest trace of sarcasm, handing it to her. 'Though God knows why you insisted on such a lavish celebration to mark the occasion.'

She opened the box and drew in a sharp breath when she saw the glittering diamond necklace and earrings. 'Oh, George, they're beautiful. Thank you, darling.' She turned away a little as he bent to kiss her. 'Mind my hair. Polly has just spent ages getting it right.' She lifted the necklace from its velvet bed. 'Would you mind?' She handed it to him and he fastened it round her neck.

'Oh, yes, they really are gorgeous.' Smiling happily, she patted the earrings then picked them up and fastened them, turning this way and that, delighted at the way they glittered as they caught the light. They would look a sensation in the new electric light George had recently had installed. She glanced up at him, opened her mouth to speak, then closed it as she saw him scowling at his reflection in her mirror. 'You're looking very smart, George,' she said mildly instead. 'But you look troubled. What's wrong?'

He drew in a noisy breath. 'What's wrong is that we should never be holding this damned affair at all,' he said tetchily. 'It should have been cancelled. Don't you realize this country is on the brink of war? This is not the time to invite half the county to some extravagant shindig. Apart from the fact that it's going to set me back God knows how much.'

Adelaide shrugged. 'You can afford it, George.' She moved her head from side to side. She liked the way the light caught the diamonds. 'Anyway, as you well know the invitations went out and were accepted long enough before all this scaremongering about war started. Don't you realize it takes months to organize a celebration on this scale? It's not something that could be cancelled at the drop of a hat. I'm surprised you could even consider such a thing. Even the Prime Minister and his wife have accepted.'

'The Asquiths are not coming. I had a telephone call this morning with their apologies.'

Adelaide stared at him in horror. 'Not coming? Why not? Don't they realize it's very bad manners to decline at the last minute? Why didn't you tell me, George? I hope they've given a very good reason.'

'Of course they've got a good reason, Adelaide. Didn't you hear what I said? The whole of Europe is in turmoil.' George's moustache twitched, a sure sign that he was losing patience. 'It's a desperate situation and the prime minister can't leave Downing Street because things are happening at such speed. Don't you realize war could be declared any day?' He didn't even try to hide the contempt in his voice.

'But why should this country be involved? I really can't see what the assassination of Archduke . . . Ferdinand, or whatever his name was, has got to do with us.' Her voice was petulant.

'I can't go into all that now, Adelaide. If you spent a little more time with the daily newspaper and a little less gazing at fashion catalogues you would know how things stood without me having to explain it all to you. Suffice it to say things are moving very quickly – so quickly that I shall be very surprised it our country is not at war with Germany by this time next week.'

She shrugged. 'I'm sure that can't be true, George. Don't you realize the king and the kaiser are cousins? They would never allow our two countries to go to war; it's unthinkable. You always were a pessimist.'

'And you've always preferred to bury your head in the sand, Adelaide. But I'd back my judgement against yours, any day.' With that he left the room, not quite slamming the door.

She sat for a long time after he left, gazing at her reflection in the mirror without actually seeing it. Twenty-five years they had been married. Twenty-five years of George looking for trouble where there was none; twenty-five years of not exactly marital bliss. She frowned. She supposed they'd been in love to begin with, she couldn't really remember now. But she'd certainly done her duty. She'd given him four children in the first five years: the two girls, Georgina and Millicent, and then the twins, James and Edward. Thank God the twins had been boys so there was an heir and a spare, as the saying went. She'd had quite enough of childbearing by the time they were born and had no desire to emulate Queen Victoria. She'd also had quite enough of George sweating and fumbling over her in bed, too, so she used the twins' birth, easy and trouble-free though it had been (although, of course, George knew nothing of that) as an excuse to banish him to his dressing room. He had never asked to return to her bed and she had never invited him. She suspected – in fact she knew – that he sought his pleasures elsewhere. Her only stipulation, after the unfortunate episode with that rather attractive housemaid, which resulted in her being dismissed for some trivial misdemeanour – all handled very quietly and satisfactorily to Adelaide's mind – was that these things should never again happen under her roof. To his credit they never had. What happened elsewhere, she neither knew nor cared.

She roused herself out of her reverie and got to her feet.

Tonight was not the night to rake over past misdeeds; tonight was the time to show a united front at their silver wedding celebrations; twenty-five years of slightly frayed and inadequately patched-up wedded bliss.

Of course, the ninety guests were unaware that the marriage was anything less than perfect as Sir George and Lady Adelaide stood smiling and greeting them as they arrived at the brightly lit house. Lady Adelaide had insisted that every electric light in the house be switched on to impress the guests, ignoring Sir George's warnings that it could cause the power to fail and plunge the whole house into darkness. Fortunately, this didn't happen. In the event, and despite George's dire prophecies, the evening went very well, as she had planned that it should.

The food was plentiful and imaginative, thanks to weeks of careful planning and days of frantic baking and preparation in the kitchen It was all laid out for inspection in the dining room on long tables covered with spotless damask tablecloths. Smaller tables, to seat four or six, were dotted around the room so that guests could drift in and out as they chose, while maids and footmen stood by to attend them and make sure their glasses were never empty. Sir George had made it his business to check that there was enough wine and champagne to mellow even the most argumentative and belligerent of the guests.

It was a colourful scene. The ladies were resplendent in gowns of every shade and hue, their jewels sparkling in the dazzling electric light, while the men provided a sober contrast in black and white evening dress. And if there was an air of reckless festivity, a sense of 'eat, drink and be merry, for tomorrow who knows what will happen?' this only served to add to the party atmosphere.

In the drawing room the furniture had been moved and the carpet rolled back to make ready for dancing. At the end of the room a small dance band – piano, clarinet, bass player and drums – played the latest tunes, 'When Irish Eyes Are Smiling', 'Oh, You Beautiful Doll', 'You Made Me Love You' and 'Peg o' My Heart', luring the younger guests in to dance and flirt the evening away while their elders won or lost money at cards in another room.

Ned Barsham dutifully danced with every girl in turn. He was a good dancer, with a natural sense of rhythm and he enjoyed dancing. But although the girls were all equally pretty, they were equally empty-headed, it seemed to him, and a few of them seemed to be blessed with two left feet. He was quite relieved when, having done his duty, he could retire to a quiet spot on the terrace to commune with the stars and a bottle of wine.

'Oh, so there you are.' James came and sat down opposite his twin.

Ned yawned. 'Yes, here I am, having done my duty and danced with every girl from here to kingdom come and several clod-hopping horses as well.' He grinned as he spoke.

'Yes, and I know which ones you mean,' James said with a laugh. 'Never mind. It's all in a good cause.'

'Is it? I'm not sure I agree. I think it's all to fuel our mother's love of ostentation, if you ask me. Bad timing, too. I expect that's why Pater's so bad-tempered.'

'Mind if I join you two chaps? I've brought my entrance fee.' A man a few years older than the twins appeared, holding a bottle of champagne.

'You're very welcome, Archie, old son,' Ned said, pushing his glass over. 'But where's our sainted sister? Shouldn't you be holding her hand since you've just become engaged to her?'

'Nice touch, that,' James said with a grin. 'Announcing it at Ma and Pa's silver wedding. Was that your idea?'

'Yes. I wanted to surprise Gina. And I did.'

'I hope you went down on one knee,' Ned said.

'What, in my best dinner suit? What do you think?'

'I think you probably did,' James guessed. 'But what have you done with her? Where is she?'

'She's doing the rounds, duty-dancing, but I've claimed the last waltz so I'm not complaining.' Archie poured drinks for all three into the wine glasses on the table. 'They're the wrong glasses, which I guess my beloved would be quick to point out. But the booze tastes the same whatever it's in.'

'I'll drink to that,' the twins said together. 'And to you, Archie,' James added with a twinkle. 'A brave man, if ever there was one, to marry our sister.'

'Amen to that.' Ned raised his glass.

'Oh, Polly,' James called to the pretty, auburn-haired maid he'd seen hurrying across the terrace with a tray of drinks. 'When you've delivered those would you bring us three champagne glasses, please.'

'Better make it four. Gina will be here eventually,' Archie added.

Polly altered course and came to the table where they were sitting. 'I'll do better than that, Mr James,' she said with a smile. 'I can leave you four glasses of champagne.'

'You're a star, Polly, you know that?' James took the glasses from the tray and looked up at her and winked.

She blushed. 'If you say so, sir.' She picked up her tray and hurried off.

Archie picked up his glass and sipped it. 'This could be the last party we'll enjoy for some time if the Kaiser has his way,' he said thoughtfully.

'Do you really think war is inevitable?' Ned asked.

He took another sip. 'Can't see anything else for it, the way the Kaiser's behaving. What do you think, James?'

'I'm inclined to agree with you.'

'Would you join up?' Archie asked.

'I guess so. I was in the Officers' Training Corps at university so if I went into the army I'd probably be commissioned,' James said. 'What about you?'

'Oh, the navy, definitely the navy,' Archie said.

'But you're an architect. Not much call for architects in the navy, I wouldn't have thought,' Ned said with a smile.

'Oh, I'm sure they'll find a corner for me. I hope so, anyway. I've always had a hankering to go to sea.' Archie turned to Ned. 'What about you, Ned? What do you intend to do?'

Ned shrugged. 'I haven't decided. But it may not happen. I'll wait till it does before I make up my mind. But here comes Gina. Let's change the subject.' The three men got to their feet as a tall, beautiful-looking girl of twenty-three, her blonde hair caught up in a midnight-blue band that exactly matched her dress, came towards them.

'Finished your duty-dancing, darling?' Archie said as he held a chair for her.

'Mm. Just about. I'm exhausted.' She slipped off a high-heeled satin shoe and massaged her toes, managing at the same time to gaze proudly at the large square sapphire ringed with diamonds that Archie had recently placed on the fourth finger of her left hand.

'Well, I hope you've remembered you've saved the last dance for me,' he said, smiling at her. 'I can hear the band playing it now.'

'Oh yes, so it is. But if you don't mind, darling, we'll sit it out.

My feet are killing me.' She glanced down at the gold and pearl watch Archie had given her as an extra engagement present. 'Oh, thank God. It's nearly eleven thirty. People will be going home soon.'

James burst out laughing. 'That's not very hospitable of you, Gina. By the way, where's Millie?'

'I'm not sure. I think she may have opted to make up a four at whist with the elderlies. You know our sister's no dancer.'

'She may be no dancer, but if she's opted for that she deserves a halo, I'd say.' James cupped his ear with his hand. 'Ah, do I hear carriages rolling? We'd better go and do our duty and bid our guests farewell.'

They all got to their feet and went inside, Archie with his arm firmly round his fiancée's waist.

A good deal later, when the last guest had gone and the rest of the family had retired, Sir George remained in his study with a few of his closer colleagues for several hours, discussing the worsening situation over brandy and cigars in an air of impending doom.

Not Adelaide. She went to bed tired but happy, smug in the knowledge that despite George's misgivings, the party had been a resounding success and with the added satisfaction that her eldest daughter was safely on the road to matrimony.

Below stairs the scene was less tranquil. All traces of the evening's activities had to be removed before those who had done all the hard work and made the whole thing happen without a hitch could even think of bed. The carpet had to be re-laid in the drawing room and all the furniture put back into place, glasses and plates collected from sometimes the most unlikely places and then washed and put away, floors swept and ash trays emptied. When it was all done to the satisfaction of Mr Walford, the butler, and only then, the staff could retire to their beds.

Polly Catchpole, Lady Adelaide's personal maid, was weary. Like all the others she had been on her feet since early morning and now she needed just five minutes to herself in the cool night air before going up to her little room under the eaves, where it was always stifling after a hot day.

She slipped quietly across the lawn to her favourite place, a seat hidden in the trees overlooking the lake. The moonlight was scattering pinpoints of light across the rippling water and it was all so tranquil she couldn't believe that all this talk of war she'd been hearing as she refilled glasses and handed round plates of pastries could be anything but that – just talk.

'Enjoying five minutes peace and quiet, Poll?' James Barsham appeared out of the trees and came and sat down beside her.

Polly immediately jumped up. 'Oh, I beg your pardon, Mr James,' she said quickly. 'I didn't realize you were there . . .'

'Oh, don't be daft, Poll, we're not up at the house now. Sit down, for goodness' sake, you must be exhausted. I know I am and I haven't been up since the crack of dawn like you.' He lit a cigarette as she resumed her seat beside him, but keeping her distance.

Theirs was a strange relationship. Ever since James was a small boy packed off to boarding school with his twin, aged nine, he had escaped as often as he could during the school holidays to Pippin Farm where Polly and her parents lived. Will Catchpole, Polly's father, was estate manager at Meadowlands and from a very early age James had enjoyed nothing better than riding round the estate with the big man, enjoying the open air and learning about the wildlife and the deer, the crops and farm management. He always returned hungry, too, ready to share a plate of Susan Catchpole's potato cakes with Polly before the two of them went off to play Cowboys and Indians in the woods with Tom Hadley, a farm worker's son who lived nearby.

As children, 'class' meant nothing to James and Polly. Although he was the elder by two years they were equals: they played together, she called him Jamie and she was Poll to him, or Polly-wolly-doodle if he wanted to tease her. Together with Tom Hadley, son of the livestock manager, when he wasn't helping his father with the animals on the farm, they had a happy and carefree childhood. Will and Susan, realizing how much this freedom meant to James, treated him as they would have done their own son (who had died before Polly was born) when he came to their house.

Polly always knew that it would be her destiny to work at the big house when she left school and privately Susan worried as to how her daughter would cope when she saw her childhood friend in his natural environment and could no longer be treated as his equal. But she needn't have worried; even at fourteen Polly accepted her position in the house and always remembered to call him Mr James and give him a quick nod when he passed. It was James who found the situation difficult. He thought the whole business of 'bowing and scraping' as he called it was hilarious and used to tease her about it until she pointed out that she could lose her place there if she didn't conform to the rules of the house. After that he was more circumspect, although occasionally he would wink at her when things were particularly formal and she would have difficulty in keeping a straight face.

But as they grew older and James and Ned, as Edward was always known, went to university, James and Polly saw less of each other and there was a subtle change in the easy relationship they had always enjoyed as children; they had grown up.

Now he offered her his cigarette case. 'Ciggie, Polly-wolly-doodle?' he asked and she could sense him grinning in the darkness.

'No, thanks. My dad would kill me if he thought I smoked; you know how strict he is. Thanks all the same. Jamie,' she added after a barely perceptible pause.

'That's better. More like old times. We had some good times as nippers, didn't we, Poll?'

'Yes, we did. And with poor old Tom, too, sometimes.'

'Mm. Funny, we always thought of him as "poor old Tom", didn't we, although he was taller and bigger than me. Well, he still is, and as strong as an ox.'

'That's because we knew his father used to beat him. Living just across the field, we could hear it sometimes, especially if Isaac had been drinking. It was awful.' She was silent for a minute, then she said, 'Did you know Mr Hadley used to hit him with a leather razor strop? He used to beat his wife, too, till one day Tom snatched the strop out of his hand and gave him a taste of his own medicine. He didn't do it after that, at least not so much.'

'Good for Tom. No, I didn't know that.'

'I expect it was while you were away at school, or university. Poor old Tom,' she said again. 'He's a lot younger than his seven brothers and sisters – I think the youngest was ten when he was born. Bit of an afterthought, you might say.'

'So by the time he was old enough to be useful the others had all left home, I suppose.'

'That's right. But I guess he felt he had to stay to protect his mother. They're very close.'

They sat in silence for several minutes, then, changing the subject, she asked tentatively, 'Jamie. All this talk of war; it seemed to be all I heard about tonight. Do you think . . .?'

He turned to her. 'Do I think there will be war, Poll? Yes, I'm afraid I do. In fact, the way things are going I can't see any way out of it.'

'Oh. Will it be soon, do you think?'

He drew on his cigarette and she saw the glow of its tip. 'Any day, I shouldn't wonder. It's affecting the whole of Europe. And now the Kaiser seems to have turned against us – even though the king is related to him, for goodness' sake. It's madness.'

'Would it affect us much? Here, I mean?' She tried to sound casual.

'Shouldn't think so. I daresay Ned and I would join the army although Archie, my future brother-in-law – I'll have to get used to calling him that – favours the navy. But we'd want to do our bit for King and country, like everyone else. It'd be a bit of a lark, I daresay.' She heard the smile in his voice.

'Oh, dear. I . . . your mother wouldn't like that. And neither would Miss Gina, not now she and Mr Penfold have just got engaged.' She turned to him. 'You don't really think it would be "a bit of a lark", do you, Jamie?'

He shrugged. 'It might not be so bad. I'd go in to train as an officer because I was in the OTC, so at least I might get a comfortable bed.' He laughed. 'And by the time the training was finished it would probably all be over, so it'd be just my luck to miss all the fun.'

'Well, going to war doesn't sound much like fun to me. All I can say is I hope it never starts.' She rubbed her eyes and tried to stifle a yawn but he heard.

'Poor old Poll. You're half dead on your feet. I'm sorry, I shouldn't keep you talking here about all these rumours of war. Go on, off to bed with you.'

'Yes, Mr James.' She got to her feet. 'And not so much of the "poor old Poll", thank you very much, Jamie Barsham,' she added with a touch of her youthful asperity of old.

As she went back across the lawn she could hear him quietly chuckling to himself.

In spite of the fact that she was so tired, Polly couldn't sleep. Her tiny room was hot, although she had opened the window as wide as it would go, but that let in the mosquitoes that bred on the lake and they buzzed round her head and bit her so she had to keep the sheet pulled up to her chin.

She smiled to herself. James calling her Polly-wolly-doodle took her back to the times they had spent playing together when they were children. Tom Hadley would come along too, sometimes, but often his father made him work, mucking out the pigsties or stables or something equally unpleasant, often till quite late at night. Although he was big and brawny, Tom was a gentle boy, very kind-hearted and devoted to his mother. He didn't deserve his brute of a father, who drank himself stupid and then blamed Tom because the place was in a mess. Polly knew that Tom was very fond of her and she was worried that he assumed that one day they would marry, although she had never given him any encouragement to think that they might. Because she knew she could never marry Tom; she liked him well enough, but not as a husband. She knew she could never, ever care for him in that way. Not in the way she cared for James. She'd been in love with James for almost as long as she could remember. Once they grew up, however, she realized that nothing could ever come of it. Sons in big houses only married servant girls in penny romances. James would no doubt marry one of the girls who had been at the party tonight – the thought of this made Polly feel a swift pang of jealousy. For her part, she was now quite convinced she would never marry at all, because in her eyes no man could ever measure up to Jamie Barsham.

With that thought she finally fell asleep.

Two

Several weeks later there was a sombre air as the Barsham family sat at breakfast in the sunny dining room overlooking the garden. Sir George was not present; he spent most of his time at Westminster now. Privately, Lady Adelaide suspected he had some little floozy tucked away there, but that was only partly true because, since war had been declared on the fourth of August, most of his time was spent at the War Office.

'I really don't understand what all this fuss is about,' she said petulantly as she attacked her scrambled eggs. 'Why we should be drawn into a little local skirmish . . .'

'It isn't little and it isn't local, Mother,' James said sharply. 'This is war. Real war. You've only got to look at the newspapers to see what's going on. The Germans have already invaded France and they've practically overrun Belgium. They've got to be stopped before there's more bloodshed like there was at Mons.'

'Men are still queuing at the recruiting office. I saw a long line of them when I was in the town the other day,' Millie said, helping herself to toast and marmalade. Unlike her siblings she was short and inclined to plumpness and cared very little about her appearance.

'I think most of them have set up camp on our lower meadow,' Gina said drily. 'There are hundreds of tents down there.'

Lady Adelaide sat up straight. 'They can't do that! It's our private property. The army can't be allowed to run riot over our land. You must go and speak to them, Ned. You're in charge since your father is not here. Go and tell them they can't stay; this is private property.'

'They're not running riot, as you put it, Mother,' Gina corrected. 'The tents are in very neat and orderly rows, hundreds of them.'

'And they've got to stay somewhere, while they're waiting to be sent to France,' Millie added. 'I believe the garrison is full to overflowing and almost every house in the town has got soldiers billeted with them.'

'That's quite right,' Ned said. 'It's no use complaining, Mother, the army have the authority to set up camps wherever there is suitable space. And for your information they did come and speak to me about it. I had to agree; our lower meadow is very spacious and very suitable. Just be thankful it isn't nearer the house.'

Lady Adelaide gave a delicate shrug. 'Well, I suppose it's some comfort that they've got so many volunteers for the army,' she said grudgingly.

'They haven't got nearly enough,' James said. 'Lord Kitchener is repeatedly asking for more volunteers and this time I intend to be one of them. I'm sure Ned will be joining me, too, won't you, Ned?'

Ned put down his knife and fork with deliberation and dabbed his mouth with his table napkin. He could never be confused with his twin. Their features were similar but Ned was a slimmer, more aesthetic-looking version of his brother. They both had warm brown eyes, but whereas James was clean-shaven, Ned wore a neat, well-trimmed moustache, and whereas James had an unruly head of dark, curly hair, Ned wore his slicked back with never a hint of a wave. Another difference in the twins was that although James was happiest outdoors, Ned preferred to be among his books, researching obscure subjects and writing about them. He would have been quite happy to pursue a career in academia.

He cleared his throat before dropping his bombshell. 'No, I don't intend to enlist, James,' he said quietly, placing his knife and fork neatly together on his plate. 'I refuse to take up arms against my fellow man.'

Gina dropped her knife. 'Ned, what can you mean?' she said, her mouth open in disbelief.

'I mean, I refuse to fight in this war,' Ned replied. He smiled at her.

'You'll be labelled a coward,' Millie said bluntly. 'As James just said, all the men are being asked to volunteer; there are placards all over the place saying' – she put on a stentorian tone – '"YOUR COUNTRY NEEDS YOU".'

'Ned doesn't have to join up if it's against his principles.' James sprang to the defence of his twin. 'There are plenty of other ways of being useful. There'll be munitions factories—'

'I'm not going to make ammunition. That's shooting people by proxy. If I won't fire a gun myself, I certainly won't load them for other people to fire. That really would be cowardly.' Ned was offended at the mere idea.

'Never mind, I'm sure Catchpole will be able to find something useful for you to do on the estate, dear,' Lady Adelaide said soothingly, helping herself to more toast.

Ned got to his feet. 'Please don't speak to me as if I was still a child, Mother. I'm twenty, which is quite old enough to make my own decisions. And I've decided it's wrong to go to war and kill people. What I shall do instead will also be my decision.'

James also got to his feet. 'I'm sorry you feel that way, Ned,' he said, putting an arm briefly round his brother's shoulder. 'But it's your choice and although I don't agree with you, I respect it. I've also made mine. I'm off to the recruiting office.'

'I hope you won't regret it, James,' was Ned's reply as they left the room together.

The three women remained at the table after the men had gone.

'What on earth did Ned mean?' Lady Adelaide asked, looking at her daughters for answers as she picked up the coffee pot.

'Nothing, Mother. Don't worry about it,' Gina said with some impatience. She sometimes marvelled at her mother's inability – or was it refusal – to understand what was going on under her nose. She pushed her cup over. 'I'll have another cup, if you're pouring one.'

'So will I, please, Ma.' Millie did the same.

'Oh, dear, it's empty.' Lady Adelaide gave it an irritated shake. 'Ring the bell, please, Millie.'

A few moments later Polly appeared, looking a little flustered.

'What's the matter, Polly? Have you been ironing and scorched a hole in something of mine?' Lady Adelaide asked, frowning at her.

'No, m'lady, I haven't been doing your ironing. I'm afraid that will have to wait till later,' Polly said apologetically. 'We're a bit short-staffed today. You see, when the butcher boy came with the meat this morning he told Cook that there were jobs going at the new factory for making munitions on the edge of town. He said they want women as well as men to work there. He said people are queuing all around the block, trying to get taken on because the money is ever so good.' She glanced briefly at the three women at the table. When they said nothing she went on: 'So I'm afraid most of the indoor staff went rushing off to try and get signed up there. They say it's to help the war effort, but I reckon it's the money they're after.' She sniffed. 'I shouldn't be surprised if most of them are back before long, though; they won't all get taken on if the queues are that long.' She put her hand over her mouth, suddenly horrified that she'd dared to speak at such length. 'Oh, I'm sorry, m'lady. Was there something you wanted?'

'Yes, we need more coffee, Polly.' Lady Adelaide indicated the coffee pot.

'Please, Polly,' Gina said, smiling at her.

'She's a servant; you don't have to grovel,' her mother reprimanded her after Polly had left the room.

'I'm only being polite, Mother. You heard what she said, the servants will be leaving in droves . . .'

Millie pealed with laughter. 'We don't have *droves* of servants. We're not Buckingham Palace, Gina.'

'All the more reason to hang on to those we do have, then. Oh, thank you, Polly,' Gina said as Polly re-entered the room.

'Yes, thank you, Polly,' Lady Adelaide said with a gracious nod. 'I'm glad to see that you haven't followed the herd and left us.'

'Oh, no, m'lady. My father would never allow me to do that. He says my place is here at Meadowlands.' She didn't add *where he can keep an eye on me* but she knew that was the case and sometimes she felt a bit stifled by his concern.

'I'm relieved to hear it.' As the door closed behind Polly, she added, 'It's a pity the rest of them aren't showing the same loyalty. I shall suggest to your father that he dismisses anyone who doesn't find work at this munitions factory. They can't be allowed to think they can leave one minute and come crawling back the next.'

'You need to be careful, Mother, or we'll end up with no staff at all,' Gina warned. 'We've already lost quite a number of the estate workers to the army, remember.'

'Just imagine if you had to do your own ironing, Ma,' Millie said wickedly.

'Don't be ridiculous,' Lady Adelaide said with a shudder. 'Drink your coffee and then ring for someone to come and clear the table.'

Later in the day, when she was taking in the tea towels that Hetty, the fourteen-year-old scullery maid, had washed earlier, Polly heard a whistle from beyond the hedge that screened the washing line. She turned and saw Tom Hadley's carroty head over the top of it.

'Tom! What's the matter?' she asked in a fierce whisper, frowning. 'You know you're not supposed—'

'I know I'm not supposed to be up at the house, Poll,' he said impatiently, 'but I couldn't go and enlist without telling you, now, could I?'

She put down the washing basket and went over to the wicket gate in the hedge. 'You're going to enlist? You never are! Does your dad know?'

He shook his head. 'No. 'Course he doesn't. He wouldn't let me go, would he? He'd say farm workers who grow food are just as important as soldiers who go and fight.'

'Well, that's true enough, I s'pose. Like coal miners. The

factories won't run if they don't have coal and people have to eat so someone's got to grow the food and look after the animals.'

'I know all that,' he said impatiently.

'Well, then, if you tell them at the recruiting office you work on a farm you'll be all right. They won't take you.'

'Don't be daft, Poll. I shan't tell 'em. I *want* 'em to take me. I'll say I haven't got a job.'

'But that's not true.' Polly looked up at her friend, puzzled. Although he was the same age as James he was nearly a head taller, with broad, muscular shoulders and big capable hands, a shock of ginger hair and weather-beaten features. While he could never be called handsome, Tom had kind eyes and a mouth always ready to smile despite the hard life his father imposed on him.

'They won't care about that. Probably won't even ask. Oh, Poll,' he said, 'don't you see? This is my chance to get away, to escape, to do what *I* want to do for a change. I don't want to spend my whole life clearing up the mess my father's too drunk to even notice.' He ran his hand across his brow. 'No, that's not altogether fair. When Dad's sober he works as hard as the next man and he loves his animals, treats them a damn sight better than he does Mum and me.' He grinned ruefully.

Polly didn't smile back. She had seen the wheals on Tom's back from the razor strop his father used to beat him with when he was younger.

'Will you do that, Poll?'

Polly looked up at him. 'Do what, Tom?'

'Oh, Poll, you haven't heard a word I've been saying.' He frowned at her. 'Listen to me. I was asking you to keep an eye on Mum while I'm away. I'm just worried Dad might take it out on her when I'm not there to look after her.'

Polly nodded and smiled at him. 'You know I will, Tom. And so will Mum. Our two mums often have a cup of tea together, you know that.' She paused. 'Does your mum know what you're planning?'

'No. I'm leaving you to tell her.'

'Oh, thanks very much.' Polly gave a sigh.

'Well, if she doesn't know, Dad can't beat it out of her and try to fetch me back.'

Polly winced. 'Don't worry, we'll look after her, Tom.' She put out her hand and he took it in his great paw. But before he could draw her to him she withdrew it. 'Now, you mind and look after yourself, Tom Hadley,' she said, keeping her voice light. 'I bet the Germans won't know what's hit 'em when you get out there.'

'Ain't you gonna kiss me goodbye, then?'

She reached up and gave him a quick peck on the cheek.

'Polly! Polly! Where are you?' came a voice from the house.

'That's Cook. I must go. Good luck, Tom. Come back safe.' She picked up the clothes basket and hurried along the path to the house without looking back. She found that for some reason she was close to tears. She had always regarded Tom as something of a big brother and she would be devastated if he should come to any harm.

But life soon became too busy to think about anything other than the next task to be done. With nearly all the indoor staff gone, either into the army or the munitions factory, Polly was run off her feet, doing the work of two housemaids as well as her regular job as ladies' maid to Lady Adelaide and her two daughters. Not that Gina and Millie were demanding; they appreciated how her work load had increased and were happy to look after themselves and each other to a large extent – unlike their mother, who expected things to go on as they always had. Polly also made time to help Mrs Bellman, the cook, when things got too much for little Hetty, although the girl was getting stronger now that she was given three good meals a day.

Mr Walford, the butler, too old for army service and with bad feet, was also struggling. He had to rely for help on Albert, the young footman who had tried to enlist but failed the army medical test. The truth was that he'd been starved as a child and consequently suffered from rickets, leaving him with weak, bandy legs; but he was too proud to admit this, claiming instead that he'd been rejected on account of poor eyesight. To prove this he went about peering short-sightedly until he found a pair of gold-rimmed spectacles in a drawer in a rarely used bedroom. The fact that wearing them gave him headaches, combined with shame at being rejected for the army, turned him into an awkward, bad-tempered young man. Polly avoided him as much as she could.

The war was not over by Christmas, as the optimistic young men who had gone off to fight it had predicted. Instead, it was turning into a protracted and bloody battle with neither side gaining much ground.

Consequently, Christmas at Meadowlands was a subdued affair. James managed to get a few days' leave because, having finished his training as an officer, he was due to be posted to the fighting zone early in the New Year.

'Do you know where you'll be going, James?' Gina asked as they took a brisk walk in the grounds on Boxing Day.

'I've not been told officially, but I'm hoping I'll join the Meadowlands Pals unit. The army have shown a bit of compassion in trying to keep men from the same villages or estates together, so that at least they are with men they know.'

'Where are they? The Meadowlands Pals, I mean.'

'Ypres, I believe. That's a town somewhere in Flanders, I'm told.' He grinned at her. 'Maybe my geography will improve once I'm out there.'

She slipped her hand through his arm and squeezed it. 'Just come back safe, Jimmy,' she said quietly. 'Never mind the geography.'

'You haven't called me that since we were in the schoolroom,' he said with a laugh. He put his hand over hers as it lay in the crook of his arm. 'But never mind me – what have you been up to while I've been away? And what's been going on here?' He paused. 'I see Ned's still around, so he hasn't had a change of heart.'

She shook her head. 'No, but he's done quite a lot to help Will Catchpole. I believe he's taken over most of the accounts and bookkeeping and goes on his rounds with him to see what needs to be done.' She sighed. 'And there's plenty to do, as you can see, since several of the farm labourers have gone.'

'Well, that'll be a change for Ned. He was never one to get his hands dirty,' James said, smiling to take the sting out of his words. 'And Millie?'

'Hasn't she told you? She intends to join the VADs and take up nursing. She did think of volunteering to drive a tram – I think she quite fancied herself as a tram driver – but then she decided on the VADs because she thought that was more worthwhile and once she'd done her nursing training there was always the chance that she might get to drive an ambulance.'

'I didn't know she could drive.'

'She can't, but she's determined to learn.'

'That's our Millie, all over. I'll tell her she can practise on my little car round the estate if she's very, very careful. That'll give her a start.'

'Really?' Gina looked at him in amazement. 'But that car's your pride and joy.'

He shrugged. 'Somehow you get to look at things differently in wartime,' he said enigmatically. 'You can drive it, too, if it's any help. And talking of you, where's Archie?'

'Well, now he's in the navy he hopes to get a commission soon. He's just finished his training so he's home for a few days. He'll be here tomorrow or the next day so you'll see him. As for me,' she sighed, 'I'm not doing anything much. Well, that's not true, I suppose. I'm kept pretty busy here. Ma seems to expect things to go on as they've always done; she forgets there are only four people to do the work of ten and both Cook and Mr Walford are near retiring age. If it wasn't for Polly I really don't know how we'd manage. She seems to be here, there and everywhere, bless her.'

'I'm surprised she's stayed.'

'Her father won't let her leave.'

'Good for Will,' he murmured under his breath.

'You know he can be a bit of a tyrant over her,' Gina went on. 'She can't do just as she likes. But she's his only daughter, so I suppose you can understand it. Not that our father had any such concern over Millie and me.' She pealed with laughter at the thought. Then she shivered. 'It's getting cold; I think we've walked far enough, James. Coming back to the house?'

'No, I think I'll walk a bit more. Store up memories of the old place to keep me going while I'm away,' he said with a smile.

Gina left him and he carried on walking until he could look over to what had always been his favourite view, the rolling parkland falling away to the lower meadow and the river beyond. Only now the lower meadow was home to several hundred army tents, laid out in neat regimented rows, with khaki figures moving between them either busily going about their business or having a quiet smoke in the winter sunshine.

He turned away, feeling like an interloper on his own land, and went back to the house, heading for the side door, then changing his mind and going in through the boot room. There he sat down on a bench and with some difficulty dragged off his boots, muddy from his walk.

'You'll be needing these, won't you, sir?'

He looked up, surprised, and saw Polly standing there with his house shoes in her hand.

'How did . . .?'

She smiled. 'I saw you go to the side door and then change your mind, so I guessed where you were going. Sir.'

'Oh, not so much of the "sir", Polly,' he said irritably. He patted the bench beside him. 'Come and sit down. I've not had a chance to talk to you since I've been home. You're like quicksilver, here one minute, gone the next.'

'There's a lot to do,' she said.

'Yes, I know. But you can spare a few minutes for your old friend, can't you, Poll?'

She flushed and nodded. 'I'll always have time for you, Jamie,' she said shyly. 'You know that.'

'Good. I'm glad to hear you say it.' He took her hand and was silent for a minute. Then he said, 'You know I'll be going to Flanders very soon?'

She shook her head, alarmed. 'Oh! No, I didn't know.' Then her shoulders sagged. 'Although I s'pose I should have done. That's where they all go when they join up, isn't it?'

'Eventually, yes. I hope to join the Meadowlands Pals, so I'll probably see Tom.' He looked at her intently. 'Shall I give him your love?'

She wasn't looking at him. She shrugged and said, 'Tell him I hope he'll come back safe,' she said. Now she turned to look at him. 'You come back safe, Jamie. Please,' she pleaded desperately. She turned away. 'I wish you didn't have to go.'

'What did you say?'

She shook her head. 'Nothing.' Reluctantly, she tried to pull her hand away but he held on to it. 'I must go. I've got jobs to do,' she said.

'Just another minute.' He smiled at her. 'I'm storing up memories for when I'm Over There,' he said quietly.

'Not much of a memory, sitting here in the boot room with me.' She tried to giggle but it sounded more like a sob.

'You're wrong there, Polly-wolly-doodle,' he said, releasing her hand. 'It'll be one of the best.' He got to his feet and helped her to hers. Then he bent and brushed her lips with his and walked quickly out of the room.

She picked up his boots and, regardless of Cook calling her, spent the next half hour cleaning them, her tears mingling with the boot polish.

Three

The year 1915 didn't start well. In January there was a new threat as the Germans began to attack from the air, sending airships called zeppelins over to bomb English coastal towns in Norfolk. Great Yarmouth and King's Lynn were both attacked with over twenty people killed and twice that number injured. And at sea, German submarines lay in wait to attack ships bringing in much-needed supplies, hoping to destroy the economy and starve the population. Already the war had claimed over 100,000 casualties.

Sir George still spent a good deal of time at Westminster. He felt more comfortable there among his cronies and deluded himself that he was indispensable at the War Office. Added to that – and if he was honest, more importantly – he had a secretary with a comfortable flat in Pimlico, a dowdy-looking woman in drab woollen suits under which he knew – because he had bought them for her – she was wearing skimpy black satin underwear.

It made little difference to the running of the household at Meadowlands whether he was at home or not. When he was there he was rarely seen, spending most of his time in his study, feeling vaguely unwell, smoking and reading *The Times* and criticizing the decisions made by the Government in his absence. These he expounded at great and boring length over dinner each night. The family were always guiltily glad when he took himself back to London.

Lady Adelaide gazed round the depleted dinner table with undisguised relief the night after he had gone after a brief foray home at the beginning of March. 'Millie's late,' she remarked as she took a delicate sip of soup from her spoon. 'Why isn't she here?'

'She's gone to Ipswich to begin her training,' Gina said patiently.

'What training?' Lady Adelaide frowned.

'She's joined the VAD.'

'VAD? What's that?'

'Voluntary Aid Detachment. It's a branch of nursing,' Gina explained patiently. 'She came and said goodbye to you before she caught the train, Mother. Don't you remember?'

'Ah, yes, of course. Come to think of it, I did think her goodbye was a little effusive for a shopping trip.' Lady Adelaide smiled vaguely.

'But you knew she'd decided on nursing.'

'Yes, but I didn't think she'd be going yet.' She put on a long-suffering face. 'I think it's very noble of her. If only I were younger I'm sure I'd be happy to do my bit for the war effort, just like Millie. And brave James, of course.'

Ned threw his spoon into his soup bowl with a clatter and pushed it away, which covered Gina's snigger of disbelief at her mother's words.

'Ned?' Lady Adelaide raised her eyebrows. 'That was rather rude.'

'Not as rude as the continuing barbs aimed at me,' he snapped.

'I don't know what you mean, dear,' his mother said, looking puzzled. 'What barbs?'

'Because I'm not in uniform like my exalted brother.'

'You're being over-sensitive, Ned. I'm sure nothing like that was in Ma's mind,' Gina said quickly.

'No, of course not, dear. You're doing sterling work helping Catchpole . . . doing whatever he does.' Lady Adelaide waved her hand vaguely, making matters even worse.

'Then what about this?' Ned reached into his breast pocket and threw a white feather down on the table. He stared at it, then said bitterly, 'Two over-patriotic, over-dressed women were handing these out to every man who was not in uniform in the town square today, saying, "Coward. Why aren't you in the army? Why haven't you enlisted?" It was humiliating.'

'It was also very stupid of them,' Gina said. 'There are plenty of good reasons why a man might not be in the army, even leaving aside the fact that he might not be fit enough to serve. Didn't you tell them you're working on the land, providing food?'

He shook his head. 'No. It wouldn't be true, would it?' He

looked up. 'The fact is, I do a bit of bookkeeping that Will Catchpole could very well manage himself and I try to look busy. But really I'm not doing anything much.'

'Oh, I'm sure that's not true, darling.' Lady Adelaide put out her hand to him.

'Yes, it is,' he said wretchedly.

Gina watched him for a few minutes. 'So what do you propose to do?' she asked quietly. 'Have you decided?'

'Yes. I've been thinking for some time that I should join the army, as a non-combatant of course. I could become a stretcher-bearer or something of that kind. I'm prepared to do anything useful that doesn't involve killing people. I talked it over with James when he was home—'

'He never told us,' Lady Adelaide said, affronted.

'No. It was just between the two of us. It was his suggestion that I could become a stretcher-bearer.' He flicked the white feather in front of him on the table. 'This has made up my mind. I shall go to the recruiting office tomorrow.'

'Oh, my dear.' Lady Adelaide clutched his arm, 'I don't think you should . . .'

He shook her off. 'There's no need to be melodramatic, Mother. I've made my decision and there's nothing more to be said.'

'I wish you luck, Ned,' Gina said, smiling at him. 'I hate the idea of both my brothers being at the Front, but I'm sure you'll be doing the right thing.'

'Thanks, sis.' Ned gave her a grim smile back. 'And don't worry, I'm under no illusions as to what I'm letting myself in for.'

Three days later Ned was in uniform and undergoing training in first aid. Three weeks later he was in Flanders.

The day after he left Lady Adelaide gazed woefully at Gina, who was carefully keeping her eyes on her plate as she ate so she didn't have to look at the empty chairs round the table.

'Oh, Gina, what shall we do? Everybody's leaving because of this wretched war. How can two women like us be expected to run an estate the size of this one with nobody to help?' she asked, as if she had the weight of the world on her shoulders.

'I expect we'll manage, Mother,' Gina said dryly. 'We're not entirely on our own anyway. We've still got Will Catchpole; he knows more about running things than anybody. And Isaac Hadley isn't likely to be going anywhere; he won't leave his animals.'

'No, I suppose not.' Lady Adelaide gave a long-suffering sigh. 'All the same—'

'I've been thinking,' Gina cut across her words. 'It might be a good idea if I—'

Now it was Lady Adelaide's turn to interrupt. 'You're not thinking of going, too!' she said in alarm. 'You can't leave me, Gina. You can't leave me to run this huge house on my own.'

'No, Mother. I was thinking it might be a good idea if I learned to drive James' little car. Apart from the two big shire horses, all our horses have been taken for the war effort so we've really no means of getting anywhere unless we go by tram.'

Lady Adelaide shuddered. 'Never!' She returned to her long-suffering expression. 'Not that I ever go far, now your father is here so seldom.'

Gina ignored her. 'I thought I might practise driving round the estate like Millie did. She didn't have any trouble handling it. In fact, I went with her several times.'

'Hm. James won't like that. Will you tell him?'

'I don't need to. He said I could. So as long as I don't crash it . . .' Gina shrugged. 'As I see it, it's either that or, if you want to go anywhere, you'll have to get yourself a bicycle,' she said wickedly.

'Don't be ridiculous.' Lady Adelaide waited until Polly had cleared the plates and brought in the pudding. Then she said, with a heavy sigh, 'Very well. But be careful.' She put out her hand. 'And promise you won't ever think of leaving me here alone.'

Gina sighed. 'I promise, Mother.' She knew that with that promise she had sealed her fate. All her ideas of learning to drive so that she could volunteer to do something useful in the war like Archie and the twins and even Millie had gone by the board, because she realized she could never leave her mother alone at Meadowlands. Yet she still felt there must be something she could do.

The solution to her problem came in a quite unexpected way.

She had gone into the town to buy some lace for her mother one rather chilly spring afternoon and was hurrying back to where she had parked the car – like Millie she had found learning to drive very easy and she loved it – when a child of not more than six years old, in patched trousers and a thin grubby-looking shirt, tripped and fell down, right in the path of passers-by.

People mostly ignored him, intent on their own interests, although one woman callously tried to push him out of the way with her foot. Annoyed at this, Gina went across to help him to his feet, noticing how thin his arms were and how pale and undernourished he appeared. She looked round to see if his mother was near, but then a girl of about twelve, barefoot and in a dress several sizes too big, hurried over and began to shake him by the shoulder.

'Frankie, you know you shouldn't run orf like that,' she began, but when the child's knees began to buckle and his face turned even whiter she stopped and put her arm round him to stop him falling again.

Gina frowned. 'Whatever's the matter with him? Is he ill?'

'No, I don't fink so. Mind you, he ain't never bin very strong.' She gave him a little shake, her arm still round him. 'You know you shouldn't run, you little silly.'

Gina was still frowning. 'Where do you live?'

The girl nodded towards a road off the square. 'Down Trinity Lane.' It was one of the poorer districts in the town.

Gina swept the boy off his feet, ignoring the fact that he was none too clean. He weighed very little. 'Come along, little one, I'll take you home,' she said gently. 'It doesn't look to me as if you're in a fit state to walk.'

'He'll be all right, miss, really he will. We ain't got far to go,' the girl was saying as she ran to keep up with Gina. 'He often falls down like that. It don't mean nothing, 'cept his belly's empty.'

'You just tell me which house,' Gina said, not slacking her pace.

'Jest here.' The girl turned a corner and indicated a house in the middle of a squalid row, where paint was peeling off every door and a number of broken windows were patched up with cardboard. A foetid stench hung over the whole area. 'You can put him down now, miss. I'll take him in.' She pushed open the door and turned, anxious to take the boy, but Gina walked past her into the house.

The door opened straight into the room. When her eyes became accustomed to the dim interior Gina saw that it was bare except

for a table and a stool. The floorboards were bare and there were
no curtains at the window, not that this last mattered because the
window itself was too grimy to see through. A woman was sitting
on the only chair by the empty grate with a baby on her lap and
four other small children clustered round her. Two of them were
crying, but they stopped in surprise when they saw the strange
person come into their house carrying their brother. The woman
tried to struggle to her feet, hampered by the gaggle of children
clutching her skirts, and Gina could see that she was again heavily
pregnant.

'No, no, don't get up,' Gina said quickly. 'Your little boy fell
in the street so I've brought him home for you.'

'Thank you very much, Ma'am,' the woman said dully. 'That
was very kind of you to take the trouble.'

Without being invited, Gina sat down on the stool by the
table, which held a candle stub in a chipped china candlestick
and nothing else. There was no sign of any food. 'Your daughter
said he fell because he was hungry. Is that right?'

The woman looked uncomfortable. 'She shouldn't hev said
that,' she said, not looking Gina in the eye.

'But why is he hungry? Is he pernickety? Won't he eat what
you give him?' she asked, puzzled.

The woman sniffed. Now she looked at Gina and her look
was scathing. 'Fat chance! He don't eat 'cause I ain't got nothin''
to give him. Thass why he's hungry,' she said angrily. 'D'you
think I'd let my little'uns starve if I'd got a morsel o' food in the
house? Pah! You rich people ain't got no idea.' She turned away
in disgust.

'Oh, I'm truly sorry,' Gina said humbly. 'I didn't realize. But
your husband . . .?' Her thoughts were racing. There must be
a husband, with all these children. Unless . . . Oh, Lord. She
was beginning to wonder what sink of iniquity she had stepped
into.

'My 'usband enlisted soon after the war started,' the woman
said with pride in her voice and Gina felt immediately guilty at
the turn her thoughts had begun to take. 'He used to be a knife-
grinder and he made a half-decent livin' goin' round the countryside
but he reckoned he oughta do 'is bit and anyway the money'd be
more reg'lar if he went to fight for King and country.' She lifted
her chin and looked straight at Gina. 'I never tried to stop him.

Charlie was always a good man and did what he thought was right and I abided by what he said.'

She waited and Gina nodded and murmured something unintelligible.

It clearly satisfied the woman because she went on: 'He got one of his mates who can read and write to send me a letter sayin' he'd allycated half his army pay to me so I should get a reg'lar income and with the money the gov'ment's s'posed to pay fam'lies of soldiers I should be pretty well placed.' She sniffed. 'I reckon I woulda bin, too. On'y trouble is, I ain't seen a penny piece of any of it.'

Gina gasped. 'But that's terrible! Why not?'

The woman ignored her question and went on proudly. 'He left me two whole pounds when he went away, two whole pounds! He'd bin savin' it up for ages in case he needed anything for his knife-grindin' bike. It was pretty old, y'see. He said, "There y'are, Lil. You take me bike money. I shan't be needin' a new bike for a while so that'll see you all right an' a bit over till me army pay come through." Them were his very words.' She gave a mirthless laugh. 'On'y, like I say, the army pay ain't never come through and I ain't had a penny from the gov'ment.' She sniffed back a tear. 'Two pounds is a lot o' money I'll grant you, an' I eked it out as best I could, but even that don't last forever when there's rent to pay an' seven mouths to feed.' She wiped her wet cheeks with the palm of her hand and looked hard at Gina. 'So now you know why my Frankie's hungry, and so are the rest of my little'uns.' She shook her head. 'And, God help me, I can't do nothin' about it. I've sold everything I've got worth sellin', 'cept this.' She twisted the plain gold ring on her finger. It looked several sizes too big now. 'I've tried to hang on to it but it'll hev to go before long, 'cause there's nothin' else left to sell an' I'm behind with the rent.' Her shoulders sagged. 'I dunno what I'm gonna do, I'm sure.' She looked up at Gina and said wearily, 'I'm sorry, miss, if I was a bit sharp with you when you first come in, but it's jest . . .' She bit her lip and her eyes filled with tears again. 'Fact is, I don't know what to do, nor which way to turn. If I can't pay me rent soon we'll be turned out an' that'll mean the Spike. Then I'd be separated from me little'uns an' I couldn't bear that an' nor could they. The on'y consolation is there's plenty more in the same boat as me. Not that thass much comfort.'

Gina said nothing for several minutes, shocked beyond words. Then she opened her purse and took some money out and gave it to the girl. 'Take this and go and get a loaf of bread and some meat pies. Quick now. And make sure you bring them back while they're still warm. Oh, and some milk for the little ones.' She turned to Lil. 'Will that do, for now?'

Tears were running unchecked down Lil's cheeks. She nodded dumbly. When she could trust herself to speak she said, 'I never thought I'd hev to stoop to taking charity, but I know I must, for the sake of the little'uns. So, thank you, miss. Thank you from the bottom of me heart.'

Gina got to her feet. 'I shall come back, Lil. And I shall make enquiries as to why your money isn't coming through. Ah, one more thing.' She scrabbled in her bag and brought out three florins, which was all she had left in her purse now. 'That will pay some of your back rent, so at least you'll keep the roof over your head.' She smiled at all the children. 'Enjoy your pies, but don't eat too much at once or you'll get tummy ache.' With that she left, hurrying away as tears blinded her eyes.

As she drove back to Meadowlands in the little car belonging to her brother, Gina's mind was busy with ideas as to how she could help Lil and the other women like her in the town who were struggling to feed their children while their husbands fought for their country.

By the time she reached home an idea had formed in her mind.

Four

It was a warm day towards the end of April. The cherry trees in the kitchen garden were full of blossom, heralding a good crop, and the blackthorn hedges at the edge of the estate were beginning to turn white with blossom – what country people called may. Daisies were already peppering the meadow underfoot as Polly hurried across to Pippin Farm to pay her mother a brief visit, and soon the golden buttercups would join them. She savoured these signs of spring and paused for a minute at the sound of a skylark singing high up in the sky. She shaded her eyes and looked up; the bird itself was barely visible but the sound of its song was clear and unmistakable. With a small sigh she hurried on, anxious to spend a little time with her mother. These days it was something of a luxury to find even an hour or so to herself in the middle of the day.

Even though there was only Lady Adelaide and Miss Gina – and very occasionally Sir George – to look after now, the house was still big and had to be cleaned; fires were still needed, there were coals to carry, beds to make – oh, the list was endless. And all with a sadly depleted staff, which Lady Adelaide didn't, or wouldn't, seem to understand. She still expected Polly to spend hours ironing her frills and fiddling with her hair. It was often midnight before she and little Hetty finally climbed the stairs to their respective bedrooms. And Hetty had to be up again at six to blacklead and light the kitchen range ready for Cook to start on breakfast, while Polly cleaned and tidied the dining room and laid the table. From then on there was no let up.

And now Miss Gina wanted more. Polly didn't like to refuse to help her, but she simply didn't see how it could be done.

She pushed open the garden gate and walked up the path. The back door was open and Burdock, the elderly black cat, was sunning himself on the step. She stopped briefly to bend down and scratch him behind his ear before stepping over him into the big stone-flagged kitchen. The delicious smell of freshly baked cakes immediately made her nose twitch.

'Polly!' Susan Catchpole greeted her daughter with a broad smile, the big, brown betty teapot in her hand. 'Oh, this is nice. And you're just in time for a cuppa. Come and sit down, dearie.'

Polly gave her mother a brief kiss, then sat down at the big scrubbed table, noticing, now her eyes were accustomed to the dimness of the kitchen after the bright sunlight outside, that Violet Hadley, a small, sharp-featured, bird-like woman with dark hair scraped back into a tight bun, was sitting there too.

'Oh, hullo, Mrs Hadley. I'm sorry, I couldn't see you sitting there,' she said. 'How are you? And have you heard from Tom lately?' Polly marvelled yet again that such a tiny woman could have produced eight children, among them such a big, brawny son.

'Yes, I had a card from him yesterday. He don't say much; he ain't much of a letter writer an' I ain't much of a reader, so I brought it over for Susan to read out for me. He says he's bin made batman to Mr James, well, he ain't Mr James now. What is he, Susan?'

'Captain Barsham,' Susan said proudly. In contrast to Violet, Susan was plump, with rosy cheeks and fading auburn hair that kept escaping from its pins.

'I ain't quite sure what a batman is,' Violet said. 'Are you?'

'I think it means Tom'll be looking after Mr James,' Polly said with a smile. She was glad to know the two men were together.

'Oh, thass all right then. They'll look after each other.' Violet didn't understand but she was satisfied.

Polly drank her tea and accepted one of her mother's currant buns. 'Oh, this is nice,' she said, leaning back and closing her eyes briefly.

'You look tired, my girl. I reckon you're working too hard,' her mother observed, topping up the teapot with water from the kettle on the hob.

'I am tired,' Polly said. She leaned forward and pushed her cup across the table for a refill. 'There's a lot to do at the house and not enough of us to do it. Now the housemaids have gone I have to do a lot of the cleaning as well as looking after m'lady and Miss Gina. Not that Miss Gina is much trouble.' She sipped her tea thoughtfully. 'Hetty, bless her, helps where she can, but she's not quite fifteen and Mrs Bellman always needs her in the kitchen.' She gave a deep sigh. 'But now Miss Gina wants to set up a sort of soup kitchen in the town and she's asked me to help her. I'd really like to, but I just don't see how I can, not with all the other things I have to do and Lady A. calling for me morning, noon and night.'

Susan frowned. 'A soup kitchen? What kind of soup kitchen?'

'I'm not really sure of the details, but apparently there are women in the town who haven't got any money so they can't even feed their children because their husbands have gone to fight the Germans.'

'But they get an allowance, don't they?' Susan asked, still frowning.

'I hevn't had anything from my Tom,' Violet chipped in. 'I don't know if I ought to, nobody's said. But Isaac's earning so p'raps I ain't entitled.'

'Well, these are women with children who've had the wage-earner taken away and now they haven't got anything to live on, so Miss Gina says,' Polly told them. She sighed. 'I said I'd like to help, and I really would, but I really don't see how I can. And when I mentioned it to Mrs Bellman, she turned the idea down flat. She said, "Doesn't Miss Gina think I've got enough to do, cooking for the family, without making soup for half the town." She was quite cross.'

Susan was quiet for several minutes digesting all this. Then she said tentatively, 'I wouldn't mind making a bit of soup. We've got spare vegetables in the garden and I daresay if we run short Old Jacob will let us have a few from the kitchen garden at the house.' She nodded towards the kitchen range. 'Wouldn't be a lot of trouble to boil it up, there's always a fire there. If it'd help, that is.'

Violet finished her tea and brushed a few crumbs from her cake into a heap as if giving herself time to decide whether or not she should speak. Having decided, she said, 'If they'd hev me at the house I wouldn't mind doing a bit o' cleaning. I love cleaning and polishing.' She hesitated. 'But I don't reckon Isaac would let me work without being paid,' she added nervously, as if that put an end to the idea.

Polly looked uncertainly from her mother to Violet and back again. 'I'd have to ask Miss Gina, first,' she said. 'But if you wouldn't mind . . .'

'I'd be glad to help. I don't like to think of people going hungry,' Susan said firmly.

'I would too,' Violet said. 'If they'd hev me up at the house. And if Isaac don't mind,' she added.

Polly smiled in delight. 'Well, that would just about solve the problem, I reckon. I'd been wondering how I could get round it because I'd really like to help Miss Gina. Thank you both for offering.' She paused. 'But of course I'll have to see what Miss Gina has to say. I'll ask her when I get back but I don't think she's likely to object.' She looked up at the clock on the wall, with its heavy brass weights and its brass pendulum ticking the seconds away. She remembered as a child trying to lift one of the weights off its chain to see how heavy it was and finding it was too heavy for her little hands to hold and dropping it on the floor. There was great consternation until everything was put back and the two weights re-balanced. She was warned of dire consequences if she ever touched the clock again. She never did. She pulled her thoughts back to the present. 'Goodness, look at the time, I must go. I'll have m'lady calling for me.'

As she got to her feet a shadow blocked out the sunlight and her father came in through the door. He was a big man with a ruddy complexion and fair, balding hair, flattened where he had just removed his hat and hung it on its peg.

'I was just going, Dad,' she said, going over and kissing his cheek. 'I expect there's still a cup of tea in the pot.'

'Good. I could do with one.' He kissed his wife and sat down heavily, giving a brief nod in Violet's direction.

'Is something wrong, Dad?' Hearing his worried tone Polly sat down again.

'Nothing for you to fret about, my girl.' He acknowledged the mug of tea his wife had poured and took several sips. 'It's just that I found a young deer from our herd had been killed in the wood – well, what was left of a young deer, I should say. Poor thing had been butchered.' He shook his head. 'I had a word with Isaac; I thought he'd likely know what might have done it. I thought a dog, maybe. I didn't reckon it was a fox, but do you know what he said?' He looked up and saw three pairs of eyes watching him. 'He reckons it was some of the soldiers from the camp on lower meadow.'

'What would they want with killing deer?' Violet asked innocently.

'What would they want? Nice bit of venison for the pot, that's what they'd want.' Will rested his head on his hand. 'Oh, we knew they'd been after rabbits, but that didn't worry us too much. Isaac even turned a blind eye when they took the odd pheasant. But young deer . . . No, we can't have that, especially the way they left the carcass. I think they thought they'd hidden it but did they think we wouldn't find it, for goodness' sake?' He took a long draught of his tea.

'So, what are you going to do?' asked ever practical Susan.

'I'll have to go and see the officer in charge. No point in troubling Her Ladyship.' He turned to Polly. 'Unless Sir George is at home?' he asked hopefully.

She shook her head. 'No, he went back to London yesterday.'

'Hm. Pity. I'd rather have left it to him, he'd have had more clout. But never mind, I reckon I can deal with it.' He swallowed the last of his tea. 'Better get on with it, I suppose. We don't usually have anything to do with what goes on in the camp, the soldiers come and go, some of them behave better than others, but they live their lives and we live ours and if there's trouble the officers sort it out.' He put his hands on the table and heaved himself to his feet. 'I hope they'll sort this out. I don't want to cause any trouble to the men – after all, they've got the prospect of fighting a war in front of them – but at the same time I can't stand by and see any more of our herd mutilated. They're all God's creatures, when all's said and done.'

'I'll walk back with you, Dad,' Polly said, linking her arm in his when they got outside the door.

'I don't want you coming anywhere near that army camp, my girl,' Will said sternly. 'There's no telling what some of those men'll get up to, given half a chance.'

'Don't be silly, Dad.' She shook his arm. 'I'm only coming as far as the kitchen gate with you. I've got too much to do at the house to bother about soldiers.'

'I'm glad to hear it. Mind you keep it that way.' He gave her a brief kiss as they parted company.

Gina was out when Polly got back and Hetty whispered to her that she'd gone for a drive with her *financy*, as she called him. 'Looks ever so smart in his officer's uniform,' she said, still whispering because Mrs Bellman was very strict and wouldn't have the staff discussing the whereabouts of the family.

'Do you know when she'll be back?' Polly whispered.

Hetty shrugged and shook her head.

'What are you two whispering about?' Mrs Bellman called from the kitchen. 'Hetty, I need you to come and prepare the rest of the vegetables. There'll be one extra tonight.'

So Miss Gina's fiancé was staying to dinner. That answered Polly's question and meant that her news would have to wait. She hurried upstairs to lay the table in the dining room. Albert was already there, peering through his useless spectacles at the whisky and brandy decanters on the sideboard to make sure they didn't need refilling. He dropped the heavy stopper from one of the decanters and it rolled across the floor, landing by Polly's foot.

She picked it up and handed it to him. 'I really don't know why you wear those spectacles, Albert,' she said, smiling at him.

'I'm sure you don't need them and you're so much better-looking without them.'

'Oh, do you think so?' He studied his reflection in the mirror over the sideboard, then whipped them off and put them in his pocket. 'There, is that better?'

She nodded. 'Much better. You look quite dashing now.'

'Oh, really?' He pulled back his shoulders and smoothed his already flat hair self-consciously. 'Then I'll have to try and manage without them, won't I?'

'I would if I were you.'

The spectacles were never seen again and breakages in the kitchen decreased dramatically.

Dinner that night was quite a simple affair with only four courses, which was Lady Adelaide's idea of economizing for the war effort. Of course, she still expected Polly to dress her even though she knew her maid was needed to help elsewhere. Tonight, for some reason quite unfathomable to Polly, she wasn't satisfied with her hair and it all had to be taken down and started again.

'I don't really like this gown,' she said, smoothing the lace at the neck of her purple silk. I don't think it suits my colouring.' She put her head on one side. 'Perhaps the yellow would be better?'

'I think the purple looks very nice, m'lady,' Polly said, keeping her temper with difficulty. 'And with your amethyst necklace and earrings . . .'

'Ah, yes. They belonged to my grandmother, you know.' Lady Adelaide lifted them out of her jewel box and Polly heaved a sigh of relief.

Gina and Archie were late back from their drive. Consequently, they had no time before dinner was served for more than a quick wash and brush up, although Archie looked very smart in his new sub-lieutenant's uniform and Gina had put on a pretty sapphire-blue blouse exactly the same colour as the sapphire in her engagement ring. In the event Lady Adelaide looked rather overdressed for an informal dinner *à trois*.

During the meal Gina tried to tell Archie and her mother about her idea for a soup kitchen in the town and the reason for it.

'What a wonderful idea. I think it's very noble of you to try to help these people, darling,' Archie said, giving her an adoring smile.

Lady Adelaide shuddered. 'I'm sure it is. I just hope you don't catch something unpleasant, Gina. Those kind of people don't keep themselves very clean, I understand. And they spend all their money on drink which is why they live in poverty.' She attacked her lamb chop with relish.

'That's just not true, Mother. They *have* no money. That's what I've been trying to tell you,' Gina said, losing patience. She raised her eyebrows towards Archie and he smiled in sympathy. 'I think we'd better change the subject.'

'Yes, we don't want to spoil your last meal with us before you go back by speaking of such unpleasant things, do we, Archie?' Lady Adelaide said. 'When is it you'll be leaving?'

'Tomorrow. Now I've finished my training I have to report to Portsmouth,' he replied.

'Oh, my dear. So brave of you.'

'Not at all. Only doing my bit,' he said, rather embarrassed by her words.

'You haven't decided to name the day yet then?' Lady Adelaide asked hopefully. She had already started looking through her beloved catalogues to find something suitable to wear for the Big Day when it arrived.

'No, Mother, not yet. Archie doesn't know where he'll be or what he'll be doing so it's not possible to fix a date at the moment, is it, darling?'

'No, not really.' As far as Archie was concerned a forty-eight-hour pass and a quick trip to Gretna Green would be quite sufficient but he knew the bride's mother would never countenance such a thing.

Gina wasn't quite sure what she wanted, if she was honest with herself. She liked the idea of being engaged and wearing her beautiful ring. In truth, she would be quite happy to carry on in that state indefinitely but she knew that sooner or later it would have to end in marriage and she would lose her freedom. She realized guiltily that that was not quite the right attitude towards matrimony and there were times when he was away that she wondered whether what she felt for Archie was quite the stuff that dreams were made of. Oh, she was fond of him, there was no doubt about that, but was that enough? At this stage in their relationship was it acceptable that she should sometimes find him just a teeny bit dull?

Five

It was the following day before Polly had the opportunity to tell Miss Gina of the help she had been offered from her mother and Violet Hadley.

'You see, I was really worried, Miss Gina. I have so much extra to do now that I couldn't see how I was going to find time to help you with your soup kitchen, and I do so want to,' she said as she was putting away freshly ironed clothes in Gina's wardrobe. 'And then, when Mrs Bellman refused point blank to help, saying where did I think she was going to find the time to make soup for half the town – well, she is very busy, I know that, but I did try to explain. I thought, well, that's that, then.' She closed the wardrobe doors, turned her attention to the chest of drawers and continued, 'I was so upset, Miss Gina, I told Mum about it when I went to see her. Mrs Hadley was there at the time and do you know, they both offered their help without even being asked. Not that I'd even thought of asking them, of course. It was like an answer to a prayer.' Polly turned to look at Gina. 'Mind you, Mrs Hadley said her husband would expect her to be paid, would that be all right?'

Gina smiled. 'You did well, Polly. And of course Mrs Hadley will be paid, there's no question about that. Your mother, too.'

'Oh, Mum won't want anything. She's just glad to help,' Polly said.

'Well, we'll see about that, but it's very kind of them both. I'll go and see them and thank them.'

Polly wasn't sure that either her mother or Mrs Hadley would feel comfortable with a visit from Miss Gina but she thought it best not to say so.

A week later everything was in place. Gina had found a room she could rent for a few coppers twice a week and she'd visited Lil to tell her what she was planning and taken her a pot of jam and a large loaf of bread and some milk for the children.

'If you know any other women with children in the same circumstances as you I'll try and bring enough soup for them, too.'

'We're all in the same boat, miss. All of us whose husbands have enlisted,' Lil told her gloomily.

'Well, I'll try and bring enough to feed the children, anyway,' Gina promised, although she was slightly worried she might have spoken rather rashly.

She was still feeling anxious as she drove into the town a few days later with Polly by her side and the large pan of soup that Susan Catchpole had made strapped into the boot.

Polly didn't share her anxiety; travelling in a motor car was a new experience for her and she revelled in it. Gina was driving extra carefully, anxious not to spill even a drop of the precious soup, so Polly, who seldom had the opportunity to come into the town, had plenty of opportunity to look around and she peered excitedly out of the car window, interested in everything she saw.

'Who are those men in light blue suits and red ties, all dressed the same, Miss Gina? They don't appear to be doing anything in particular, just walking about. Oh, look, there's one on crutches. Oh, poor man, he's only got one leg. And there's another with his arm in a sling. Do you know who they are, Miss Gina?' she asked, puzzled.

'Yes, I do, Polly. They're all soldiers who've been wounded in the war. They were brought back from Flanders to the military hospital and now they're convalescing so they're allowed into the town. When they're fit enough they'll be sent back again.'

'Oh, that's dreadful.' Polly was silent. This was an aspect of war that hadn't occurred to her. She'd seen the posters with Lord Kitchener telling men their country needed them and she'd seen the cheerful ranks of men with their little cardboard suitcases going off to be issued with their uniforms. Even seeing the soldiers – probably some of those same men – drilling down at the camp on the lower meadow at Meadowlands hadn't prepared her for the grim reality of war – that not only did men die, but that some would sustain terrible injuries that would be with them for the rest of their lives. 'Surely they won't send back that man who's lost a leg.'

'No, he'll be invalided out.'

'What does that mean?'

'He'll have to leave the army.'

'You mean they'll turn him out?'

'That's what it amounts to, yes. Ah, here we are.' Expertly, Gina turned the little car down a side street but she couldn't get far because of the crowd of pale, shabby women blocking the road, their equally shabby offspring clinging to their skirts. 'What on earth's going on here?' she said, frowning and sounding the car horn.

Suddenly, Lil pushed her way forward. 'I'm really sorry, miss,' she said anxiously. 'I only told my neighbour you was coming, I swear I never told nobody else. But word got round there'd be soup for the littl'uns. I couldn't stop 'em coming.' She was wringing her hands, fearful she had jeopardized her own children's chance of food.

'No, of course you couldn't. No mother wants to see her children hungry.' Gina smiled at her reassuringly. 'I just hope I've brought enough soup so they can all have some. But I can't do anything for anybody until I can get to the room I've rented.' She raised her voice. 'Could you let me pass, please, so I can get to the door?'

They still crowded round, those at the front reluctant to lose their place and those further back afraid of being left out.

'There'll be no soup for anybody if you don't let me through.'

Like the parting of the Red Sea the crowd immediately stood back to let the car through.

Five minutes later Gina had managed to persuade them all into some kind of ragged queue, children at the front, older siblings looking after their little brothers and sisters, while Polly began to ladle out the nourishing vegetable soup her mother had made. Soon the children – hundreds of them, it seemed to Polly, although in fact there were about thirty – were guzzling soup out of any kind of container their mothers had been able to lay their hands on: chipped china cups, equally chipped enamel mugs, basins, jugs, one child even had a teapot with half the spout missing, the older ones making sure the little ones didn't miss out. Not until they had all had their share – one ladle-full and half a slice of bread from the loaves Susan Catchpole had made that morning – did the mothers come forward, and even then, by mutual consent, those who were pregnant or with babies at the breast were given priority. In the end there was just enough for everyone, although the last four women had very small helpings and the bread had long gone.

'Next time we must try to bring milk, too,' Gina said to Polly as they cleared up and put the things back in the car. 'I wish I'd—' She stopped as she felt a tugging at her sleeve.

A young woman who had been pretty once was standing beside her, a baby in her arms and two small children holding on to her skirts. The little ones were still licking the last of the soup from their cups and the baby was lying apathetically in his mother's arms.

'I'm sorry to trouble you, miss, but could you do suthin' for me?'

'I will if I can,' Gina said, making sure to smile at her, but puzzled as to what she could possibly want and secretly worried that she might have landed herself more deeply into the situation than she had intended. 'What is it you'd like me to do?'

'Could you write to the 'thorities for me?' the woman asked. 'Y'see, I ain't much of a one with pen and paper meself, but I'm at me wits' end to know what else to do.' She rocked the baby in her arms as she spoke. 'I've tried to talk to people but nobody seems to want to listen.'

'Come back inside and talk to me. I'll listen, but I don't know if I'll be able to help,' Gina said, leading the way.

The woman's story, told in a rambling, garbled manner, with frequent pauses to wipe her eyes on her apron, was the same as Gina was to hear repeated many times over the next weeks. Her name was Mrs Hunter and she had never received the separation allowance she was entitled to when her husband joined the army, which was a paltry one shilling and a penny a day for herself and twopence for each of the children.

'Thass one and sevenpence a day I should be hevin',' she said. She frowned, concentrating. 'That would be ten shilluns and elevenpence a week, by my reckoning. Is that right?'

Gina nodded.

'That'd pay the rent and leave some over for food. Least, it would if I'd ever got it. But I ain't had a penny piece. And I was s'posed to get a 'llowance from my Alf, too. He said he'd allycate half his pay to me, but he ain't never bin given the form he's got to fill in before it can be stopped from his pay. He's worried sick because I ain't getting the money, he's afeared I think he ain't bothering about me but I know he's a good man and it ain't his fault.' She sniffed. 'Would you write and tell them and ask what's happened to the money, miss?'

Gina nodded. 'I'll certainly see what I can find out,' she promised. 'What did you say your name was?'

'Mary. Mary Hunter.' Her chin lifted with pride. 'My husband used to be a cobbler before he enlisted. He made a good living and we was thinking of moving to a better area. We'd even saved a bit, too.' Her chin sank and she gave a sigh. 'Good job we did; that money's all I've had to live on since Alf went away. But it's all gone now and the rent's behind. I used to work at the clothing factory but Alf said I should stop when the children came along, and I couldn't go back now, not with Sidney here being so sickly.' She indicated the baby, who was beginning to grizzle.

Saddened by what she had heard and promising again to do what she could to help, Gina locked up the rented room and went back to the car where Polly was waiting. On the way home, neither of the women spoke, each preoccupied with what they had seen and heard.

When they arrived back at the house, Polly went straight upstairs to put on her uniform and take up her domestic duties again and Gina went to her room, calling in at her mother's sitting room on the way to tell Lady Adelaide she was back.

'Ah, Gina, do come in and meet my guest,' her mother said in the tinkling voice she reserved for people she wanted to impress.

Gina frowned. She felt tired and a bit grubby and her mind was still reeling from the deprivations she had witnessed. What she wanted most was to wallow in a hot bath and change her clothes, not to sit and be polite to one of her mother's affluent friends, who had nothing better to do than sit and drink tea and talk inanities. She couldn't even see who it was because the guest was sitting on a settee overlooking the garden with her back to the door. On the other hand, the thought of a cup of tea – she could see the tray on the little table in front of her mother laden with the silver tea set and best china – was very enticing.

But to her surprise, as she advanced into the room a tall figure in the uniform of an army officer stood to greet her.

'This is my daughter Georgina, Major Palgrave,' Lady Adelaide said with a little simper. She clearly expected the major to gallantly express surprise at such a youthful-looking lady having a grown-up daughter.

He didn't.

He advanced towards Gina and held out his hand. 'Andrew Palgrave.' He inclined his head. 'I'm very pleased to meet you, Miss Barsham.'

Gina managed to hide her surprise and said what she hoped was the right thing, then, fearful that this man had come with bad news about James or Ned, blurted out, 'Are you here with news of my brothers, Major Palgrave?'

He smiled and she noted that he had a very attractive smile and warm grey eyes.

'Oh, no, indeed not. I promise I'm not the bearer of bad tidings.'

'Thank goodness for that.' She sat down on the nearest chair and accepted the cup of tea her mother had poured.

He resumed his seat, explaining, 'No, I've come to apologize for the behaviour of the men under my command. They had been told that all the land beyond the lower meadow was out of bounds so they should never have been in the wood at all.'

'Ah, you're thinking about the young deer that was killed the other day,' Gina said. 'Yes, I heard about that.'

'You didn't tell me,' her mother said sharply. 'I knew nothing about it.'

'It's not something you would normally concern yourself with, Mother,' Gina said without looking at her.

'Then I apologize for speaking to you about it, Lady Adelaide,' the major said. He turned back to Gina and explained, 'In truth I hadn't realized that Sir George wouldn't be here. I came to pay him a courtesy call after your estate manager visited the camp complaining of my men's behaviour. I wanted to assure him that such . . .' He hesitated, searching for a word that wouldn't offend her sensibilities and not finding one, then went on: 'Such behaviour would not happen again. Naturally, when I learned that he wasn't at home I would have left, but the young footman insisted I should see Her Ladyship instead and she graciously offered me tea.' He smiled and nodded his gratitude in her direction. 'However, this particular unit will be moving in a day or two so there should be no more trouble.'

'Where are they going?' Gina asked. 'Or aren't you allowed to say?'

'They're being sent to Ypres.'

'Oh, how brave.' Lady Adelaide laid her hand theatrically over her heart.

'It's not a matter of bravery. They don't have any choice in the matter,' Major Palgrave said bluntly.

'Are you going, too?' Gina asked. She realized she would quite like to get to know this young man better.

He nodded. ''Fraid so.'

'Then perhaps you would do us the kindness of having dinner with us tonight,' Lady Adelaide said quickly.

'I'm sure Major Palgrave has far better things to do than have dinner with you and me, Mother,' Gina said. She was becoming irritated by her mother's rather flirtatious attitude to this young man who was almost half her age.

'Indeed, no. I should be delighted to come,' he replied politely.

'That's settled, then. Shall we say eight o'clock?'

Later, after a long, relaxing bath, Gina was sitting at her dressing table unsuccessfully trying to persuade her hair to stay up in its loose knot on the top of her head, when Polly came in after a brief knock.

'Shall I do that for you, Miss Gina?' she asked. And without waiting for an answer she came over and expertly twisted and pinned it firmly in place.

'Thank you, Polly,' Gina said. 'I wasn't going to bother you tonight. I knew you'd be worn out after today's venture – I'm sure I was – and I'm sure you've had more than enough to do downstairs, since we've got a guest for dinner tonight.'

'Yes, Mrs Bellman's not very happy about that. She doesn't like extra people being sprung on her at the last minute.'

'I expect she'll cope. She always does.' She smiled up at Polly. 'Thanks. I can manage for myself now. Oh, do you think the pale blue or the apricot? The blue has sleeves so perhaps it's a little less formal . . .'

'Yes, I think the blue would be very suitable. Shall I fetch it for you?'

'No, I can manage, thank you. You'd better go and placate Mrs Bellman. We don't want the potatoes burnt.'

'I'll do that later. I've got to see to Her Ladyship first,' Polly said.

Later, as she went down the stairs in her second-best pale blue evening gown, Gina noticed as she glanced at her hand on the banister that she had forgotten to replace her engagement ring, which she had removed as looking a little ostentatious before going on what she was beginning to call in her mind 'the soup run' earlier in the day.

Lady Adelaide had anticipated a quiet evening with Major Palgrave – hoping Gina might be tired after her day of do-gooding and prefer a tray in her room. With Polly's assistance she dressed in one of her favourite gowns, the rose-coloured one which, although requiring firm and slightly uncomfortable corsetry, made her waist look smaller and pushed up her bust in what she considered to be a youthful way. She hadn't yet caught up with the latest fashion of slightly less figure-hugging styles. Garnet earrings and necklace set the dress off quite nicely. Studying her reflection in the mirror she was not displeased by what she saw.

But disappointment mingled with annoyance in equal measure when she made her entrance and saw that Gina was already there and talking quite animatedly to Major Palgrave.

Dinner went off smoothly and Lady Adelaide accepted Major Palgrave's compliments on the meal graciously, although she'd had absolutely nothing to do with its preparation, nor in fact with the choice of menu, since Mrs Bellman had declared, 'If I'm supposed to provide a special four-course meal I need more than a couple of hours' notice. I'll just have to stretch the beef into beef wellington and add a bit more stock to the soup. I've already made the lemon sponge so they'll just have smaller helpings and there's plenty of cheese and fruit so they'll not starve.'

Her Ladyship found it more than a little irritating that Gina kept monopolizing the conversation. Even though she herself constantly tried to steer the conversation on to topics that she thought interesting, somehow it always ended up in a sometimes quite animated discussion between Gina and the major on a different subject altogether. She rang for coffee rather more forcefully than was strictly necessary and they moved to the drawing room.

Albert was just pouring the coffee when the door opened and Sir George walked in.

'Oh, we weren't expecting you, my dear, or we would have waited dinner,' Lady Adelaide lied as he gave her a brief peck on the cheek. 'I'll ring for Mrs Bellman to rustle up something for you.'

'No need. I ate on the train.' He turned to Albert. 'But bring another cup, Albert, I could do with more coffee.'

After being introduced to Major Palgrave he sat down and accepted his coffee.

Lady Adelaide then began a rambling tale about deer and the reason for the major's visit as if she knew all about it, till Gina managed to get a word in and assure her father that Will Catchpole had dealt with the matter in his usual efficient manner.

'My visit was simply a courtesy call to apologize for my men's transgressions and Her Ladyship was kind enough to invite me to dinner,' the major finished.

'Glad to hear it.' Sir George passed a hand over his brow and nodded absently.

'George, are you ill? I don't believe you've heard a word we've been saying,' Lady Adelaide said sharply.

He looked up. 'No, I don't believe I have. I'm sorry.' He glanced up. 'You obviously haven't heard the terrible news. The *Lusitania*'s been sunk. She was torpedoed by the Germans off the coast of Ireland early this afternoon. It was in the stop press of the late edition of the evening paper.'

'Are you quite sure, George?' Lady Adelaide asked, as if there could be any doubt. 'You can't mean the big Cunard liner. You must be mistaken.'

'I do indeed mean the big Cunard liner, Adelaide,' Sir George said tetchily. 'It's hardly something I would make up.' He shook his head, as if he could hardly believe it himself. 'Imagine, a ship of that size. She was carrying nearly two thousand people on board and she went down in less than twenty minutes. They fear that some fourteen hundred people have been drowned, but of course they can't be sure of the figures yet.'

'We know German submarines patrol the coast looking for merchant ships, to try and cut off our supplies, so no doubt one would have been tracking her,' the major said. 'But not to sink her! I thought there was an agreement that passenger liners wouldn't be attacked.'

'They say all's fair in love and war,' Sir George said wearily. 'But this is beyond belief. There were apparently over a hundred American citizens on board, which I suppose is hardly surprising since the ship had come from New York. The enemy must have known this, so why . . .?' He shook his head.

'Maybe this will alter the president's neutrality policy,' the major said thoughtfully.

'That remains to be seen.' Sir George held out his cup for more coffee, obviously shaken by the news he had just imparted. The major drained the last of his and got to his feet.

'I think, under the circumstances, I should take my leave,' he said. 'Thank you for your hospitality, Your Ladyship.' He turned to Gina. 'And you, Miss Gina. I hope we may meet again under happier circumstances.'

He left and Sir George left with him to go to his study.

Huffily, Lady Adelaide got to her feet. 'I think I shall retire. The news has quite upset me, and quite spoilt the evening,' she said.

Gina watched her go. Sometimes, her mother could be quite insensitive and she obviously thought Major Palgrave ought to have been more interested in her chatter than having a conversation with Gina. Gina smiled to herself. She had really enjoyed talking to Andrew Palgrave and would enjoy meeting him again if the opportunity arose. She went to twist the engagement ring on her finger, a habit she had acquired since Archie had placed the large sapphire there nine months ago, only to remember that she had forgotten to replace it after the soup run. Forgotten? Or had it been unconsciously deliberate?

Six

When Sir George was at home Reg Walford, the butler, made it his business to iron the morning papers before they were taken to him in his study. Doing this made sure that he was the first to read any interesting items and if they were suitable pass them on to the rest of the staff at breakfast. If Sir George was in London, Walford didn't bother with the iron, assuming, quite rightly, that Lady Adelaide never picked up a newspaper and it was beneath his dignity to iron newspapers for anyone else. He simply read them and left them on the hall table.

On the day following the loss of the huge ocean liner *Lusitania* there was much to impart – in fact Mr Walford had been so engrossed in reading all the details that he had scorched the edge of the newspaper with the iron and had had to cut it off before taking it to the study for his employer to peruse.

'Very grave news in *The Times* today,' he said as he took his seat at the head of the kitchen table, which was always covered for meals with a clean, blue-checked tablecloth with matching napkins, and accepted a cup of tea from Mrs Bellman, seated behind the big enamel teapot on his right.

'You mean about the *Lusitania* being torpedoed by a German submarine, Mr Walford?' Albert said, unable to attack his boiled egg until the butler was seated and now doing so with relish.

'Where did you hear about it?' Mr Walford was clearly put out at not being the first with the news.

'The army gentleman, Major somebody-or-other, who was here last evening, told me about it when I handed him his cap as he left. Dreadful tragedy, by all accounts. I couldn't sleep for thinking about it.'

'Indeed, it is a dreadful tragedy,' Mr Walford agreed. He elaborated: 'There were nearly two thousand people on board, apparently, but less than six hundred of them survived.'

'Oh, what terrible loss of life, Mr Walford,' Mrs Bellman said, shocked. 'All those people drowned.'

'Indeed it was. There were some very prominent people on board, too, according to the newspaper – over a hundred of them Americans, including Alfred Vanderbilt, the millionaire yachtsman, and also some close friends of President Woodrow Wilson,' Mr Walford said. 'But it doesn't say who they were.'

'My uncle's on the *Lusitania*.' Hetty spoke for the first time. She blushed as she realized that for once she had the attention of everyone at the table. 'At least I think it's the *Lusitania*,' she added uncomfortably. 'Or it might be the other one . . .'

'The *Mauritania*,' Albert prompted. 'That's the sister ship to the *Lusitania*.'

'*Mauritania*. That's it.' Her brow furrowed as she tried to think. Then she shrugged. 'Well, it's one or the other, I can't remember which. Anyway, he's a stoker. We was ever so proud to think he was on board such a luxury ship and he said what it was like on board – he got to sneak a look before the passengers arrived. He said it was like a palace and ever so big.' She paused. 'I think it might be the *Mauritania* he's on.'

'Let's hope it is,' Mrs Bellman said. 'He wouldn't have stood much chance if it was the other one.'

'He certainly wouldn't,' Mr Walford agreed. 'The ship sank in less than twenty minutes, by all accounts, which was why there were so few survivors.'

'Do you think the Americans will join the war now, Mr Walford?' Polly asked. 'You said a lot of Americans had drowned.'

'I wouldn't be surprised. I believe there had been an agreement that passenger ships wouldn't be attacked, but since the Germans blatantly disregarded this, and with so many important Americans on board . . . but we'll just have to wait and see.' Mr Walford looked at his watch and got to his feet. 'That's enough speculation, there's work to be done. Albert, collect up the silver and take it to the butler's pantry.'

Albert groaned as he got up from his chair. He hated cleaning the silver.

Gina was just finishing her breakfast as her father came into the dining room.

'Oh, has everyone else finished?' he asked, surprised.

'There isn't anyone else these days, Father. Only Mother and me and you know she usually has her breakfast in bed.'

'Hm. Yes, of course. Ugh. This scrambled egg is cold,' he complained as he helped himself from the dishes on the sideboard.

'It's been there for over an hour, Father. Even the hot plate won't keep it hot for that long.'

'No, I suppose not. I've been reading the newspapers and lost track of time. Dreadful business, the *Lusitania*, dreadful business. Can't get it out of my mind.' Nevertheless, he didn't let it affect his appetite and managed to eat his cold scrambled egg with relish before going on to several slices of toast and marmalade.

Gina waited until he had finished, then poured him a second cup of coffee before saying, 'As I don't often get the chance to speak to you privately, Father, could I ask your advice on something that's troubling me?'

'Oh, yes? And what might that be, my dear?' Ready to don the mantle of paternal concern he regarded her benignly over the gold-rimmed spectacles he had forgotten to remove before coming to the dining room,

Gina launched into a passionate resumé of her experiences at the soup kitchen and the dire problems of Mary Hunter and hundreds of women like her.

'So I promised Mrs Hunter I would do what I could to help,' she finished, 'but I really don't know where to start, or who to write to. What would you advise, Father?'

'I'd advise you not to worry your pretty little head about it,' he said firmly, words above all others to set Gina's teeth on edge.

She removed her hand from where it lay on the table before he could lean over and pat it and, holding her temper with difficulty, said coldly, 'My "pretty little head", as you so patronizingly call it, is neither here nor there, Father; I do worry about it and I'm determined to do what I can for those helpless women.'

'Believe me, you could be stirring up a hornets' nest if you go interfering with the wheels of bureaucracy, Gina,' he warned. 'You must let those who know what they're doing get on with it. You won't be popular if you start complaining about the way things are run.'

'But they're not *being* run. They *don't* know what they're doing! They take men away from their families without any thought of how they'll manage with no breadwinner. Meantime children are starving!' Gina was horrified at her father's callous attitude.

He didn't answer but patted his moustache with his napkin and laid it on the table, then pulled his gold hunter out of his waistcoat pocket and looked at it as he stood up. 'Goodness, I'm late. I must get back to my study. I've got some papers to look through before I return to London.' As he passed her chair he gave her shoulder a little squeeze. 'I'm sure you and your friends are doing sterling work with your little soup kitchen. Keep up the good work.'

With that he left the room, humming a little to himself, little knowing how close his daughter had come to throwing the coffee pot after him.

Undaunted, one afternoon a week later Gina went to the public library in the town to see if she could get any help with people she might contact. Having had no luck, and preoccupied with her lack of success, she left with an armful of books for both her mother and herself, missed the bottom step coming out of the library and careered straight into a passing army officer, dropping the books on the pavement.

After he had steadied her and as he was helping her to stow the books safely in the basket she had brought with her for the purpose, Gina said with a rueful laugh, 'That'll teach me to put the books away before I leave the counter instead of trying to do it as I go along. I really am most awfully sorry. I hope I didn't hurt you when I barged into you like that.' She glanced up at him, then sat back on her heels and looked again. 'Goodness! Major Palgrave! I didn't realize it was you! Well, at least I didn't barge into a total stranger.'

He grinned down at her. 'I wondered how long it would take you to realize it was at my feet you'd fallen, so to speak. Are you hurt, Miss Barsham?'

'Only my pride at being such an idiot,' she answered cheerfully as he helped her to her feet.

'But I'm sure you must at least be shaken up,' he insisted.

She dusted down her dress. 'No, I'm perfectly all right, I assure you.'

'In a desperate hurry, then, Miss Barsham?' the major persisted.

Gina laughed. 'No, I'm not in any particular hurry, I was just being careless in not looking where I was going. Why do you ask?'

'Because I'm desperately trying to find an excuse to ask you to have tea with me,' he said, slightly embarrassed. 'Jacklins is just up the road and I'm told they do a very nice line in toasted teacakes.'

'Then I think the very least I can do is accept your kind offer, Major Palgrave, since if you hadn't been passing at such an opportune moment I should very likely have measured my length on the pavement,' she said with a smile. She put her head on one side. 'Perhaps, should anyone ask, I do feel slightly shaken,' she admitted conspiratorially, her smile widening.

'Then may I offer you my arm?'

'I think better not. I don't think I can admit to feeling that shaken.' She laughed again and fell into step beside him.

They conversed easily, like old friends, as they made their way to the tea shop, a rather smart affair with crisp white damask tablecloths and napkins and discreet silverware. By the time their order arrived they were on Christian-name terms.

'My goodness, Andrew, these look delicious,' Gina said, drawing off her gloves. She picked up the teapot. 'Shall I be mother, as they say, and pour the tea?'

'Yes. Please do.' He nodded, smiling, then his expression changed. 'Gina, you didn't tell me . . . I didn't realize . . .'

She looked up, puzzled, then realized his eyes were on her left hand. She followed his gaze and saw the engagement ring glittering on her finger.

'Oh, I'm sorry, Andrew. Didn't you know?' she said.

He shook his head. 'How could I? You weren't wearing it the other night. I particularly noticed.'

'Wasn't I?' She frowned. 'Oh, no, that's right, I'd forgotten to put it back after doing the soup run.'

'I would hope any fiancée of mine wouldn't forget to wear the ring I had given her,' he said dryly.

'It was an oversight,' she explained, blushing as she realized that it made the matter even worse. She ploughed on. 'Archie is in the Royal Navy. He's just been promoted to sub-lieutenant on board HMS *Invincible*. I'm very proud of him.'

'And madly in love with him?' he asked, quirking an eyebrow.

She hesitated. 'I'm very fond of him. I've known him since his younger brother was at school with my brothers. My sister Millie and I used to go over to their house with the twins and play tennis in the school holidays and Archie always managed to be there.'

'So you couldn't exactly call it love at first sight?'

'Not really. I seem to remember the first time I met him his young brother was trying to put a frog down my back.' She chuckled. 'And I went to hit him with my brother's cricket bat, missed and caught Archie instead. He was very good about it considering I caught him quite a whack on the side of his head.' She sighed. 'Archie's very long-suffering. It's just that there's so much going on at the moment now that I've started the little soup kitchen that I don't have much time to think about him.' With something of a shock she realized that this was true.

'I can't imagine I would ever stop thinking about a girl I was in love with, whatever I was doing,' he said thoughtfully. 'She would always be on my mind, always be part of me.'

'Would? I take it you don't have someone special waiting at home for you?'

He shook his head. 'I'm never in one place long enough. I've been too busy forging my career in the army.' He was quiet for a minute, then, 'Do you believe in love at first sight, Gina?' He smiled at her, a quirky little smile.

She stirred her tea, carefully not looking at him. 'I'm not sure. I suppose it's possible . . .' She looked up. 'What about you, Andrew? Do you?'

He nodded and again smiled the quirky little smile. 'Yes, I think perhaps I do. But I guess I'm just a sentimental fool. Tell me about this soup kitchen; it sounds intriguing.'

He listened, watching her intently and, feeling on safer ground now, Gina told him all about the women and children she was trying to help. By the time she had finished the butter had congealed on the teacakes and the tea was cold.

He called the waitress and asked for fresh tea, at the same time keeping his eyes on her as she told him of her father's lack of interest in her project. 'He told me not to bother my "pretty little head" about it,' she said in disgust. 'I nearly threw the coffee pot at him.'

'I can imagine.' He smiled at her. 'Did you know your eyes go a deeper blue when you're animated? You've got beautiful eyes, Gina.'

She blushed. 'Thank you. What a really nice thing to say. And there's me thinking you've been hanging on to every word I've spoken,' she added lightly.

'Oh, but I have. Every single word.' He still didn't take his eyes off her face. 'In fact, I believe I might be able to help. I'll give you a couple of addresses I think might be useful: there's the Soldiers' and Sailors' Families Association, and also the National Relief Fund. They are supposed to help families in distress.' He scribbled the addresses down on the back of an envelope he had in his pocket. 'There you are. Now may I ask a favour of you? Will you write to me and tell me how successful you are in getting help?'

She laughed. 'But you're only on our lower meadow. Why do you want me to write?'

'Because I'm not going to be there for much longer. My battalion is being posted to France next week.'

'Oh.' She felt a sudden sharp stab of disappointment. 'Well, of course I'll write, Andrew, if you'd like me to.'

'I would, Gina. Very much.' He scribbled another address down. 'This should find me.'

In bed that night Gina went over the conversation with Andrew. They had talked easily about every subject under the sun, agreeing and disagreeing good-humouredly, for far longer than it took to consume tea and teacakes. They had even talked on the dangerous subject of love at first sight, which she had never believed in. But, heaven help her, she did now. And she had more than a fleeting suspicion that Andrew Palgrave did, too.

But it was too late. She was going to marry Archie – dear, dependable Archie – who was at this moment out on the high seas risking his life. Andrew Palgrave knew this and would forget her soon enough. If only she hadn't agreed to write to him. That had been a mistake. Yet she couldn't bring herself to regret it.

Seven

The weeks passed. Andrew Palgrave and his troops left and more soldiers arrived on lower meadow, staying for an equally brief sojourn before they too were thrown into battle to replace those who had gone before. The war raged relentlessly on.

Gina wrote to every government official who might have the remotest ability to help her cause and also to the addresses Andrew had given her. Whilst waiting for replies, which were a long time coming – if the letters were acknowledged at all – she continued doing what she could for the poor unfortunate women and children who were in such desperate need. But, as she was the first to admit, she didn't work alone. Polly was always by her side; she was the one who doled out soup and kept the stronger and more aggressive children at bay so that the smaller and weaker ones got their share. Because they all loved Susan Catchpole's soup.

For her part Susan was thoroughly enjoying using her culinary skills making tasty soup by the gallon. When she had raided her husband's vegetable patch as much as he would allow she went to Jacob, Head Gardener at Meadowlands, and begged more from the kitchen gardens there, which were always overstocked. With bones provided by the butcher and now and again the odd rabbit that Will had snared, Susan's soup was both filling and nourishing and the children began to look slightly less starved as the weeks went on.

But although Susan refused payment for her soup, Gina realized that the little ones needed milk, and this had to be paid for. She funded it out of her own pocket for several weeks but she knew this couldn't go on. Then she had the bright idea of inviting all her friends and acquaintances for afternoon tea.

It was a beautiful sunny afternoon and she arranged for tea to be on the lawn. Then, as the elegant and well-dressed ladies were busily tucking into scones and fresh cream, strawberries and chocolate éclairs, she began to tell them about the conditions and deprivations of the people she was trying to help. Even as she talked several people reached for their purses and she had no trouble in getting them to part with money so that she could continue to buy badly needed milk for the children and nursing mothers. There were, of course, exceptions. One elderly dowager, the mother of one of Gina's friends, declared that any deprivations these people suffered were self-inflicted, the result of drinking and loose morals. Gina, keeping her temper with difficulty, asked the old lady if she would like to accompany her on her next visit to Trinity Row and see for herself the conditions, but at that point the old lady was forced to rummage in her reticule for her smelling bottle, saying the sun was too hot, making her feel faint, and made no answer to Gina's suggestion.

Meantime, what had begun as a desperate effort on the part of Gina and Polly to try to save a few families from starvation was gradually turning into something of a social club, a place where the women and children from Trinity Row − and further afield as the news spread − could congregate for a cup of soup and a cup of tea and increasingly, as time went on, for help and advice.

Sometimes Gina was asked to read letters by poor women embarrassed to admit they couldn't read but desperate to know how their husbands were faring. It was often not easy to decipher the scrawl of these men, who were often almost as illiterate as their wives, but she did her best, and wrote replies from these wives, the replies dictated in little more than a shame-faced whisper. Understanding their embarrassment Gina brought along a folding screen that had been relegated to the attic back at home to offer a little privacy. From then on she was kept busy most of the time either reading or writing letters whilst Polly ladled out soup for the children and poured tea for the women and afterwards organized little games for the children to play so that their mothers could sit quietly nursing the smallest ones and talking over their troubles and exchanging what news they could glean about their menfolk, glad that at least they were all in the same Pals Unit.

When at last the money they were owed began to trickle through – although not fast enough and not nearly as much as they were entitled to – the women were almost pathetically grateful to Gina and insisted that it must have been her influence that had done it. Those that were able even insisted on paying a ha'penny for their tea, so anxious were they to ensure that the little soup club continued.

Millie came home on leave in July. She had lost weight and looked fit and healthy although her hair was still its usual untidy frizz.

'Oh, Gina, I don't have time for fancy hair-dos,' she laughed as they went in to luncheon and Gina teasingly remarked on it looking more like a bird's nest than a hair style. 'I'm far too busy. In any case, my hair has to be crammed under my cap out of the way, so nobody sees it. Not that anybody will care when I get to France.'

'France? When are you going to France?' Lady Adelaide perked up at the word France as she shook out her table napkin and spread it carefully over her third-best maroon grosgrain dress.

'Next month, probably. Didn't I tell you, Mother? They're getting short of wagon drivers to take the wounded to the field hospitals, so I volunteered.'

'I'm surprised they accepted you. Surely that's no job for a lady,' Lady Adelaide said, horrified.

'It is if there aren't enough men to do it,' Millie said, tucking into lamb stew with relish. 'Mm, this stew is lovely. We don't get food like this at the hospital.' She turned to Gina, anxious not to give her mother the opportunity to question why there weren't enough men. Sometimes, as she well knew, Lady Adelaide could be very obtuse.

After luncheon Gina and Millie took a walk in the grounds. Gina tucked her hand through her sister's arm. 'Oh, Mill, I do miss you. Ma can be very hard work at times.'

'I know she can. I miss you too, Gee, and I'm sorry I've had to leave you to cope with her. But I really enjoy what I'm doing in the hospital. I feel as if it's worthwhile. And some of the poor buggers who get sent home wounded . . .' She gave a deep sigh. 'Do you know, Gee, there are times when I look at some of those poor mutilated sods and wonder if they wouldn't have been better off if they'd been killed outright.'

'Millie! That's a dreadful thing to say!' Gina said, shocked.

'I know it is. But you haven't seen them, Gina.' Millie quickened her step and changed the subject. 'It's a lovely day,' she said brightly. 'Let's walk to the lake before we go back to the house and you can tell me what you've been doing while I've been away. This soup club you've talked about in your letters. It sounds intriguing and well worth doing.'

It took the whole of the walk to the lake and then back to the house for Gina to explain what she and Polly had set up.

'The letters I've written to various authorities seem to be bearing fruit at last, at least some of them do,' she finished. 'The women are beginning to get their allowances as army wives, which is a shilling and a penny a day for the wives and tuppence a day for each child, which isn't a lot, but at least it means they can pay their rent and don't risk losing the roof over their heads, so that's one worry gone. But they should get more. They should get the extra money their husbands have allocated them from their pay, because the men have already had it deducted. But it doesn't always come through, which is a scandal.'

'No doubt you're writing strong letters to the Powers That Be over that,' Millie said, squeezing her sister's arm.

'Of course I am. It's only by badgering that you get things done, it seems to me.'

'I'd really like to come and see what you've been doing at this soup kitchen. When do you next go?'

'Well, I'm supposed to go tomorrow, but as you're only home for a few days and I don't want to waste a minute . . . Unless you'd like to come too?'

'Just what I was going to suggest.'

The next morning Millie squeezed into James' little car with

Polly and the vat of Susan's delicious-smelling soup and Gina drove to the room in Trinity Row that she was renting. The women and children were already there, waiting for the door to be unlocked, but when they saw Millie the mothers became agitated and anxious to keep their children quiet, clearly over-whelmed by the sight of another 'posh lady' and fearful that she had come to close their little club down.

Gina quickly reassured them and introduced her sister, telling them that she was a nurse on leave, shortly to be going to France. As for Millie, she soon put them at their ease, talking to them and asking about everything she saw. With pride they told her that they took it in turns to fetch kettles of water from the tap in the yard to boil for the tea and the washing up – and often to wash the grubbiest of the children too – pointing out with pride that there was actually a gas ring in the corner, a luxury few of them enjoyed in their own homes.

'Although,' one confided, 'Agnes don't like it. She's afeared it'll blow up and ketch us all alight. But she ain't all that bright,' the woman added matter-of-factly.

Later, Millie went round and talked to each woman individu-ally, listening to their problems and giving them advice where she could.

'Not that I could offer much more than common sense,' she said with a yawn as she reclined on Gina's bed later.

'Sometimes that's all that's needed,' Gina replied. 'Just someone to talk things over with.'

'Mm. Who was that young woman in the corner I was talking to? The one in the green dress. She looked a bit better dressed than some of the others and so did her children.'

'Oh, that's Maudie. She "goes with soldiers", I was informed in hushed tones. The others don't approve but they take it in turns to look after her children while she's "working", as they call it, because she pays them.'

'That raises a few interesting questions,' Millie said thoughtfully.

'What do you mean?'

'Well, they say they don't approve of what she's doing yet they're happy to share in what she earns. If they really didn't approve they wouldn't take her money.'

Gina nodded. 'Yes, I can see that. On the other hand, can you blame Maudie? It wasn't until she was on the point of being turned out of her house for being behind with her rent that she turned to prostitution. And the reason she was behind with her rent was that she wasn't getting any of the army pay she was owed. You could say she was driven to it.'

'Isn't she worried she could catch something unpleasant?'

'I mentioned that to her but she said she's careful. I don't know exactly what she meant by that and I thought it better not to ask.'

'You'll just have to keep an eye on her. If you're concerned, try and get her to see a doctor.' Millie sighed. 'It's a bugger, isn't it, when women have to resort to prostitution to feed their children simply because the government drag their feet in handing over what's due to them?'

Life seemed flat after Millie's leave was over, and Gina felt sad and rather lonely. She knew Archie was somewhere in the Atlantic on HMS *Invincible* but had no idea when she would see him and letters from him were few and far between, although full of assurances of his love when they did come. She sent equally loving letters back to him, although he seemed more and more a remote figure and she had to keep taking out the photograph he had given her, resplendent in his sub-lieutenant's uniform, before he left, to remind her of him, because for some strange reason it was Andrew Palgrave's face that sprang to her mind when she tried to think of Archie.

Towards the end of the summer Ned came home on leave. He looked grey and haggard and thinner than ever. For the first three days he did little but sleep and after that he took to walking for hours about the estate, avoiding company. By the time he went back he looked refreshed but had said little about his life. Gina was the only person he talked to at any length; his mother's constant questioning and inconsequential chattering got on his nerves and caused him to clam up.

'Is it very bad over there, Ned?' Gina asked one day when he accepted her offer to accompany him on his walk.

'Pretty grim,' he answered shortly.

'The men you work with, are they . . .?' She broke off, not knowing how to go on.

'Decent blokes? Oh yes, most of them anyway. The one I work

with all the time, a chap called Patrick, a corporal, is a really good bloke, always ready with a laugh. We get on well together.'

'Can't be much to laugh about,' Gina observed.

'They call it gallows humour. It helps us . . . well, it keeps us going.'

'Have you managed to catch up with James?'

'Not yet. But I hope to if his unit gets sent to France, which it probably will. Then if we can both get a forty-eight-hour pass we might be able to meet and catch up with each other's news. What about your Archie? Where is he now?'

'Somewhere in the Atlantic, I think. It's very hard to get news because obviously they don't want to let the Germans know where they are or what they're doing. It's worrying, though. If they could sink a huge ship like the *Lusitania*, a battle cruiser doesn't stand much chance, does it?'

'I wouldn't say that, Gee. Don't forget, a battle cruiser is armed so it can fight back.'

She tucked her hand into his arm and squeezed it. 'I know, but I still worry. Just as I worry about you and James.'

'I know you do.' He put his hand over hers as it lay on his arm. 'Your Archie's a lucky bloke, Gina, you know that?'

She squeezed his arm. 'And she'll be a lucky girl who marries you, Ned.'

'Oh, I don't think I'm very likely to blight some poor damsel's life by marrying her.'

'Don't be too sure. One of these days you might find—'

'I notice Will Catchpole's daughter is still with us,' he interrupted, cutting across her words. 'I always thought James had a bit of a thing for her. She's certainly a pretty girl, with all that auburn hair.'

'James? Did you really?' She digested this for a moment. 'Well, you'd know, of course, being his twin.'

'Not necessarily. We've never been that close that we share our every thought. It's just that I've noticed one or two things. Anyway, it must be nearly time for luncheon, and for once I'm starving.'

'So your leave has done you some good. I'm glad about that, Ned.' She squeezed his arm again. 'It's a pity you've got to go back so soon, though.' She laid her head against his arm. 'Keep safe, Ned,' she whispered. 'You must keep safe and come back when this dreadful war's over.'

'I promise,' he said, dropping a kiss on her forehead. He looked round at the rolling meadows and green trees. 'How could I not come back to this, Gee? It's the thought of it that keeps me going through the mud.'

After Ned had gone back, life seemed flat for Gina. She missed her brothers and sister more than she would have thought possible and prayed for their safety every day. She was anxious about Archie, too, somewhere out in the Atlantic. At least, she supposed that was where he was but she had no way of being sure because his letters were few and said little. She had briefly exchanged letters with Andrew Palgrave but it felt somehow disloyal to Archie to write to another man and gradually her infatuation – for that was what it was – died.

Then suddenly, it seemed, autumn arrived in a blaze of colour before the leaves fell, leaving the trees bare before freezing into winter. And still the war raged, with little gain on either side and far too much loss and mutilation of lives.

Christmas was spent quietly at Meadowlands. Sir George was at home, which didn't add much to the festivities because he found fault with practically everything Lady Adelaide said or did. On Christmas Day the family paid one of their rare duty visits to church, whilst back at Meadowlands elaborate preparations for Christmas luncheon were going on, even though there would only be three people at the table. That was, of course, unless Her Ladyship picked up any rich strays at church who were looking for a meal. As it happened, in her role as the Lady Bountiful she deigned to invite the churchwarden and his wife, who were quite well-heeled, but happy to defer their turkey until Boxing Day, and the curate, who was slightly down-at-heel and had been hoping for an invitation somewhere.

Mrs Bellman wasn't worried; she always over-catered so that there would still be plenty left for 'downstairs'.

Gina was relieved at how well luncheon went. Bernard Finch, the curate, was a surprisingly articulate young man and she enjoyed some very pleasant and quite heated exchanges with him. It was with mild astonishment that she realized how late it was when he left to visit one or two elderly and lonely people, the churchwarden and his wife having already gone home. Privately, she promised herself to go to church some time when he was preaching; she imagined his sermons could be quite interesting.

Downstairs, Mrs Bellman, Mr Walford, Polly, Albert and Hetty enjoyed their roast turkey and Christmas pudding a little later, but with no less relish than the family. After the Christmas crackers that Lady Adelaide had provided – she didn't believe in lavish presents for the servants – were pulled and the washing-up done, Polly and Hetty were given the rest of the day to themselves.

As Polly was putting her hat on, ready to go home and see her parents, Albert called, 'Come and have a look at this, Polly.'

Frowning, she went to where he was standing and was amazed when he took her in his arms and gave her a lingering kiss. She pushed him away. 'What do you think you're doing . . .?' Her voice trailed off as her eyes followed where he was pointing to the bunch of mistletoe over their heads. 'Oh, I really got caught there, didn't I?' she said with a giggle. She wagged her finger. 'But don't do it again, Albert Jones.'

He grinned. 'Only at Christmas. Now, where's Hetty? I want to catch her.'

'And don't forget Mrs Bellman – for goodness' sake don't leave her out,' Polly whispered in his ear. Then she pulled on her gloves and hurried out of the door, laughing.

Eight

Will and Susan Catchpole were waiting anxiously for Polly to arrive on Christmas afternoon. They knew that she couldn't leave the house until everything was cleared away and everywhere was spotlessly tidy after Christmas luncheon was finished; it wouldn't be fair to the other servants. But they still kept glancing at the clock, for in spite of going to chapel in the morning for the Christmas Day service and enjoying the capon Susan had roasted for their own midday meal, their celebrations didn't really begin until their only daughter arrived home.

It was four o'clock. Susan had the kettle on and Will had put chestnuts in the fire to roast when they heard the latch and Polly came in, bringing a blast of cold air with her.

After greeting her parents with Christmas kisses she went over to warm her hands at the fire before even taking off her coat. 'I could hear the soldiers at the camp singing Christmas carols as I walked over,' she said, giving a little shiver. 'I reckon they wish they were at home with their families instead of camped in those canvas tents on lower meadow. Especially if it starts to snow.'

'It won't snow,' Will said, in the slow, ponderous way he had of speaking, as he filled his pipe. 'Wind's in the wrong direction. Might rain, though.'

'Well, that's nearly as bad, under canvas,' Susan said. 'I wonder if we ought to have invited one or two of them to share Christmas with us,' she added thoughtfully. 'There was plenty of meat on that capon.'

'No, is the answer to that,' Will said firmly. 'For one thing, how would you choose who to invite? And for another, how would you know what sort of riff-raff you might be letting into the house? We don't know where they've come from.'

Susan clamped her lips tightly together. She knew better than to argue with her husband even if she didn't agree with him. Sometimes, though, she felt that Will's dogmatic approach to life, what he called his Christian principles, didn't accord with her ideas of what she called Christian charity, which she had learned at her mother's knee and not by listening to some ranting preacher a bit too fond of the sound of his own voice. Christmas and Easter were the only times Susan could be persuaded to accompany her husband to church and she felt no better for going. She felt no worse for staying away, either, although she didn't tell Will that.

Polly took off her coat and hat and hung them both on the hook behind the door. As it was Christmas a fire had been lit in the front parlour and they all went through, Susan carrying the teapot and Polly with the tea tray with cups and saucers and Christmas cake. Will followed behind with the chestnuts on a shovel, to be put in the parlour fire embers.

Polly gave a little shiver. 'Not quite so warm in here as it is in the kitchen,' she remarked in a masterpiece of understatement.

'No, but it's Christmas,' Susan said, as if that explained everything.

'Takes three days to get the chill off this room,' Will said as he settled himself in the tall red plush-covered armchair beside the fire.

'Oh, it's not as bad as that,' Susan admonished him, although she was careful to drape a shawl round her shoulders before she sat down opposite him in the smaller, matching armchair.

Polly made herself as comfortable as she could on the horsehair settee that, together with six dining chairs, all covered in red plush, completed the suite. Will had dragged it forward so that she would get some benefit from the fire but she had taken the precaution of putting on her thickest jumper and skirt, knowing what it would be like in the room where a fire was lit only about twice a year.

As they drank tea they exchanged their Christmas gifts; Polly had saved up and bought her mother a new apron and her father an ounce of his favourite tobacco; Susan had knitted Polly a warm scarf and mittens to match and Will had carved her a squirrel out of wood; it was sitting up on a log and holding a nut between its paws and he had polished it and painted the nut a darker brown. When they had all expressed delight at their respective presents Polly produced another parcel from her carpet bag.

'This is a special present from Miss Gina, Mum,' she said proudly, handing it to her mother. 'She says it's to thank you for all the delicious soup you've been making. They all love your soup, you know, Mum, 'specially the children.'

'Well, it's little enough to do for the poor mites,' Susan said with a shrug. 'I can't bear to think of little ones going hungry.' As she spoke she unwrapped the parcel Polly had placed in her hands very carefully and took out a pair of china ornaments.

'Oh, my goodness! Just look at these!' she said, flushing with delighted surprise. 'Oh, Miss Gina shouldn't have . . . There was no need . . . How did she know I've always wanted a pair of Staffordshire dogs?'

'Reckon a little bird told her, don't you, Mum?' Polly grinned. 'She said she wanted to give you something since you wouldn't let her pay you, so she's given you a present instead. She said to tell you that she couldn't have done what she's done for those poor women and children without your help.'

'Oh, that's rubbish,' Susan said over her shoulder as she stood up to place the two black and white china dogs at each end of the mantelpiece, which was already overburdened with small china fairings and the large, imitation marble clock that was always twenty minutes fast. But Polly could see how pleased she was because she couldn't stop smiling.

They spent a happy evening together, drinking tea, eating large slices of the Christmas cake Susan had made and eating the roasted chestnuts Will had gathered in October and kept for the occasion.

'There's not as much fruit in the cake as I'd have liked,' Susan apologised. 'I've been saving it up, because it's hard to get hold of these days.'

'Well, there's a war on,' Will said, holding out his plate for more.

'Tastes all right to me, Mum,' Polly said, gathering up the last of the crumbs on her plate. 'I can taste you didn't stint with the brandy.'

'I thought I could spare a drop or two from the bottle we keep in case there's illness in the house,' Susan said with a wink. 'Seein' as it's Christmas.'

'Yes, and seein' as it's Christmas, how about a game of dominos?' Will said, getting to his feet and fetching them. Will loved a game of dominos.

Reluctantly, the two women left the warmth of the fire and went to the table.

'I wonder how Mr Ned and Mr James are spending Christmas,' Polly said thoughtfully when it wasn't her turn to play. 'And Tom, of course, but he'll be all right; he'll be looking after Mr James, as he's his batman.'

'Do you reckon the twins will manage to meet up for Christmas?' Susan asked, following her train of thought.

Polly shrugged. 'I don't know. I don't think the family hear from either of them very often. From what I can make out it's quite difficult to get letters through. Last I heard they were in different places.' She tried not to sound too concerned, although in truth every morning she surreptitiously checked the post to see if James' distinctive handwriting was there. If it was she shamelessly listened when Lady Adelaide and Miss Gina discussed it over breakfast, as she knew they would, to glean what she could of his whereabouts and wellbeing. On occasion she had also asked Miss Gina, quite casually of course, if she had heard anything of the twins, usually being told that 'as far as we know they're well, but as you know, news is hard to come by'. James, of course, never wrote to her personally; he had never said he would and she didn't expect him to. But he was never far from her thoughts.

Will won two domino games, as he always did, then Polly looked at the clock. 'It's nine o'clock, time I was getting back,' she said, doing rapid mental calculations to allow for the twenty-minute discrepancy. 'It's been lovely being home for a few hours.'

'It's been lovely having you home, dearie,' Susan said warmly. 'Even though we know you're never far away.'

'I'll walk back with you,' Will said, getting to his feet.

'There's no need, Dad. There's a moon, so I'll be able to see my way.'

'I know. But I don't want you wandering about in the dark with all those soldiers about on lower meadow. You never know what they'll—' He broke off as there was a frantic hammering on the back door. 'What in the name of . . . who can that be at this hour? On Christmas night, too.'

'Better go and see, Will,' Susan said, alarmed. 'Take the poker with you.' They rarely had visitors and never at this time of night.

Will didn't take the poker; he took the lamp and went to the back door.

'Oh, my goodness me, Violet, you'd better come in,' they heard, then in a louder voice, 'Susan, it's Violet. She's hurt.'

Susan and Polly exchanged worried looks and both hurried through to the kitchen.

Violet Hadley was already sitting huddled on a chair by the table, with blood streaming from a cut on her head and a purple bruise already forming on the other side of her face and her eye swelling and rapidly closing. Her lip was cut and bleeding and she was dabbing at that and the eye that wasn't swollen alternately.

'I thought he was gonna kill me,' she said in little more than a whisper. 'I had to get out. I hope you don't mind.'

''Course we don't. I've told you before you can always come to us, Violet,' Susan said, busying herself with warm water and a cloth to wash away the blood. 'Isaac on one of his rampages again?'

Violet gave a brief nod and a sigh that was half a sob. 'He hasn't been like this for a long time, not since Tom went away. Tom made him promise not to drink because he knows it makes him violent and Tom's the only one who can do anything with him. He promised . . .' She drew in a quick breath as Susan touched a raw spot while cleaning her wounds. 'But he got all miserable because it's Christmas and Tom's away – he's fond of that boy, though you'd never know it – and started on the whisky he won in the horseshoe pitching competition at the Horse and Groom last summer.' She closed her good eye briefly – the other was so swollen it had closed itself – and continued, 'Once he started on the bottle he couldn't stop. I tried to take it away from him but he punched me and started blaming me for all his troubles – not that he's got any troubles, far as I can see, leastways no more than anybody else. But he kept on lambasting me, saying it was all my fault, and I was a stupid bitch. Then he hit me so hard I fell and hit my head on the corner of the dresser. I think he thought he'd killed me. He just stood and stared at me, the bottle in his hand. I think in a way it sobered him up, but I didn't stop to see. I got to my feet and ran out. Didn't even stop to get a coat.' She hugged herself and shivered. 'It's freezing out there.'

'You'd better give Violet a drop of your medicinal brandy, Susan,' Will said. 'She looks as if she could do with it.' He winked at Polly. 'If you didn't put it all in the cake.'

''Course I didn't.' Susan gave him a scathing look. 'Come on, Vi. Draw up to the fire and drink this, it'll warm you. You can have Polly's old bed for the night.'

'No, I'll go back in a bit, when he's had a chance to sober up and realize what he's done.' She took a sip of brandy and coughed. 'I ain't used to alcohol,' she said apologetically. 'Can't see why Isaac's so fond of it.'

'We'll wait and see how you feel,' Susan said, pursing her lips.

Will nodded. 'Meantime, you sit there and collect yourself, Violet, while I walk back to the house with Polly,' he said. 'And on the way back I'll look in and see how Isaac is; time enough then for you to decide what you want to do, whether to stay or go.'

Violet nodded. 'Thanks, Mr Catchpole.'

Will lit the lantern and together he and Polly went out into the night. Polly's assertion that there was a moon may have been true but tonight it was hidden behind thick rain clouds that were already producing a fine, cold drizzle and this turned into a steady downpour before they were halfway to the house.

'You go back, Dad. You'll get drenched,' Polly pleaded. 'I haven't got far to go now.'

'I shall see you to the door, so save your breath and don't argue,' he replied, holding the lantern high enough to make a circle of light on the ground in front of them to show them the way. 'I don't know why young Tom saw fit to go off and join the army the way he did,' he went on. 'He didn't need to go. All he needed to say was that he was wanted on the land. The good Lord knows there was no lie in that; his father struggles without him.'

'That's why he went, Dad. To escape the drudgery of life with his father. If Mr Hadley had treated him better he might have thought twice before enlisting. I just hope Tom is having a better time where he is now than he did at home with his father.'

'I don't think that's very likely, my girl. Not from what I've been reading in the newspaper.' He stopped as they reached the back gate. 'Well, here you are, my lovely, back safe and sound.' He bent and kissed her cheek. 'Goodnight and sweet dreams.'

'Goodnight, Dad. Thanks for walking me back.' She hurried up the path to the back door as he held the lantern high for her. Not until she was safely inside did he turn and retrace his steps the way they had come.

All the way back he was rehearsing in his mind what he would say to Isaac Hadley. Although he knew it was none of his business to interfere between husband and wife, he felt somebody needed to put in a word for Violet now that Tom wasn't here to protect her. When he arrived at Riverside Farm he had to plough through the ankle-deep straw and filth in the yard to reach the back door. There he hammered on the door with his fist, although the barking of the old dog chained up by his kennel was sufficient warning in itself that someone was there.

Will waited, then hammered on the door again. When there was still no sound from inside he tried the door and pushed it open. He looked round. The kitchen floor was spotlessly clean except for where Isaac had walked over it in his filthy boots and a trail of blood spots where Violet had run out of the house. Everything on the dresser was neat and tidy, copper jelly moulds gleamed on the top shelf and such china as they had left that Isaac hadn't smashed in a rage was displayed on the lower ones. On the mantelpiece, along with some cheap but carefully placed ornaments, was a card from Tom and the clock on the wall ticked the seconds away. On the table, the cat was enjoying an uninterrupted feast of roast chicken carcass beside Isaac, who had been seated there but was now sprawled across it in a drunken sleep.

Will shooed the cat off the table and put the chicken in the meat safe, then managed to pull Isaac to a sitting position in order to half-lift, half-drag him over to the horsehair sofa by the wall. There he dumped him, draped a coat over him and left him, after standing over him and telling him exactly what he thought of his behaviour. Isaac's only thanks was an enormous, reverberating snore.

Disgusted, Will went home.

Susan and Violet both looked up when he pushed open the door.

'Oh, Will, look at you, you're soaked!' Susan said, shocked. 'I didn't realize it was raining.'

Violet said nothing, but looked at him expectantly.

'Yes, I've been,' he said, answering her unspoken question. 'He's dead to the world. I've covered him up and left him snoring. Heaven knows what time he'll wake.'

'Six o'clock,' Violet said. 'On the dot.'

'You haven't seen him, he's as drunk as a lord. He'll have a head the size of a haystack and twice as thick. He'll never wake at six.'

'He will, I tell you,' Violet argued with a sigh. 'I've seen it all before and it's always been the same. Never mind how drunk he's come home, he's always been up at six to go and see to his animals. He wouldn't neglect his animals if he was dead on his feet.'

'What about you, Vi?' Susan asked.

'Me?' She gave a mirthless laugh. 'I've learned to keep out of his way. He'll be like a bear with a sore head in the morning. Then he'll come over all maudlin and say he's sorry and he'll never do it again.'

'He might mean it this time when he sees your black eye and that plaster Susan's put on your head,' Will said grimly. 'If he's got any sense he'll realize he could have killed you.'

'One day he probably will,' Violet said, getting to her feet.

'Aren't you going to stay here the night, Vi?' Susan said anxiously. 'I've told you . . .'

'No. I'd better get back. He won't like it if I'm not there.' Violet smiled at her. 'Thanks all the same, Susan.'

'I'll walk you back,' Will said, shrugging on his wet coat again. He picked up the lantern. 'Don't wait up for me, Susan.'

After they'd gone Susan raked the dying embers of the fire and sat down beside it. What a way to end Christmas Day! She was thankful she had such a good and caring husband.

Nine

There was little to celebrate as 1915 turned into 1916, another year that didn't begin well. There was worrying news from the French front at Verdun and in England there was news that the Government was planning to introduce conscription for single men between the ages of eighteen and forty. If the target for conscriptions wasn't reached, it was announced, it would then be extended to married men, according to their circumstances. At the same time the upper classes were urged to release some of their below-stairs staff to the war effort.

'I hope they're not suggesting we should let even more of our staff go, George,' Lady Adelaide said to her husband when he imparted this news on one of his infrequent visits home. 'Heaven's sake, most of our indoor staff have already gone, they volunteered ages ago, which means we're already hopelessly understaffed. Poor Polly is run off her feet doing the work of a housemaid when she should be attending to my needs. And Gina tells me we're even employing that little woman – what's her name – Mrs Hadley, from Riverside Farm, to help with the cleaning several mornings a week now. On a temporary basis, of course.' She ran her hand over the little polished table beside her, searching for dust. 'She's very good,' she admitted thoughtfully, finding none. 'It might be a good idea to keep her on permanently.'

'Polly. Isn't that Will Catchpole's daughter?' Sir George asked. He'd noticed her because she was a pretty little filly.

'That's right. And that's another thing. When Polly should be doing the work she's paid for, Gina keeps wearing her out by taking her off to this soup kitchen thing she's set up for the poor.' Lady Adelaide made a moue of distaste.

'Ah, yes, I must have a word with Gina about that.' Sir George got to his feet. 'She's making my life very difficult in the House of Commons with all these letters she keeps writing about women and children starving because they're not getting money that's owed to them, or some such. Doesn't she realize there's a war on? MPs have better things to do than sort out the money worries of people too idle to work, and I've got better things to do than apologise for her making a nuisance of herself.' He took his gold hunter out of his pocket and looked at it. 'Better still, you have a word with her, Addy. I've got a train to catch.' He dropped a kiss on her forehead and left the room.

Below stairs the bell rang and Polly hurried up to Lady Adelaide's sitting room to be told that Sir George had left so there would be one less for dinner.

'And whilst you're here would you fetch my embroidery, Polly? It's over there, on that table.' Lady Adelaide waved her hand towards a little table not quite within her reach.

Polly handed it to her and hurried back to finish the ironing that Her Ladyship entrusted to nobody else.

When she got back to the kitchen she found that there was a strange woman standing just inside the door. She was tall and gaunt and her face under her hat was a funny yellow colour. Hetty had gone back to her task of cleaning the knives after answering the door to her and Mrs Bellman was sitting in the rocking chair by the fire enjoying her afternoon rest and looked none too pleased at being disturbed.

'Good afternoon, can I help you?' Polly asked, since Mrs Bellman didn't seem interested.

'Hullo, Polly,' the woman said. 'Don't you recognize me?'

Frowning, Polly shook her head. 'No, I'm afraid not. Should I?'

'Reckon so. We shared a bedroom when I worked here.' The woman smiled. One of her front teeth was missing. 'I'm Ruby. Surely you haven't forgotten me.'

'She wants her old job back,' Mrs Bellman said with total lack of sympathy. 'She's got a cheek, if you ask me. She was quick enough to leave so that she could go to that munitions factory; now she wants to come crawling back.'

'Can I sit down a minute, Mrs Bellman?' the girl said. 'I can't stand up for too long these days.'

'You won't be much use here, then,' Mrs Bellman said, waving her to a chair.

'Did you get the sack?' Polly asked, pouring her a cup of tea from the pot on the stove and then resuming her place at the ironing board.

Ruby shook her head. 'Oh, no, nothing like that. I had to get out because it was killing me. The stuff they have to work with at that place makes everybody ill. It's horrible there.'

'What's horrible about it?' Hetty asked, looking up from her knife cleaning, her face alight with interest. She risked a glance at Mrs Bellman. 'I was thinking of applying for a job there,' she whispered behind her hand. 'I've heard they pay ever so well.'

Ruby took several sips of tea. 'That's as maybe, but it ruins your health, that's what,' she said. 'Look at me. My skin's gone yellow as mustard and that's on account of the explosive stuff we have to put in the shells. The whole place stinks of it. They say it's harmless, but how can it be harmless if people faint and have to be carried outside till they revive? And that happens all the time. And if you take too long to get back to work or if you pass out too often they dock your pay.'

'A lot of people work there, though,' Hetty said, unconvinced.

Ruby nodded and drank more tea. 'Yes, well, we all went there with big ideas about doing our bit to help our boys out there fighting. And as you say, the pay's good so nobody complained when the hours got longer and longer. But although it's all hushed-up or put down to other causes I know for a fact people have died, poisoned by that stuff that goes into the shells. It gets into the liver and shrivels it up, so I've heard, that's why people's skin goes a funny colour.'

'Like yours,' Hetty said, agog with interest.

'Don't be rude, Hetty,' Mrs Bellman said, but Ruby didn't seem to mind.

'Oh, there are plenty worse than me. That's why I wanted to get out before I got ill.'

Hetty's eyes were round as she took this in. 'I've seen women in the town with skin the colour of mustard. I wondered what was wrong with them.'

'Well, now you know.' Ruby nodded sagely. 'But it's not only that. I've heard rumours about big explosions where people have been killed in factories just like ours in other places in the country. So far nothing's happened at our place, touchwood.' She knocked on the table with her knuckles. 'But there's always the chance. Mind you, they're very strict. We all have to wear special clothes and caps, and rubber-soled shoes. And we mustn't take matches in, nothing that might make a spark – as if anybody would, if they'd got any sense, with all that TNT about. So, there you are,' she finished grimly. 'That's what it's like. And if you take my advice you'll steer well clear of the place.'

'So. Still think you want to work there, Hetty?' Mrs Bellman asked.

Hetty shook her head. 'No, not likely! Not after what Ruby's just said.' She got to her feet and in a rare burst of willingness said, 'I've finished the knives, Mrs Bellman. Shall I start on this washing-up?'

'I think you'd better,' Mrs Bellman said, her expression one of smug victory. 'And then you can begin to prepare the vegetables for tonight.'

'Yes, Mrs Bellman.'

'I'll give you a hand,' Ruby offered.

'Just you wait a minute, missy.' Mrs Bellman held up her hand. 'You haven't got your job back yet. It's not my place to hire and fire. You'll have to speak to Miss Gina about that.'

Ruby got to her feet. 'When can I see her? You see, I've got to find work. My dad was furious when I left the factory. He's says he's not having me at home not paying my way, although God knows he took enough off me when I worked there. And tipped most of it down his throat,' she added bitterly.

'She's in her room. I'll just go up and find out if it's convenient to see you,' Polly said.

'I'll come up with you and wait outside. It'll save you making two journeys,' Ruby offered, following her.

'I hope Miss Gina will take you back,' Polly said, smiling at her as they went up the back stairs. 'We could certainly do with another pair of hands and . . . ah, here we are. Good luck, Ruby.'

Fifteen minutes later Ruby returned to the kitchen, wreathed in smiles. 'Miss Gina says she'll be glad to have me back and I can start right away, if I want. So what would you like me to do, Mrs Bellman?'

'You can help Hetty with the vegetables.'

In spite of her previous sharp words Mrs Bellman was very kind to Ruby. In her first weeks back she gave her plenty of milk to drink, which Ruby said had been recommended at the factory – and sometimes even provided, to counteract the toxic materials they had to work with. She also gave her as many sedentary tasks as she could until the fainting fits faded. Gradually, away from the factory and with good food, the yellow hue faded from Ruby's skin, she began to put on weight and her stamina returned, but it took several months before she fully recovered.

In April Gina received news that Archie's ship had docked and he had been given seven days' leave. Full of excitement, she put on her green skirt and matching three-quarter length coat and a darker green velvet head-hugging hat, which she knew he liked, and drove in her brother's little car to meet him. As he got down from the train she just managed to register that he was looking bronzed and fit after months in the Atlantic, and leaner than when she last saw him, before he swept her into his arms and kissed her as if he would never let her go.

'In front of all these people, Archie,' she managed to murmur, giggling and holding on to her hat as they came up for air.

'I can't help that. I've waited far too long for this,' he said, bending his head and kissing her again.

'I've missed you so much, darling,' he said, when at last he released her.

'Me, too.' She hugged him. 'Oh, Archie, it's so good to have you back again.' It was true. As soon as he'd stepped off the train all her previous doubts dispelled and she knew with absolute certainty that this was the man she wanted to spend the rest of her life with and that it had been nothing more than loneliness that had briefly attracted her to Andrew Palgrave.

They spent his leave hardly out of each other's company. They went for long walks, they drove to little out-of-the-way pubs for quiet meals and all the time they talked, often about nothing in particular, simply delighting in being together.

The only place he didn't accompany her to was her 'soup run', which was as much a tea club as a soup run now.

'I'm afraid it's a women and children only morning,' she told him as they sat holding hands in the sunshine on the bench overlooking the lake at Meadowlands. 'I can't let them down, darling, it's a lifeline for them although I begrudge any time I have to spend away from you.'

'I expect I'll survive,' he said, grinning at her. 'Anyway, from what you've told me in your letters it's hardly the place for a humble sailor.'

She leaned away from him, smiling. 'Why? Are you afraid they might mob you?'

'I don't think there'd be any danger of that. Not with you there to protect me.' He pulled her close again and his voice dropped. 'But they might corrupt my mind,' he whispered darkly.

'Ah, yes, my innocent boy, there's no telling what you could learn from those poor souls,' she agreed, matching his tone. Then she became serious. 'You really don't mind, then, Archie?' She looked up at him.

'Not at all, darling. As you said, you can't let them down. Obviously they depend on you in all sorts of ways and it's amazing what you've managed to do for them. I've loved reading in your letters about your battles with the authorities.'

'Oh, I hope I haven't bored you,' she said quickly.

'Never. I'm proud of you, darling. You've done things for them that they could never have done for themselves. You should get a medal. Or, better still, a kiss. Or several.' A good deal later he said, 'You go and look after your soup club, my darling, and I'll spend some time catching up on family news with Ma and Pa.' He grinned ruefully. 'It's time I did.'

The soup club followed its usual pattern. They were all waiting for Gina and Polly to arrive in their little car and the routine was so well established now that the whole thing was set up in a very short time. Polly dispensed the soup so that everyone got their fair share but the women took it in turns to brew the tea and preside over the teapot. The few pence that some of them insisted on contributing when they could were used to buy the luxury of a penn'orth or so of broken biscuits from the Home and Colonial grocers to share round between them, although the children ate most of them. Gina was only too well aware that this was an important oasis in their lives of grinding poverty and hardship.

Polly was busily doling out soup into proper mugs, most of

which had come from the back regions of the dresser in the kitchen at Meadowlands, when she said, 'Teddy Baxter, you've already had your share. Come on now, love, don't be greedy, there's others in the queue.'

Crestfallen, Teddy turned away.

'He never 'ad 'is. 'E took it 'ome for 'is dad,' said the next in line, a little dark-haired girl.

'Shut up, Meggy Perkins. Don't tell tales,' said another, bigger girl, pushing her out of the way.

'Well, it's true. I seen 'im.'

There was a scuffle before Polly managed to get them all back in line and after that she was kept busy until all the soup was gone. It was not until they were on their way home in the car that, weary and feeling in need of a bath, Polly remembered the incident and related it to Gina.

'I know they don't always tell the truth, but I've never heard that one before,' Polly said, yawning. 'I don't know if I did right but I gave him another half a mug as we'd got plenty today. But if they start telling tales like that to get extra we won't have enough to go round.'

'It wasn't a tale, Polly. It was quite true. His father is at home,' Gina said. 'And that soup was probably all the poor man's had to eat for several days. Annie Baxter, his wife, came to me today to ask if I could do anything to help them. Percy Baxter lost a leg at Ypres and so of course he's been invalided out of the army.'

'Oh, poor man.'

'Yes, but that's not the half of it. Because he's no longer in the army he doesn't get his army pay and for the same reason his wife doesn't get her army allowance. So they've had all their money stopped, they've got nothing to live on and he can't get work.'

'That's awful,' Polly said, shocked. 'So what will they do, Miss Gina? How will they live? And with four children, too. Oh, it's cruel. And him wounded fighting for his country. It's not fair.'

'No, it's not fair, Polly. Annie's going to try for work at the munitions factory, but that means he'll have to look after the children and the little one is not yet two.'

'But Ruby said that factory is a dreadful place.'

'I know. I've heard that, too. And Annie Baxter is already

consumptive. But when the alternative is to starve . . .' Gina gave a deep sigh. 'Of course, I shall write to the powers that be but what good it'll do heaven only knows. They neither seem to know nor care what happens to these poor men. Yet they're asking for more and more men to enlist. Oh, how much longer will this wretched war go on for?'

It was a question she repeated when she saw Archie that night. She'd bathed and washed her hair as she did after every soup run and put on a blue dress that matched her eyes, one that she knew he particularly liked.

After dinner, at which Lady Adelaide bored them endlessly with the imaginary deprivations she was suffering because of the war, Archie rescued Gina for a walk in the grounds.

'I know she's your mother, but I think you must be a saint to put up with her,' he said, his arm firmly round her waist.

'It's a small price compared with some of the things I've heard today,' she said with a sigh.

'Want to tell me?'

'Not really. It's just so sad . . .' Nevertheless she found herself telling him about the plight of the Baxters. 'I'm worried that working in that munitions factory will kill Annie Baxter,' she finished. 'She's already consumptive.'

'Oh, my poor darling. You really do have to deal with the most tragic things. No wonder you're looking tired tonight.'

She shook her head. 'It happens all the time. It's just not fair. I'm sorry, darling, I shouldn't be burdening you with the Baxters' plight but I can't get it out of my mind. Oh God, I wish this war was over.' She laid her head wearily on his shoulder. 'I often imagine how it will be, Archie. When it's all over we'll be able to get married and have our own home . . .'

'We don't have to wait till the war's over to get married,' he said quietly.

She lifted her head. 'But how can we plan a wedding? There wouldn't be time to make all the arrangements.'

'I've been into all that. We could be married by special licence on my next leave. That's what one of my fellow officers did.'

'But how? You never know when you'll get leave, Archie,' she said, puzzled.

'That's just the thing. As long as we have the licence we'll be able to marry at quite short notice. Oh, we won't have all the trimmings, big wedding, hundreds of guests—'

'Which would be what my mother would want, of course.'

'Never mind your mother, what about you, Gina? How would you feel about a quiet wedding?'

She squeezed his arm. 'Deliriously happy. I just want to be your wife, darling. I don't care about trimmings.'

He gave a great sigh of relief. 'And to think I've been trying to pluck up the courage to ask you ever since I've been home.'

She held up her face for his kiss. 'Well, now you've asked me and I've said yes. Please.'

When he released her she said thoughtfully, 'How long do you think we'll have to wait? Can we marry before you go back?'

'No, it takes a bit longer than that, darling.' He kissed the tip of her nose. 'But we'll put the wheels in motion before I go back and next time I come home . . .'

'When will that be?'

'When the Admiralty says so. Depends where my ship gets sent next.'

'Well, put in a word so that it doesn't get sent too far for too long.'

He grinned at her. 'Getting impatient?'

'Of course I am. I can't wait to be Mrs Penfold.'

Ten

After Archie had gone back to his ship, which was now somewhere in Scotland, Gina alternated between being bereft at his absence and bubbling over with excitement at their secret plans. They had agreed to tell no one their intentions in case the news leaked to Lady Adelaide, who would be appalled at the idea of a quiet wedding.

'Can't you just imagine my mother's reaction?' Gina had giggled (she'd done a lot of giggling in her excitement) safely encircled in his arms.

'What will the neighbours say?' Archie hazarded a guess.

'I hope you haven't been misbehaving yourselves.' Gina had mimicked her mother's most frosty tone.

'Fat chance, since I've been on the other side of the world.' He'd pulled her even closer. 'But I'm more than happy to make up for lost time . . .'

In fact, it had seemed quite natural and not like misbehaving at all.

Relying only on his letters to discuss their plans now, Gina hugged her news to herself. But in the end her excitement bubbled over and she confided her secret to Polly as they drove to the soup club one brilliantly sunny day at the end of May.

'Oh, Miss Gina, how wonderful,' Polly said, her excitement matching Gina's. 'When do you think the wedding is likely to be?'

'As soon as possible. Next month with any luck, but obviously it depends when Archie is able to get leave and he can't say when that's likely to be. Now we've got this far I can't wait to be his wife.' She gave Polly a sideways glance. 'You promise you won't say anything to anybody.'

'I promise. Cross my heart.' She made the appropriate gesture. 'As if I would, Miss Gina. You ought to know me better than that.'

Gina was glad she had shared her secret with Polly, for it meant there was someone to whom she could show the pretty – and rather expensive – blue and cream silk dress and the extravagant blue wide-brimmed hat trimmed with cream-coloured roses she had bought to be married in. Also the cream satin shoes with rather uncomfortably high heels.

'Oh, Miss Gina, you'll look so beautiful, and the blue matches your eyes,' Polly said when Gina showed them to her.

'And I thought I'd carry cream roses.' Gina stroked the fabric lovingly.

'Perfect, Miss Gina.' Polly's eyes sparkled.

Since journeys to and from the soup club were the only times Gina was able to speak about her impending wedding and Polly was as eager to listen as she was to talk about it, these excited conversations were a good antidote to the troubles they had to deal with at the soup club. At the same time, they were full of admiration and amazement at how stoic the women were in the face of all their problems.

Annie Baxter, whose husband had lost a leg and been invalided out of the army with no pension, had been taken on at the munitions factory, although she could only work for half a day at a time.

'I dunno how long they'll keep her on,' one of her friends said. 'I don't think they like part-timers, but she ain't got the strength to do a full day.'

'She ain't got the strength to do half a day, if the truth be told,' another one said. 'I don't think she'll last long there. I said she shoulda told them she'd got a nasty cough so they'd put her on lighter work but she said she wouldn't hev got took on at all if she'd told 'em that. I 'spect she was right, even though they're still cryin' out for workers and she's got to get money from somewhere.' She sighed and shook her head. 'Hev you heard anything from the authorities about her husband's disability pension, Miss Gina? I think it's shameful. That poor man lost a leg in the war and they sent him home with no money and no pension. They didn't even give him a pair o' crutches so he could get about and look for work.'

It was Gina's turn to sigh and shake her head. 'No. I'm sorry, Vera. All I hear is that it will be dealt with. They don't say when, they simply say cases are dealt with in the order they are received. That's always the answer I get when they bother to answer my letters, which isn't all that often. Nevertheless, I keep pestering them although I truly believe they are swamped with applications for help. And it's help that should be awarded automatically, not begged for. It's outrageous and I'm just really sorry I can't do more.'

Vera laid a hand with black and broken fingernails on Gina's arm. 'We understand. We know you do what you can, miss, and we're grateful,' she said.

Going home in the car Polly said, 'I heard what they were saying about Annie Baxter's husband not having crutches so he can get about, Miss Gina. Surely there's plenty of wood on the estate that could be used for that. I reckon my dad could make a pair of crutches; he's ever so good at making things. Or he could get one of the men who repair the fences and suchlike to do it.'

'I don't think it's quite like mending a fence,' Gina said with a smile. 'They'd have to be the right length, for a start. But I'm sure there must be someone who'd know how to go about it. Yes, that's a good idea, Polly. Have a word with your father, see what he says.' She heaved another weary sigh. 'And I'll write yet more letters.'

She turned the car into the square and as they drove through the newsboys were shouting the headlines and waving the latest editions of the newspaper.

'They're making more of a racket than usual. I wonder what all the excitement's about.' Gina frowned and wound down the window.

'Perhaps we've won the war,' Polly said hopefully.

'No, I don't think it's that, people aren't exactly throwing their hats in the air. Here's a penny, hop out and get a paper, then we'll find out.'

Obediently, Polly got out of the car and went to the news stand. 'Read all about it! German fleet routed at Jutland!' the boy was shouting. She handed over her penny and got back into the car.

'He's shouting something about the German fleet being routed. I don't know what that means,' she said without much interest.

'I guess it means the German fleet has been forced to retreat. Well, that's good. But what else did he say?' Her eyes were on the road as a stray dog ran across so she could only manage a brief glance at the newspaper. 'Where did it happen? And what British ships were involved?' Her knuckles were white as she gripped the steering wheel.

'He was only shouting the headlines, Miss Gina,' Polly reproached her. 'But I think he shouted something about Jutland, wherever that is. Is it a country?'

'I think so. My geography's not that good. But what about British ships? Does it say which ones were involved?' she asked urgently.

'I'm sorry, Miss Gina, the print's too small for me to read while we're going along,' Polly said. 'All I can read is "Sea Battle off Jutland" because that's written big.'

'Never mind, I just hope and pray my Archie wasn't there.'

Polly did her best to peer at the small print to see what else she could glean but the motion of the car was making her feel sick so she had to give up.

As soon as they reached Meadowlands Gina stopped the car and grabbed the newspaper. She remained in the driving seat and read in large black letters that the British Grand Fleet had won the battle against the German Navy at Jutland. Impatiently, she skimmed the details – all she needed to know was whether or not *Invincible* had been there. It had. Her heart in her mouth, she read on until she came to 'Losses sustained'. Ignoring the ones on the German side, she read that the battle cruiser *Indefatigable* had been blown up and sunk with the loss of a thousand lives. On the next line the colour drained out of her face as she read that the battle cruiser *Invincible* had also been sunk, with very few survivors.

'Oh, God.' She leaned her head on the steering wheel.

So Archie must have been in that battle. And she'd been deluding herself that he was safely in harbour somewhere in Scotland.

Helplessly, not knowing what else to do, Polly laid an arm round her shoulders. Once the car had stopped she'd managed to see the words Gina had just read.

At her touch Gina raised her head. She sat staring out of the window, part of her mind numb, while another part was frantically trying to think, to decide what to do to find out if he was one of those few survivors. She looked down at her hands and saw that she had automatically crossed the fingers on both hands. 'Oh, please God, he's alive,' she whispered, over and over again. Then she turned to Polly. 'How can I find out if he's safe? I don't know what to do, Polly.'

Polly had never seen her young mistress so undecided and lost. 'What about Mr Penfold's parents? Would they know?' she suggested tentatively.

Gina's tense shoulders relaxed a little. 'Yes, of course. That's the obvious answer. Why didn't I think of it? Thank you, Polly.' She gave her a brief smile. 'Just crank up the car again for me, will you, and then you can go and have lunch. I'll drive over to Enderby Hall and see if there's any news.'

Polly did as she asked and went into the house. As she entered the kitchen the bell from Lady Adelaide's room was jangling and she hurried to answer it. Lunch would have to wait.

Gina drove the four miles to Enderby Hall at breakneck speed, screeching to a halt at the front door. She got out of the car and hurried up the steps to ring the bell.

'Oh, Parker,' she said breathlessly as soon as he opened the door. 'Can I see Mr or Mrs Penfold, please?'

'They're both in the small sitting room, Miss Barsham, but I don't think—'

'Thank you, Parker.' She didn't wait for him to finish but hurried past him and knocked at the appropriate door and went in.

It was a room she'd been in many times with Archie: a pleasant, light room, with settees place strategically round the fire, today unlit and masked by an intricately embroidered fire screen. Along one wall a large mahogany sideboard carried heavy cut glass dishes and vases and a tantalus containing amber liquid; small tables holding photographs of members of the family stood about the room and a whatnot in the corner held small china ornaments. A large marble clock and more china ornaments stood on the mantelpiece and heavy velvet curtains were pulled back from the windows, which were open to let in what breeze there was.

The sight that met her eyes told her all she needed to know. Winifred Penfold was sitting on a settee opposite the door, weeping uncontrollably and her husband, ashen-faced, was holding her, helpless against such heartbroken grief – a grief that he shared but, as a man, dared not give rein to.

He released his wife gently and got to his feet and came and took Gina's hands in his. 'You've heard, then?'

She shook her head, desperately looking from one to the other. 'No, I came to see if you knew . . . But I can see . . .'

'We only got the news about an hour ago. They didn't contact you as well, my dear?'

She shook her head dumbly. 'At least, I don't think so. I've only just got back. I came straight here. I didn't go into the house.'

Winifred Penfold lifted her head for the first time. 'They wouldn't contact Gina, would they? She's not his next-of-kin,' she said, her voice flat.

'No, I suppose not. Nevertheless . . .' He put his arm round Gina in a simple, fatherly gesture and led her to a chair.

'We were going to be married on his next leave,' Gina said, her voice little more than a whisper. 'We'd planned . . .'

'Really? Archie never mentioned it,' Winifred paused in the act of wiping her eyes yet again, her tone faintly disbelieving.

'No, it was a secret. We were going to be married by special licence . . .' Her face crumpled. 'I only bought my dress last week. It's beautiful, blue and cream silk . . . Now I'll never wear it.' Suddenly she put her hands over her face and began to sob. 'I loved him so much,' she wept, 'and now he's not there any more.'

'I know you did. And he returned that love,' Hubert answered quietly. Like all men of his time he regarded it as unmanly to show his feelings, but his heart was bleeding for his son and for this young girl who had loved him.

Gina tried to pull herself together and glanced at Winifred, who was again weeping into her handkerchief. 'I'm sorry. I should go now. I don't want to intrude on your grief.' Still weeping herself, she got to her feet.

'It's your grief, too, my dear. We understand that,' he said. 'Now, sit down again and I'll ring for Beatrice to bring in some tea. The cup that cheers, as they say.' His mouth twisted. 'Not that it will bring us much cheer today but just the same I think we all need it.'

He rang the bell, then went and sat beside his wife and took her hand.

'We should tell the others,' Winifred said, trying equally hard to pull herself together.

'All in good time, my dear. All in good time.'

Beatrice brought in the tea and a plate of biscuits.

'Cook says she'll delay luncheon until you're ready, madam,' she said quietly.

'Thank her, Beatrice. We'll let her know,' Hubert said, answering for his wife.

'Luncheon?' Winifred looked up, puzzled, her handkerchief still shielding most of her face. 'Is it time for luncheon, then?'

'It's nearly two o'clock,' Hubert said. He turned to Beatrice. 'I think, on second thoughts, you'd better tell Cook we'll forgo luncheon and have dinner early. We don't want to inconvenience her too much.'

Beatrice bent her knee in a little bob. 'Whatever you wish, sir. Downstairs we're all very sorry and upset about the dreadful news. We were all fond of Mr Archie.' Unable to say more, she put her hand to her mouth and stumbled from the room.

Winifred blew her nose and lifted her head to give Gina a watery smile. 'Would you mind doing the honours, dear? I fear my hand is not quite steady enough at the moment.'

'Of course.' Gina did as she asked and Hubert handed the tea and biscuits round. They talked a little and wept a little and drank several cups of tea which helped a little but not much.

'I feel so empty,' Gina said, her voice wobbly. 'I can't see a future without him.'

Hubert laid a hand over hers. 'Don't look into the future, Gina. Don't look further than tomorrow, in fact; concentrate on getting through the next hour, the next few minutes, even. I've found that's the best – the only – way to cope with tragedy. It's how I managed when my favourite brother was thrown from his horse and killed. But it's hard. Very hard.' His voice broke. 'Especially when it's your son.'

Winifred looked up and held out her hand towards Gina. 'You'll come and see us again, Gina, won't you? We'll let you know when the f—'

'There won't be a funeral, my darling,' Hubert interrupted gently. 'Archie's ship was sunk. In those circumstances . . .' He said no more.

'This *bloody* war!' Coming from Winifred, who had never been known to use even the mildest expletive, the word shocked them all, even Winifred herself. 'I'm sorry,' she muttered, 'but it's how I feel.'

Hubert's eyes widened but he said nothing.

'Oh, you're so right, Mrs Penfold. It's how we all feel,' Gina said. Her voice dropped. 'Now I begin to understand how those poor women at my soup club are feeling. I sympathize with them and do what I can to help them but until now I couldn't know the depth of their suffering. And they have the added worry of little or no money and children to feed.'

Suddenly, speaking about it jogged her memory and she looked down at her dress, which was crumpled and a bit dusty and dirty from her morning's work at the soup club. 'Oh, I'm really sorry,' she said, looking up at them, horrified. 'I've been there – at my soup club – all morning and when I read the headline in the newspaper I came straight here without stopping to change my clothes. So I'm afraid I'm a bit dirty and probably carrying the aroma of the place, which isn't exactly ashes of roses, although we do try to encourage cleanliness as far as we can. But it's difficult for them with only one outside tap between six houses and no . . . Well, it's difficult.' She stood up and put her hand to her head. 'Oh, I'm sorry. I'm prattling. I do apologize. I should go and get myself cleaned up.'

'It's perfectly all right, my dear,' Hubert said. 'We understand completely.' He sighed. 'Under the circumstances I don't think we'd have noticed if you'd come wearing a sack.'

Winifred gave a ghost of a smile. 'Now you come to speak of it your hat is slightly awry, but I hadn't noticed until you spoke.'

'I think that must have happened when one of the children tried to stroke the feather.' Gina put up her hand to straighten it.

'You're doing admirable work there, Gina,' Hubert said. 'Archie told us a little about it when he was last home. He was very proud of what you were doing. You must keep it up; it'll help you to . . . to cope.'

'You could stay and have lunch with us, Gina.' Winifred frowned. 'Is it lunchtime, Hubert?' she asked for a second time. 'I don't know what time it is.' She shook her head as tears welled in her eyes again. 'I can't think of anything except my poor boy.'

'I've told Cook we'll forgo lunch and have dinner early, my dear. Unless you're hungry?'

She shook her head again. 'No, but I'd like more tea. Will you stay and have more tea, Gina?'

'Thank you, no. I really must go and get myself cleaned up.'

'I'll ring for Drummond to take you home, Gina,' Hubert said.

'Thank you. That's very kind.' She shook her head. 'No, I'm sorry, I forgot. I've got my car so there's no need. But thanks all the same.'

'Well, drive carefully, my dear.' He bent his head and kissed her forehead. 'You brought my son a great deal of happiness and for that I thank you, Gina.'

Eleven

Gina went straight to her room when she arrived home; she couldn't yet face telling her mother the dreadful news and having to listen to her sympathetic prattling, well-meaning though she knew it would be. She was grateful that Polly, ever thoughtful, had hot water ready so that she could wallow in her bath and try to come to terms with her grief undisturbed.

She wept for a long time, in rage at the futility of a war that had taken her beloved Archie from her; in sorrow that his life had been cut so cruelly short when they had planned such a wonderful future together; and partly, as she finally realized with a pang of guilt, in self-pity because of the loss and suffering she was forced to bear.

At that realization she thought of the poor, poverty-stricken women at the soup club and the way they faced their troubles with such stoicism, helping each other where they could and finding something to smile about in even the direst situations. While their husbands were away fighting and sometimes dying for their country, and their problems so often ignored by the authorities, their concerns were never for themselves but only for their children; to keep a roof over their heads and their bellies filled. They had so little, these women, yet they struggled on, making the best of what they had. Thinking about them and the hardships they were forced to endure and how little they complained made Gina feel ashamed at her own weakness and made up her mind that she would follow their example and be strong, too. Her grief would be hidden in hard work; she alone would know that a part of her had died with Archie.

She climbed out of the bath and called Polly to help her to dress in her most sober dress, a dark green cotton check with white collar and cuffs, which Archie had always liked.

'I shall go down to dinner tonight, Polly,' she said firmly. 'I have to tell my mother what's happened sooner or later.'

'M'lady already knows, Miss Gina,' Polly said. 'Sir George telephoned from London with the news and to say he'll be home shortly. She keeps asking where you are. I told her you were taking a bath, otherwise I think she would have come to your room.'

'Thank you for that, Polly.' Gina gave her a little smile. 'I needed time to gather my strength and try to come to terms with the black hole that's opened up in my life.' She paused and bit her lip against the tears that still threatened. She took a deep breath and continued, 'Do you know, it was thinking about the women at our soup club that helped me most. It helped me to somehow get things in perspective, to realize that I'm not the

only one suffering like this. Can you understand what I'm trying
to say?'

Polly nodded, frowning slightly. 'Yes, I think I can, Miss Gina.
Those women are so strong, aren't they? Whatever happens to
them they just keep going.' She finished gathering up the towels.
'Now is there anything else, Miss Gina?' She put her head on
one side, frowning at Gina's reflection in the mirror. 'A little
rouge? You're dreadfully pale, if you don't mind me saying so,
Miss Gina.'

'No, I don't think so, thank you, Polly. I don't want to look
like a wooden doll, with two spots of colour painted on a white
face.' She managed another little smile.

'Oh, Miss Gina, I'm sure you'd never look like that!' Polly was
quite shocked.

When Gina arrived in the dining room her mother got to her
feet and came and kissed her. 'I'm so sorry, my darling. Archie
was such a lovely man,' was all she said but there was a wealth
of love and compassion in her tone. She handed Gina a glass of
sherry. 'I think your father will be home soon, so we'll wait for
dinner. I hope you'll manage to eat a little. You need to keep
your strength up.'

'Yes, I think I shall,' Gina said. Then added, with some surprise,
'In fact, I think I'm quite hungry. I can't remember when it was
I last ate.'

'That's good. I'm glad you've got an appetite.'

Sir George came in very soon after. He too kissed Gina. 'Keep
your chin up, my dear,' he said gruffly, never a man for emotional
outpourings. He then greeted his wife before pouring himself a
whisky and downing it in a gulp.

During dinner he told the two women what he knew of the
battle that had cost Archie his life.

'There were heavy losses,' he said sadly. 'It's estimated over
six thousand men died and we lost seven ships. But we crippled
the German fleet. I don't think they'll trouble us a lot more in the
North Sea.'

'Oh, is this dreadful war never going to end?' Lady Adelaide
sighed. 'There'll be no young men left if it goes on like this.
Then where will we be?'

'We'll be a nation of spinsters, so I shall be in good company,'
Gina said bitterly. She put down her spoon and fork, her plum

tart half eaten. 'I think I'll go to my room now, if you don't mind, Mother,' she said, getting to her feet. 'Perhaps you'd ask Polly to bring coffee to me there.'

'Of course, my darling.' She waited until Gina had left the room, then turned to her husband. 'It was very brave of her to come down to dinner and I was pleased to see that she managed to eat a little. She was very fond of Archie, you know.'

Sir George nodded. 'Is she hoping against hope he might have survived? Because it's a forlorn hope. I've seen the list of survivors from *Invincible*; there were only about half a dozen and Archie's name wasn't among them.'

'No, I think she accepts that he's never coming back. Poor girl. Our eldest child, George; she was such a happy little girl.'

'Please God she will be again in the fullness of time.' He dabbed his moustache with his napkin. 'I must write to the Penfolds. One can only imagine their devastation. If it had been one of our boys . . .'

'Oh, George, don't! I can't bear to even think of such a thing.'

Gina went through the next days and weeks like a zombie. The only thing that sustained her was her soup club, where she was with women who had faced loss too, and understood what she was going through, but they had the added burden of poverty and children to care for. Seeing the way they coped with their troubles through their resilience and fortitude gave her the strength to keep going.

What depths of misery and despair she plumbed during sleepless nights she alone knew and Polly, who watched over her like a hen with a wounded chick, could only guess.

Then James arrived home unexpectedly, unshaven and looking thin and tired and ten years older than his age.

'I was given a few days' leave and the transport was there so I took advantage of it to return to civilization,' he explained cheerfully, unaware how his altered appearance shocked his mother and sister. 'I couldn't wait to get home and sleep in a proper bed, with clean sheets and blankets.'

He slept solidly for two days and two nights and eventually emerged from his room looking more like his old self, although this only served to emphasize how thin he had become.

Mrs Bellman prepared all his favourite food, to which he did more than justice, but loud noises, even the noise of a lid replaced heavily on a vegetable dish, made him start and begin to shake for several minutes, composing himself again with obvious effort. Tactfully, the others pretended not to notice and he never referred to it.

The weather was hot and sunny and he spent long hours walking in the grounds, on his own, or sometimes with his sister. As he wandered through the woods with Gina one afternoon he lifted his head and sniffed the air. 'Lord, if you knew how often I've thought of this, the green everywhere, the fresh smell . . . I'll never take the beautiful English countryside for granted again. Now I'm home I can't get enough of it. Beats barbed wire and desolation into a cocked hat,' he added with an attempt at humour.

'Was . . . is it very bad over there?' she asked since he had provided an opening for her to broach the subject.

'Pretty bloody. Not really a subject for discussion on a summer afternoon in an English country garden,' he replied briefly. 'Let's go and sit by the lake.'

They walked through the wood towards the lake in silence. The shutters were up. He wasn't going to talk about his experiences and Gina realized she had made a mistake in thinking that he might. She put her hand through his arm and squeezed it to show that she understood. 'Oh, it's so good to have you home, Jimbo,' she said, using the name he hadn't heard since their nursery days.

'It's good to be home,' he said on a sigh. 'I can't tell you just how good.'

They reached the lake and sat down on the seat overlooking the water. 'One of my favourite spots,' he said, drinking in the scene. After a while, he turned and looked at her.

'I'm really sorry about poor old Archie, Gee. It must have been bloody awful for you, old girl, losing him like that. And you'd only been engaged such a short time, too. He was a good bloke, Archie. Bloody shame. All the best blokes—'

'Don't, James. Don't say it,' she said fiercely. 'I couldn't bear it if . . .' She bit her lip, unable to speak again for a minute. Finally she said, her voice flat, 'At first I kept thinking he'd come back, that it wasn't real. Everybody thought I was being brave, but I wasn't; I was just waiting for him to turn up and tell me it was all a mistake and he hadn't been on the ship at all. But of course he never did and gradually I've come to terms with the fact that he never will.' She paused, then when he didn't speak she carried on sadly, 'We'd planned to get married on his next leave. I've even bought a dress and hat to wear.'

'I didn't know that!' he said, surprised.

'No, we hadn't told anybody. Now, of course, there's no point.' She shook her head and her voice brightened a little. 'But I don't look ahead, not any more. Archie's father told me to take one day at a time and not to look to the future, so I don't. It was good advice. I take each day as it comes and every night I thank God I've managed to get through it. I even begin to think it's getting slightly easier, or perhaps it's that I'm learning to live with the hurt. Polly's been marvellous, I don't know what I'd have done without her. She even makes me laugh sometimes.'

'I'm glad to hear it. Laughter is a great safety valve.' He turned and looked at her. 'How is Polly, by the way? I've hardly clapped eyes on her since I've been home. No, that's not quite true. I keep seeing her but she's always disappearing round a corner or into a room. She's like quicksilver.'

'She's that all right, but I guess she has to be to get her work done and still have time to run the soup club with me. We're pretty short-staffed, you know. Most of the servants are either in the army or the munitions factory, although Ruby – you remember Ruby?' He nodded so she went on: 'She went to work there but had to leave because it was making her ill, so she came back to work for us.'

'Ah, yes. I've heard a bit about this soup club, here and there. Tell me about it. You say Polly helps you to run it?'

'She did at first. Now we run it together, which is a little different, more of a partnership. She doles out the soup and keeps the children in some kind of order, the women themselves look after the teapot and most of the time I simply listen to their problems and try to do what I can to help them.' She paused. 'Although just recently they've helped me as much if not more than I've helped them,' she added thoughtfully.

'It sounds like a really good thing, Gee.'

She laughed, the first time he'd heard her since he arrived home. 'Pa doesn't think so. He keeps telling me to stop writing to MPs. You see, they all know he's my father so they keep badgering him to try and stop me being such a nuisance. I suppose they think he has influence over me.'

It was James' turn to burst out laughing. 'They obviously don't know you.' There was admiration in his voice.

She shrugged. 'It's the only thing I can do to help these poor women to get what they so desperately need. They can't do it for themselves, most of them are illiterate. And if those stupid men in Whitehall only realized it, the best way to stop me writing letters is to act. I'm only asking for what these women are entitled to. Heaven's sake, they were anxious enough to get men into the army but they didn't give a thought to how their families would fare, left without a breadwinner.' She shuddered in frustration. 'Oh, let's not talk about it. It makes me furious.' She looked at her watch. 'And talking of letters, I've got several to write so I'd better go in. Coming?'

'No. I think I'll stay here a bit longer and enjoy the scenery. Then I must go and see Isaac Hadley and his wife. Tom asked me to let them know he's all right. He's not much of a letter writer, so they'll be worrying about him.'

'Mm. It's nice Tom is with you. Do you see much of Ned?'

He hesitated a moment, then replied, 'Not really. France is a big country, you know.'

'Yes, of course. Silly of me to ask.' Satisfied with his answer Gina went back to the house.

James remained sitting by the lake for a long time, drinking in the peaceful stillness, the sound of the birds singing and the breeze gently moving the leaves on the trees, thinking about his twin and imagining how shocked Gina would have been if he'd told her about his last meeting with Ned.

It was after a particularly bloody battle; there were so many men lying wounded out on the battlefield that more stretcher bearers were called in. Ned was among them, although James hadn't known it at the time. It was only afterwards, when James was sitting in his bunker writing his report, that Ned had staggered in, exhausted and covered in mud from head to toe.

He'd got to his feet immediately. 'Ned! I didn't know you were here! God, you look a mess! Sit down and I'll get Tom to rustle up something to eat and some hot water so you can clean yourself up a bit. Oh, I can't tell you how good it is to see you, old chap.' He'd wrung his brother's hand in delight.

'I couldn't go back without seeing you. They said I'd find you here,' Ned said, sinking down on to a bale of hay that served as a seat and leaning his head wearily back against the wall. 'God, what wouldn't I give for a nice cup of English tea.'

James handed his brother the lukewarm remains of his mug of tea. 'Best I can manage, I'm afraid. I'll get Tom to heat up a tin of Maconochies for you,' he'd said, referring to the canned stew that could be heated to provide a hot, if not very appetizing meal.

Ned had shaken his head as he drained the tea. 'No hurry. I just need to . . .' He'd leaned back again and closed his eyes. 'I'm so bloody tired, James. Exhausted from going out there time after time, fetching back poor buggers who've been blown up, whose lives'll never be the same again, or who won't even live till we can get them to the ambulance station. And all because of this bloody, senseless war. And now my best mate Patrick's copped a packet. He stood on an unexploded shell and got blown to bits. I can't believe he's gone, even though I saw it happen. I actually saw it happen. Couldn't believe my eyes at first.' His head rolled from side to side. 'God, it's all such a bloody nightmare.'

'Patrick?'

'My mate, my buddy. My partner. I've told you about him. We hit it off from the first time we met and we've always worked together . . . laughed together . . . done everything together, really. He made this whole mess bearable for me. God, I'm going to miss him.' He'd dashed his hand across his eyes as he spoke.

James remembered then that Patrick had been Ned's particular partner in the stretcher-bearing unit. This usually comprised six men to a stretcher, or only four if things were particularly busy, and they tended to work in pairs. Patrick and Ned had always worked together, being fellow 'conchies', as conscientious objectors were called, doing the dangerous, filthy, exhausting task of rescuing men out in the field of battle, men who were too badly wounded to help themselves, and carrying them back on the stretchers, often under fire and through thick, knee-deep mud, to be transported to the nearest field hospital.

'I'm sorry, Ned.' It had seemed such an inadequate thing to say.

'Thanks.' Ned had moved his head a little. 'We had such plans, Patrick and me. After the war we were going to start a convalescent home for poor bastards like the ones we were saving from extinction, who could never live a normal life . . . We were going to . . . Oh, what's the use. It'll never happen now. I can't do it without him. I don't have the heart.'

'Things change, Ned. After this bloody war's over . . .'

Ned had opened his eyes and looked straight at his brother. 'Not everything, James. Patrick was special.'

As their eyes met James understood perfectly what he was saying and the colour drained from his face.

'Christ, Ned, keep your voice down. If you're saying what I think you are . . .'

Ned nodded, his face expressionless.

'My God! You could land yourself in prison. Look what happened to that writer chap, Oscar Wilde. Dreadful scandal, by all accounts. People still talk about it, even now, although it all happened before our time.'

Ned had only shrugged. 'No danger of that now Patrick's not here.'

Looking back, James remembered the mess and muddle of emotions that had gone through his mind as he sat watching his distraught brother trying to come to terms with the death of his friend. His first reaction had been to go over and put his arms round his twin, to try to comfort him, but shock and revulsion at what Ned had revealed held him back and kept him rooted to his seat, his head in his hands.

Finally, he'd looked up. 'Can't you . . .? Isn't there some kind of . . . I dunno, cure?' He hadn't known how to phrase it.

'Oh, for God's sake, James, spare me that.' Ned had cut him off sharply. 'It's not important any longer. Patrick's dead. There'll never be another like him so you don't have to worry about me disgracing the family. I wish now I hadn't told you; I don't know why I did, except you're my twin, so I suppose I thought you'd understand. Not that there's any reason why you should . . .'

'Good God, no!' It had come out more vehemently that James had intended.

'I thought not.' Ned got to his feet. 'Well, perhaps it's as well I've told you because now you know the continuation of the family name is going to rest on your shoulders so you'd better come through this lot alive, brother mine.' His mouth twisted in some semblance of a smile. 'Well, maybe not on your shoulders, exactly, but you know what I mean. It certainly isn't going to rest on mine, so I hope you've got someone in mind to share the burden with.'

'Can't say I have,' James had replied, although for some inexplicable reason a picture of Polly Catchpole had sprung into his mind. He got to his feet and shook Ned by the hand. 'I'm sorry, Ned, if I reacted badly. I'm afraid I haven't been much comfort to you, but the shock . . .'

Still clasping his brother's hand Ned clapped him on the shoulder. 'I do understand, Jimbo, and I guess if the boot had been on the other foot I could well have behaved in exactly the same way. But in a funny way I'm glad I've told you, although I guess I wouldn't have said anything if we'd been living in normal times.'

'And now I've got over the shock I'm glad, too,' James said.

They had hugged each other spontaneously and with a muttered 'Good luck' they had parted.

James had never told a soul what had gone on between him and his brother that day and he was certain he never would.

He remained there, thinking about his brother and gazing over the lake for a long time. Eventually he got to his feet and, hands in his pockets, walked the half-mile to Riverside Farm to tell the Hadleys that their son Tom was alive and well.

Twelve

Polly finished the last of Lady Adelaide's ironing. She had hoped, once Ruby was reinstalled as a general duties maid, that this was one of the tasks she would be able to relinquish, but m'lady insisted that she could always tell if somebody else had ironed her things because nobody else paid such meticulous attention to her frills and flounces as Polly did. Hearing this, Polly was tempted to retaliate by scorching a nightgown or leaving a few creases, but it was not in her nature to give less than her best, so the task of ironing remained with her.

Not, in truth, that she minded. It was quiet and peaceful in the ironing kitchen, giving her precious time to think her own thoughts with no fear of interruption, which was something of a luxury. She was particularly glad of this now that Master James was at home because she needed a bit of time and space to sort out her feelings. It had been a shock when she first saw him; she guessed it had been the same for the family because nobody had expected him home. But when he'd walked in the door he looked so tired and haggard that her heart went out to him. Fortunately, it was Mr Walford who had opened the door to him so he hadn't even noticed Polly crossing the hall and she was able to slip into the dining room under pretext of looking for table napkins, should anyone have asked. Since then she'd managed to keep avoiding him, she wasn't sure why. No, that wasn't true, she knew exactly why. She was afraid – afraid if he spoke to her he would see in her face what she felt for him; that she wouldn't be able to hide how desperately she had longed for his return; that she prayed for his safety every night. She knew only too well that their childhood carefree days as equals were gone forever; inevitably he had grown up and away from her. Yet somehow she was sure that underneath the veneer of army life the Jamie she knew and loved was still there. But she had grown up too, and in truth she was shy; she didn't know how to behave in his presence, so she kept out of his way. It was enough to know that he was here, under the same roof; that he was safe.

She finished her ironing and put everything away, then looked at the kitchen clock. She was free for the next hour, time enough to slip across for a cup of tea with her mother, who would probably have some of her favourite cakes waiting for her. She hung up her apron and, with Mrs Bellman's blessing, put on her hat and hurried across the lawns to Pippin Farm.

'I'm home, Mum,' she called as she went in at the open door. 'I hope you've got the kettle on.'

'Tea's already brewed,' her mother called back. 'You're just in time.'

It was their usual greeting. Polly suspected her mother kept the kettle at the ready all day. She went through to the kitchen and stopped short as she saw James sitting at the table.

'Oh!' Her first instinct was to turn and go out again but she realized how silly that would look so instead she turned and hung her hat on the back of the door. After that she smoothed her hair to give the colour that had flared in her face time to die down before advancing into the room.

Then James looked up and smiled at her, the same heart-warming smile she knew so well. 'Ah. Polly-wolly-doodle,' he said. 'Just like old times, meeting in your mother's kitchen over a cup of tea – and look, she's even baked some of her special cakes for us, just like the old days.'

It was easy, after that. They dropped into their old familiar bantering ways while a beaming Susan made sure there were plenty of cakes on the plate and their teacups were refilled. Nearly an hour later, a precious hour that had seemed more like five minutes, Polly stood up to leave.

'I'll walk back with you, Poll,' James said, getting up too. 'I should spend a bit of time with my mother before I go back to France.'

'When will that be?' Susan asked.

'Tomorrow, unfortunately,' he replied with a sigh, adding, 'Not a prospect I relish.'

They left together and Polly made to set off across the lawn, the shortest way back to the house, because now there was just the two of them her shyness had returned. But James turned off towards the woods.

'I thought you wanted to go back to the house so that you could spend time with your mother,' Polly said, puzzled and slightly alarmed at the direction he was taking.

'I'll be spending all evening with her; that'll be quite enough, thank you.' His next remark justified her apprehension. 'I just thought it would be nice to walk through the woods since it's such a lovely day, to recapture some of the memories of my – our – youth.' He grinned at her. 'We spent a lot of time in these woods when we were nippers, didn't we, Poll?'

She tried to match his nostalgic mood, but she found it difficult because for some reason her mouth had gone dry and her heart was hammering. 'Yes,' she said with a nervous little giggle, 'playing cowboys and Indians . . .'

'And pirates. I was very proud of that eye patch I found . . .'

'Except that it kept slipping down because the elastic was worn out.' She burst out laughing. On old, familiar ground she felt safer, so she began to relax.

'Ah, you would remember that, Poll! And to think I imagined I cut quite a dash as a pirate.'

'Oh, you did. Quite a swashbuckler.' She gave a sigh. 'But it never seemed to matter whether it was pirates or cowboys and Indians, I remember it was always me that ended up being taken prisoner.'

'That's because you were a girl. But I always came back and rescued you, didn't I?'

She nodded. 'Eventually. Although you once threatened to leave me there all night. I was petrified.'

'But I didn't leave you, did I? I came back and untied you. Remember?'

Oh, yes, she remembered. She remembered how frightened she'd been when the light began to fade and how she'd cried and clung to him in her relief and he'd hugged her and promised he'd never leave her like that again. As they walked on without speaking she wondered if he was remembering, too. She risked stealing a glance at him but his jaw was set and he was staring straight ahead.

They reached a clearing and she paused and looked up. 'Tom fell out of that tree,' she said.

He glanced up briefly. 'Yes, so he did. Fancy you remembering that.'

'Well, he was only showing off, so it served him right. He was always showing off, daft thing.'

'He wanted to impress you; that's why he did those things.'

'Do you reckon?'

'He tells me he's planning to marry you when he gets back.'

'Oh, does he, indeed! That's the first I've heard about it.' She glanced up at him, expecting him to smile with her but his mood seemed to have changed, grown sombre. 'Jamie?' The childhood name came quite naturally. 'What is it? Have I said something wrong?'

He gave her a quick, nervous smile. 'No. No, of course not, Poll, just . . . Is there a log or something where we can sit for a minute? I'm not feeling . . .' He began to tremble violently.

She looked round and saw a fallen tree. She took his hand and led him across and he sat down, still trembling, his face ashen and his teeth chattering.

She sat on the grass at his feet, still holding his hand, looking up at him.

'I'm sorry. Don't look at me. I'll be all right in a minute. It's just . . . didn't you hear it?'

'Hear what?'

'The guns.'

'Oh, that. It's the soldiers on lower meadow doing target practice. It happens so often I don't notice it most of the time. Did it alarm you?'

'I . . . it reminded me . . . there's always so much noise. It never stops.' He pulled his hand away from hers and covered his ears, rocking back and forth. 'It never stops,' he said, grinding his teeth.

Without stopping to think she got up and sat beside him on the log and put her arms round him and held him close, stroking his hair as he clung to her. 'It's all right, Jamie, you're quite safe here with me,' she whispered. 'We're in the wood, where we used to play as children. You and me and Tom.' She said it over and over until his trembling ceased. Even then she didn't release him, but held him, savouring the moment, the closeness of him, the feel of his arms round her, holding her as tightly as she was holding him. It was a moment she would cherish forever.

She didn't know how long they stayed locked in each other's arms but at last his hold slackened and he pulled away from her.

'I'm sorry, Poll,' he muttered, embarrassed, taking out a handkerchief and mopping his face, half turned away from her. 'It's just . . . it's that noise. It gets to me.'

'It's all right, Jamie. I understand.' It was true, she understood that he was trying to tell her that those few moments had meant less than nothing to him, she had simply been something to cling to in his fear, nothing more than that. *Nothing* more than that. To let him know that she had got his message she stood up, smiling brightly. 'Are you feeling better? Do you want to walk back now?'

He got to his feet and stood looking down at her. Suddenly he realized that what he wanted more than anything else in the world was to take her in his arms and kiss her, to stroke her hair and tell her how much he loved her, had always loved her. But they were no longer children and the gulf between servant and master had widened with the years so that he was afraid she would think he was simply trying to take advantage of her, as so often happened in big houses, which was something he would never do. And then of course, there was Tom . . .

He nodded and turned away. 'Yes. Let's go back now.'

They walked back, saying little, and when they reached the

house they went their separate ways, Polly to the kitchen and
James up the steps to the front door.

The next day James returned to France and life at Meadowlands
returned to normal, or what passed as normal in such troubled
times.

Gina and Polly spent ever more time at what was still called
the soup club although it had gradually blossomed into a kind of
social club where the women could go for a cup of tea and a chat
as well as for help and advice. But the main attraction, especially
for the children, was always the precious soup.

There were other advantages. Once it became more widely
known what Gina was doing, several of her friends and acquaintances began offering help – not at the club itself, which would
have been a step too far for most of them – but by giving provi-
sions, mainly tinned food or vegetables that their gardeners had
grown, and cast-off clothing that they had tired of or their children
had outgrown. Someone had even discovered an old sewing
machine in an attic and it turned out that one of the soup club
women had actually been a seamstress before an early marriage
and too many pregnancies had put a stop to a promising career.
She was only too glad to earn a few coppers altering garments to
fit for those who could afford to pay even a tiny amount because
her husband had been discharged from the army a nervous, trembling wreck quite unfit to work – although the authorities disagreed
with this, saying that since he was still in possession of all his limbs
there was no reason why he shouldn't look for employment.
Consequently, no pension was forthcoming and without the soup
club and what little she could earn, the family would have starved.

There were other signs of the good work that Gina and Polly
were doing. After some persuasion from Polly, Will Catchpole had
sent one of his workers to measure Annie Baxter's husband for a
crutch, which had been duly made and delivered. Now Percy Baxter
was able to stand on the corner of the street selling matches, which
shamed him beyond words because it was a far cry from his trade
as a bricklayer. But it earned him a few coppers to keep his family
just above starvation level so he forced himself to swallow his pride
and stand there, day after day with his tray of match boxes and
safety pins hanging round his neck as people he knew either walked
by or bought his wares out of pity for him. He couldn't spare the
money to travel daily to a town where he wasn't known.

Still grieving for her beloved Archie, Gina threw herself wholeheartedly into her work at the soup club, writing letters, most of which were never even acknowledged, and listening to endless tales of hardship although there was never any lack of support for her in her own sadness. Polly watched over her and worried as she grew thin but there was little she could do to prevent her working longer and longer hours for families who were coming from further and further afield as news spread of what 'the posh lady' was doing to help.

'I'm sorry we were so late leaving, Polly,' Gina said wearily as they drove home one day as autumn was beginning to slip into winter. 'I know we're only supposed to be there from ten till one but did you see the queue? Some of those women had walked for four miles to ask for help. I couldn't turn them away, could I?'

'No, Miss Gina, of course you couldn't.' Polly stole a glance at her. 'But I'm going to make sure you have something to eat and a rest before you start writing letters.'

Gina smiled. 'And what about you? You must be exhausted, keeping all those children in order.'

'Oh, they're no trouble once they get a mug of soup inside them. The little ones often go to sleep and I'm teaching a few of the older ones their letters,' Polly said proudly.

'What a good idea!' A wide smile spread across Gina's tired face. 'I'll see if I can find some of my first primers, I expect they're still somewhere in the schoolroom. If they can read and write a bit it'll give them a better chance in life.'

'That's what I think. But some of them really aren't well enough to concentrate. They often fall asleep, once they get a mug of soup inside them, just sitting cross-legged on the floor, poor mites. And have you seen how bow-legged a lot of them are?'

Gina frowned. 'I think that's caused by rickets, but I'm not sure.' She sighed. 'Oh, I wish my sister Millie would get leave; she'd know about these medical matters.'

'Where is Miss Millie now?'

'Working in a field hospital somewhere on the Somme, I believe. She's not likely to get leave; from what I can make out from the few lines she manages when she writes home they're far too busy.'

'Is that where Mister Ned and Mr James are, too?'

'I think so.'

'I hope they'll be able to see each other sometimes.'

'Yes, I hope so, too.'

They reached home and both climbed wearily out of the car. Gina patted the bonnet. 'Thanks little car. We could never keep doing what we do without you.'

'What a good thing Master James said you could drive it,' Polly added.

'Indeed it is. We'd be sunk without it.' Gina looked at her watch. 'Oh, we're far too late for lunch. Do you think Mrs Bellman will have saved us some?'

'If not I'll make you some scrambled egg and bring it to your room.'

'Lovely. Make sure you bring some for yourself, too. Put it all on a tray. We'll eat together.'

'Oh, I couldn't, Miss Gina!' Polly was horrified.

'Nonsense. We're partners at the soup club so why shouldn't we eat a spot of lunch together? Do as I say and don't argue.' Her smile took the sternness out of the words.

Over lunch any awkwardness Polly might have felt was quickly dispelled as they discussed the impossibility of getting medical treatment for the people they were helping.

'The trouble is, medicines have to be paid for and any money we get has to go on food for the growing numbers of people who come to us for help,' Gina said, running her fingers through her hair wearily.

Polly nodded. 'And you hear such dreadful tales. Maisie Bullock told me her neighbour's husband was sent home from the Front too ill to work. She said he should never have been called up in the first place because he was already consumptive, but then he got gassed so they had to discharge him.'

'Oh, dear.' It was a tale that was becoming all too familiar.

'That's not all,' Polly went on. 'Maisie said the doctor came and ordered him to have some kind of expensive medicine, which he couldn't afford because he's got no pension.'

Gina frowned. 'But . . .'

'It's true. When he was discharged from the army they said he wasn't eligible for a pension because he was already consumptive before he joined up and they only pay a pension for war wounds.'

'But that's iniquitous!' Gina was horrified.

'So his wife's been selling her furniture, bit by bit, to buy it for him. Not that it does him any good, Maisie says.'

'Oh, dear. That's terrible. Why hasn't she come to us?'

'Maisie says she won't leave him.'

'Are there children?'

'Yes, three. Sometimes Maisie brings them with her so they can have a mug of soup.'

Gina gave Polly a tired smile. 'I hope your mother realizes how many people her soup has saved from starvation, Polly.'

'Oh, yes, she does. And now that Ruby is back here and Tom's mother is not needed so much to help with the cleaning and polishing, Mum has enlisted her to make some soup. Hadn't you noticed we take nearly twice as much as we used to?'

'Come to think of it, yes, I had noticed the saucepans were bigger.' Gina laughed. 'I'm not very observant, am I, Polly?'

'You've got a lot of other things on your mind, Miss Gina.'

'Yes, and I must get my pen and paper out while it's all still fresh. I'll certainly make a complaint about the treatment of that poor man. The Government are desperate to call men up to fight, whether they're fit or not, but it's obvious they don't care what happens to them, or their families when they're no longer able to work. Now, where are my notes?'

Polly began to gather up the remains of their belated lunch. 'Yes, and I must go and tackle m'lady's ironing.'

'I shall have a word with my mother about that,' Gina said sharply. 'I'm sure Ruby is quite capable of taking that off your hands.'

Polly made a face. 'I wish you would. You see, m'lady insists that I do it. She says Ruby doesn't do it right.'

'Well, there's a war on and we all have to make sacrifices. My mother can put up with a few creases in her laundry here and there as her sacrifice. She hasn't given up much else.'

Thirteen

It was a cold, wet and windy day in November, which meant the soup club would be extra busy, because in bad weather more women and their children came to enjoy a little warmth as well as to be fed and their grievances heard.

Gina made a right turn from the square into the road where

the soup club was held and saw a man on crutches in a long mackintosh and bowler hat trying to shelter in the doorway of the room they rented.

'Oh, heavens,' she groaned. 'I don't think we can cope with men! Why doesn't he send his wife like the rest of them do?'

'Perhaps he hasn't got one. Anyway, he doesn't look like he needs help. Look at his clothes; he looks very smart,' Polly replied, trying to peer through the raindrops on the windscreen. A sudden thought struck her. 'Oh, Miss Gina, I hope he isn't from the Authorities, come to close us down.' To Polly 'The Authorities' was like some mythical ogre, bent on their destruction, or at least on making life as difficult as possible for all concerned, and particularly Miss Gina, who battled with them on a daily basis.

'Don't be silly, Poll, he can't have come to close us down. We pay the rent regularly and we're not a nuisance to the neighbourhood.'

'Quite the reverse, I'd have said,' Polly remarked primly. 'And I shall tell him that, if he says that's what he's going to do.'

'Well, we won't know if we don't get out and ask him.' Gina opened the car door and put up her umbrella. 'Can I help you?' she called to him as she went across to unlock the door.

'Miss Gina Barsham?' he asked.

She nodded curtly.

'My name is Max Rodwell.' He bowed his head slightly in a polite gesture. 'I'm sorry I can't doff my hat but as you can see I'm a little incapacitated.' He indicated his crutches with a pleasant, slightly apologetic smile. 'Your sister Millie suggested I should come and see you.'

She didn't return his smile. 'You'd better come in, then. We can't stand here talking in the rain.' At the mention of Millie's name Gina felt a little less hostile to the man but she was not prepared to let her guard down until she knew a little more of him. She was puzzled, too, as to how he could possibly know Millie.

They had hardly got inside the door when a crowd of women and children appeared as if by magic. It appeared they all had their allotted tasks, supervised by Polly. Three or four women carried the precious pans of soup in, several others put up tables and laid out mugs for the soup and cups for tea. Another one brought in water and put the big kettle on the gas ring to boil for the tea, whilst yet another shepherded the children into some kind of order.

Two more rolled in the milk churn that was left on the step each day by a farmer they had never yet managed to meet and thank for his generosity and that was, miraculously, never touched until Gina arrived. Polly wielded the soup ladle.

'Goodness, you're very well organized.' Max Rodwell looked round admiringly as he followed Gina to the screened-off corner where she spent most of her time listening to and trying to help with problems.

'So we should be. We've been doing this for quite some time,' Gina replied, her voice crisp and still a little frosty. She sat down behind the little card table, her usual position, and indicated that he should take the other chair, which he did with some difficulty. There was no space for anything else so she waited while he folded his wet mackintosh and put it on the floor beside him with his bowler hat on top. Then she said, 'Now, how can I help you, Mr Rodwell?'

He smiled again and despite her misgivings she found herself smiling back.

'I rather think the boot is on the other foot, Miss Barsham. I've come to see if I might be of some assistance to you,' he answered. 'I am actually *Doctor* Rodwell, Max to my friends. Millie is a very good friend of mine; we worked together quite a lot in the field ambulance service. When she knew there was a chance I would be in this area she suggested I might be of some use to you whilst I convalesce from my brush with the enemy.'

'It's very kind of you, Doctor Rodwell, but much as we could do with your help I'm afraid we don't have any money to pay for it.' Gina's regret was genuine.

'I was not asking for payment, Miss Barsham, I was simply offering help,' Max Rodwell said sharply, clearly offended. He began to struggle to manoeuvre his crutches so that he could stand. 'But if you don't want my services I won't waste your time any longer. I can see you're a busy lady so I'm sorry to have bothered you.'

Gina got to her feet so quickly that her chair would have fallen if there had been room and she held out her hand. 'No, no, please don't go. I've obviously got it all wrong and I do apologize,

Doctor Rodwell. We do desperately need your help for these poor people. Please, stay and have a cup of tea so that you can see what we're trying to do and if you're still prepared to help us we would be most grateful.' She found she was twisting her hands together nervously and holding her breath, afraid he would walk out of the door and they would lose him.

He stood, balanced on his crutches, regarding her thoughtfully. 'If you don't soon take a breath you'll fall down, Miss Barsham,' he remarked drily.

She flushed. 'But will you stay and help us? Please? I'm truly sorry that I insulted you by getting off on the wrong foot.'

'On the contrary, I think it's me that's on the wrong foot, Miss Barsham,' he said gravely. 'But unfortunately, it's the only one I have. I was forced to leave the right one and half my leg in a shell hole on the banks of the Somme.'

'Oh, I . . .' She looked up at him and saw a twinkle in his eye. 'You're laughing at me.'

His face broke into a boyish grin. 'Yes, I rather think I am.'

She relaxed and laughed out loud. 'Well, I deserved it.' She became serious. 'I'm really sorry about your injury.'

He shrugged. 'It could have been so much worse. With any luck they'll fit me up with an artificial leg eventually, but it won't be yet. Till then I manage quite well on these.' He held up a crutch briefly.

'Please, can we start again? Won't you sit down again and I'll get someone to bring you a cup of tea, Doctor Rodwell.'

'Max. Please call me Max. And I'd love a cup of tea but if you don't mind I'd prefer to have it out there with the children.' He jerked his head towards the room where there was quite a hubbub going on. 'I don't wish to offend you, Miss Barsham, but I need to gain their confidence if I'm going to do anything for them.'

'Of course. I understand.' She edged round the table and laid a hand on his arm. 'I can't tell you how sorry I am that I was so rude to you, Doctor . . . Max, nor how grateful I am that you're here.'

He smiled. 'That was a really gracious apology, Miss Barsham.'

'Gina.'

'Gina.'

'And Polly is my right hand – my partner in this. We work

together and I truly couldn't manage without her. Come and meet everybody.'

At first there was a wary silence as Max was introduced and his role explained, but one by one the children's curiosity got the better of them and before long they were bringing him their peg dolls and toys from the box in the corner – toys that had been discarded from the nurseries of Gina's well-to-do friends and acquaintances – and fighting over who should sit beside him.

At the end of the morning, when everything was tidied away and the mothers had taken their children and gone back to the squalid rooms they called home, Gina set out three chairs.

'I think we should all sit down and take stock,' she said, taking the chair in the middle. 'Yes, you too, Polly,' she added as Polly hung back. 'We're all equals in this venture. Now, Doctor – Max, what are your thoughts about our soup club? And I'm not looking for glib compliments, I want the truth, because we're not doing this as some kind of conscience-salving, do-gooding enterprise; we really want to help these poor people.'

'I think you're doing absolutely the right thing,' he replied. 'I've heard nothing but praise from everyone I've spoken to today. The children clearly idolize Polly.' He smiled at her. 'And the women are more than grateful for your advice and the letters you write on their behalf, Gina. One of the things I heard most was that you *listen* to them and that's so important.' He spread his hands. 'So, what more can I say? Except that I hope you'll allow me to add my efforts to yours whilst I'm in the area. There's quite a lot of infection among the children that I'd like to try and clear up, for a start. And they could do with a few lessons in hygiene.'

Gina rolled her eyes. 'Couldn't they just! But it must be so difficult when they have one privy between four or six houses and every drop of water has to be carried from the communal tap.' She gave a huge sigh. 'But thank you, Max. You're an answer to our prayers. We need your help. These women – and hundreds like them – have been badly let down.'

He nodded. 'I've certainly heard some harrowing stories this morning.'

'I'm sure you have. You see, right from the start of this war all the effort was put into getting men into the army. Precious little thought was given to the families left behind with no breadwinner. When we set up our soup club the women and children who came to us were all on the point of starvation. It was truly awful.' She shrugged. 'We can't do much, I'll admit, but a mug of soup – which Polly's mother makes by the gallon for us – a cup of tea and someone to listen to their troubles and try to get something done for them, does at least help to show that they're not entirely forgotten. And sometimes the letters I write actually get results and something is done. But not often enough,' she added, shaking her head.

Going home in the car the conversation was naturally all about Max and his timely arrival at the door of the soup club.

'You said he knew Miss Millie, was that how he found out about the soup club?' Polly asked.

'Yes. Apparently they worked together in a field hospital on the Somme, so now we know where Millie is,' Gina replied. 'Right in the thick of it.'

'Along with Mr James and Mr Ned.' Polly gazed out of the window and quietly offered up a prayer for their safety and an end to the carnage of this disastrous war.

That evening, for something to talk about over supper, Gina told her mother about Max Rodwell turning up at the soup club. Not that she expected Adelaide to show much interest. She was never very sympathetic towards the affairs of the poor; she knew they existed but didn't wish to be reminded of the fact, particularly over supper. So Gina was surprised when her mother paused, her fork halfway to her mouth.

'*Doctor* Rodwell, did you say?' she asked with interest.

'That's right. Doctor Max Rodwell. He knows Millie; she told him about our soup club and he wants to help.'

'Good,' she said absently. Then, with more animation, 'We must invite him to dinner. I'm sure your father would like to meet him.'

'Father's rarely here.'

'All the same, I think we should invite him. He may have news of Millie.'

'Not recent news. I think he's been in the military hospital here for at least the past eight weeks. He lost a leg in the fighting.'

'Oh.' Adelaide made a moue of distaste. 'Even so, it would be polite. And perhaps he wouldn't mind taking a look at my toe . . .'

'*Mother!* If Max Rodwell comes to this house it will not be to look at your toe!' Gina was disgusted at her mother's self-centredness. She relented. 'Well, perhaps, if he isn't going home to wherever he lives we could invite him for Christmas. If he's still with us, of course.'

'That's six weeks away.'

'We don't want to appear too pushy. And father will be home, so the numbers will be even.' Gina was anxious to avoid her mother making a fool of herself over Max as she had over Andrew Palgrave. Briefly, she wondered where Andrew was now. Their exchange of letters had petered out after a few months but she still thought of him from time to time.

Max soon became a firm favourite at the soup club. He quickly identified which of the children needed to be given extra milk and he discouraged the mothers from sewing their children into their clothes for the winter. This had begun when Gina persuaded her friends to donate warm winter clothes that their own children had outgrown to the soup club. The habit of stitching children into their clothes for the winter was common practice in a good many working-class families, together with rubbing children's chests with camphorated oil or hanging little bags containing camphor blocks round their necks. This was all done in good faith, believed to ward off the winter coughs and colds that frequently proved fatal. There was no mistaking children who received this treatment. They carried their own miasma of unwashed body and camphor wherever they went. Schools could be particularly pungent and the soup club was becoming equally aromatic until Max gently put a stop to the practice.

Christmas came and at the soup club they had a little party. The mothers decorated the room with sprigs of holly from the hedgerows and Polly's mother supplied warm mince pies. From somewhere – Polly suspected it was her own pocket – Gina had managed to find money to buy tiny gifts for each child together with a few sweets and afterwards Polly lined them all up to sing 'Away in a Manger', which she had spent weeks teaching them, along with the Christmas story.

Before they all left, Gina was given a patchwork bag.

'Aggie here, wot's got the sewin' machine an' makes over all the clo'es you bring us, she made it up from scraps. Ain't she clever?' said Maudie Hinchcliffe, who made the presentation, in admiration. 'Thass to thank you for wot you do for us, Miss Gina. We're ever so grateful, ain't we, gals?'

There was a chorus of assent and then someone shouted, 'Three cheers for Miss Gina . . .'

'And Miss Polly,' someone called.

'Thass right. An' Doctor Max. Hip, hip . . .'

'Hooray.' They all shouted, and it was difficult to know whether the women or the children shouted the loudest.

Then everyone went back to their bleak little homes full of Christmas cheer.

On Christmas Day, Max arrived at Meadowlands, immaculately dressed in a dark grey suit, the right leg of the trousers pinned up below the knee, a spotless white shirt and maroon tie. He was driven in a smart Ford car by a young ex-soldier he called Thurlow, who had also been recently discharged from the army with a dreadful, bubbling cough through having been quite badly gassed in the trenches. Max brought with him whisky for Sir George and chocolates for the ladies, including Polly, who he was clearly puzzled to see later waiting on table.

Over lunch, Max told them he had decided to remain in the area now he was no longer in the army. He had found himself a flat and was employing Thurlow as his driver and man servant.

'Poor fellow nearly went down on his knees with gratitude,' he said sadly. 'He had envisaged spending the rest of his life begging in the streets. But I'm giving him something to help with his cough and with plenty of fresh air and the right food he'll manage perfectly well as long as I keep an eye on him.'

'That's very noble of you,' Gina remarked.

'Not at all. I need him as much as he needs me. I think we shall get along very well.'

'You're staying in the area, then. Does that mean you'll be setting up in practice?' Adelaide said, adding archly with her habitual lack of tact, 'No ties elsewhere?'

'Yes, yes and no, in answer to your questions,' Max replied briefly, a disarming smile robbing his answers of any curtness, at the same time discouraging any further probing into his affairs.

'What are these new-fangled weapons they're talking about now, Rodwell?' Sir George asked, immersed in his own train of thought and completely oblivious to the previous conversation.

'Tanks, they call them, don't they? They run on caterpillars, or some such. Can't see they'll ever be much use.'

'Oh, but they will, Sir George,' Max replied with enthusiasm. 'They're armoured, so the men inside are protected from bullets, and the metal caterpillar allows the tank to traverse rough ground that an ordinary wheeled vehicle would get bogged down in.'

'Oh, George, *must* the conversation always be either the war or politics when you're at home?' Lady Adelaide asked plaintively.

Sir George put down his napkin and got to his feet. 'Apologies, my dear. Most insensitive of me to bring the outside world into your dining room. Come, Rodwell, we'll take our coffee in my study. I've got some rather good brandy to share with you and I'd like to know what you think of the new prime minister. It seems people either love or hate Lloyd George but the general opinion seems to be that Asquith was far too indecisive.'

Max picked up his crutches and got to his feet.

'Excuse me, ladies,' he said, having no choice but to follow Sir George and seeming quite happy to do so.

'Afternoon tea will be served at five,' Gina called after him. 'I hope Father will release you from his clutches for that.'

'I might even join you,' Sir George said genially.

'Oh, Lord. I hope not.' Lady Adelaide raised her eyes towards the ceiling.

'Mother! It's Christmas,' Gina hissed, envisaging a dull afternoon with her mother discussing dress patterns and the latest fashion to raise skirts to above the ankle, which Lady Adelaide thought quite scandalous.

Below stairs, once the ice was broken, Brian Thurlow had a thoroughly enjoyable time. Without breaking any confidences he was able speak of his gratitude at being taken on by Dr Rodwell, and being given his own quarters in the large flat at the edge of the town.

'Nice man, the doctor. Very nice man. Real gentleman,' was his verdict. 'Gets a lot of pain from that leg, though, even though most of it isn't there any longer. Funny, that.'

Polly longed to ask him if he knew Mr James or Mr Ned but he seemed more intent on impressing Ruby with his tales so she kept quiet. In any case, he'd only been a corporal so he was unlikely to have known them.

After lunch and when everything was cleared away, a trolley was laid for afternoon tea and cold platters left for supper, then everyone was free to go home or visit relatives. Mrs Bellman and Mr Walford stayed behind; they each had their own private sitting rooms. Polly and Ruby went to see their respective families so Albert volunteered to take Brian home with him, which was not an entirely altruistic offer since he had high hopes of a ride in the smart Ford car.

Fourteen

Christmas afternoon, when Lady Adelaide went up for her quite unnecessary afternoon rest, Gina went to sit by the fire in the drawing room with Somerset Maugham's latest book, *Of Human Bondage*, which had been one of her Christmas presents. But she didn't open the book; instead she sat staring into the fire, thinking of Archie and what might have been, remembering the way his hair curled at the nape of his neck, how much she had loved him and the life together they had planned. They should have been spending this Christmas happily married, even possibly looking forward to the birth of their first child if it hadn't been for the bloody war, she reflected savagely as her eyes filled with tears over what might have been. She put her hand on her flat stomach. She couldn't imagine what it must be like to have a baby growing inside her and now she would probably never know. This war had changed, and was changing, people's lives in unimaginable ways, most of them not for the better. She gave herself a mental shake at the thought, dried her eyes and opened her book.

She had hardly read two lines when there was a tap at the door and Max put his head in.

'Ah, there you are, Gina. Do you mind if I join you?'

'Please do. Mother's gone for her rest and I was just sitting here gazing into the fire, thinking, instead of reading my book. It'll be a relief to have someone to talk to.' She smiled up at him. 'How did you manage to escape from Pa? He can be like a leech when he gets hold of someone to listen to him. He does rather pontificate, as you've no doubt discovered.'

He gave a wry grin. 'Well, he sort of nodded off so I left him to it.'

'Very sensible of you. Do come and sit down by the fire. Since we're both "off duty", so to speak, it'll be a relief to have a conversation about something other than what's going on at the soup club. For a start I'm anxious to hear a bit more about my sister, since you've obviously seen her over there. What's she doing? Is she happy – well, as happy as anyone could be, under the circumstances? I do miss her, you know, and her letters when we get them are so sketchy . . .'

'Letter-writing isn't easy, where she's working.' He lowered himself into an armchair facing her and placed his crutches on the floor beside him. Then he said, 'When I saw her last she was absolutely fine, although I have to admit I was not.' He made a sketchy gesture towards his empty trouser leg. 'But I'd known her for some time before that as we'd worked quite a lot together in various places. At the moment she's attached to a field ambulance up near the Front. That's where they receive the wounded and patch them up and either send them back to their unit, or on to the casualty clearing station. Not a nice place to be; some of the things they have to deal with are – well, not pleasant, as you can imagine. They're all dreadfully overworked there but Millie's always cheerful and doesn't let it get her down.'

'Sounds like Millie. She obviously hasn't changed much,' Gina said with a smile. 'And she's well?'

'Oh, yes. In fact, she seems to thrive on what she's doing.'

'She's found her vocation, would you say?'

'Mm. You could say that.' He steepled his fingers, his mind clearly elsewhere. 'There is one thing . . .' He hesitated and she looked at him in alarm. 'No, no, it's not anything dreadful, quite the reverse, in fact.' As her look turned to a puzzled frown he smiled in embarrassment. 'Sorry, I'm not doing this very well, am I? But as I told you, we've known each other for quite a while and become friends – well, more than friends.' He took a deep breath. 'I'm sure she won't mind me telling you, and I guess you won't be surprised, that we're unofficially engaged to be married. Although I'd prefer it if you kept it to yourself for a while, in case she wants to spring it on you all as a surprise when she comes home.'

'Of course.' Gina's shoulders sagged with relief, then as his words sank in her face lit up. 'Oh, Max. That's absolutely wonderful! I'm so pleased. For both of you.'

'We won't be married until the war is over, of course. But that's the main reason I've decided to settle in this area, so that she won't be too far from her family. You, in particular. She's always telling me how marvellous you are.'

'Rubbish.' She clapped her hands. 'Oh, what a lovely Christmas present. And to think I was beginning to wonder if Millie would ever settle down. She's such a scatterbrain.' She got up and went over to him and shook his hand warmly. 'Congratulations, Max. I can't tell you how pleased I am.' She laughed delightedly. 'Oh, you'll be my brother-in-law, won't you? How nice. I think, under the circumstances, I'm allowed a chaste kiss.' She bent and gave him a swift peck on the cheek.

'Thank you, Gina.' He smiled up at her. Then he rubbed his chin thoughtfully. 'There's something else I feel I should tell you . . .'

'Yes?'

'I have been married before. My wife, Margaret, was killed two years ago in one of the first zeppelin raids. We'd only been married a year and she was pregnant with our first child. I'd suggested she should go back and live with her parents in King's Lynn while I was away. I was sure she would be safe there, in Norfolk. How wrong can one be?' He shook his head. 'I never ever thought I would fall in love again, let alone contemplate marriage.'

Gina nodded. 'I can understand that.'

'I thought my world had ended. I didn't care what happened to me, so I immediately volunteered for Ypres and after eighteen months or so was sent to the Somme, which is where I met Millie and against all my expectations – or, if it comes to that, my inclinations – I fell in love. She's a remarkable woman, your sister, Gina.'

'She is, indeed.'

He was silent for several moments, then went on: 'Naturally, I shall never forget Margaret, she'll always have a special place in my heart, but grieving forever won't bring her back. Life has to be lived, one has to move on. Your sister taught me that, although she probably doesn't realize it.'

'She knows, though, about your wife?'

'Yes, of course. I wouldn't have let our relationship develop without telling her about Margaret. Millie's very understanding. She's also very down to earth, which I very much appreciate.'

'Thank you for telling me, Max, and I really do understand because Archie, my fiancé, was lost on the *Invincible* at the battle of Jutland. Maybe Millie told you.'

He nodded. 'She did. I'm sorry.'

'As you say, life moves on. In my case it moved on to the soup club. I often think that soup club saved my life, or at least my sanity, and helped me get things in perspective. So many women came to us there in dire need of help, with nobody to listen to their problems, that I felt compelled to do what I could for them. Yet they were so resilient and stoical even though they had such harrowing stories to tell, that they made me ashamed that I'd been sitting at home wallowing in my grief.' She smiled. 'But you've seen them, Max, you know how it is.' She glanced at her watch. 'Goodness, I must go and fetch the tea trolley. Ruby and Polly will have left everything ready so I only have to brew the tea.'

He frowned. 'No, hang on a minute, Gina. There's something I don't quite understand. I thought you said that Polly was your partner, and she certainly acts like it at the soup club, yet I saw her waiting on table at lunchtime and now you say she's prepared the tea trolley. Who, exactly, is she? Or rather, what is her position in your family, if it's not a rude question?'

She smiled. 'No, of course it's not a rude question. Polly is quite remarkable. She appears to slip quite easily between roles. Her father is our estate manager so she was born here and went to the village school. When she was fourteen she began work here as kitchen maid. But she's an intelligent girl and soon worked her way up in the below stairs hierarchy. Now she acts as ladies' maid to my mother and me, although with most of our staff having left to do war work of one kind or another she'll turn her hand to anything. My mother can't, or won't appreciate this and she still expects Polly to wait on her every whim. Mind you, I have to admit I take up a lot of Polly's time, too, but it's with the soup club, not with being fussed over.'

'I see. That explains a lot.'

Gina absently smoothed the cover on the book she was holding. 'The funny thing is,' she mused, 'although she always calls me

Miss Gina, her attitude towards me is quite different here to what it is when we're working together at the soup club, where we're more or less partners. And she never, ever mixes the two roles up; she's always deferential here at the house, whereas at the soup club she's never afraid to say what she thinks and she'll argue her point if she feels something very strongly, which she would never do here. She's a remarkable girl; I'm very fond of her. I regard her as a friend as much as a maid.' She looked up as the door opened. 'Ah,' she said quietly, 'Mother's arrived in time for tea. She usually surfaces at around this time. I'd better go and fetch it.' She got to her feet, smiling at Max. 'I'll leave you to her tender mercies. No, don't get up, I'm sure she'll understand.'

The rest of the day passed pleasantly enough, ending with a game of cards which Lady Adelaide was quite gleeful at winning.

As she walked up the stairs to bed, with Gina by her side, Lady Adelaide remarked, 'Doctor Rodwell – Max – seems an exceedingly pleasant young man, doesn't he?' She turned and looked her daughter up and down. 'If you play your cards right, my dear . . . Oh, not yet, of course,' she added hurriedly as she saw the expression on Gina's face. 'But in the fullness of time . . .' She raised a questioning eyebrow.

Gina shook her head. 'Oh, no, Ma, I don't think so. I'm not looking for a husband. Nobody could replace my Archie. After all . . .'

'I know, my dear, it's only just over six months since he died. It was very tactless of me.' She laid a hand on Gina's arm. 'Nevertheless, I do hope you will marry, eventually. And Max Rodwell is very . . .'

'If I ever marry, Mother, and it's a big IF, it won't be to Max Rodwell, I can assure you of that,' Gina interrupted her firmly. But she didn't say why.

As 1917 began there was no sign of a let-up in the fighting although neither side gained much ground. After six months and the use of tanks by both sides, the battle of the Somme still raged, cold and wet, bogged down in mud, claiming more and more lives.

At sea, German submarines were making a concentrated attack on English shipping. In the Mediterranean at the beginning of January the Cunard liner *Ivernia* was sunk with the loss of over

150 lives and in the Atlantic later in the month another 350 died when HMS *Laurentic* was sunk by a mine. The enemy submarines were everywhere, all round the coast and into the Atlantic, claiming hundreds of ships and lives practically unhindered. But when a hospital ship with its red cross signs illuminated was torpedoed, claiming more lives, it provoked outrage. The Germans claimed that British hospital ships carried munitions but this was firmly denied by the Government.

In the United States of America the mass-production methods of the car industry were brought into use in the shipbuilding, aircraft, and munitions industries, creating prosperity for all, although they had not yet officially joined the war against Germany.

In England, Prime Minister David Lloyd George, and Andrew Bonar Law, Chancellor of the Exchequer, announced that the war was now costing over five million pounds a day and encouraged the entire population to subscribe to the new five-shilling 'war loan' to help to finance it.

Most of the women at the soup club could neither read nor write but they somehow managed to get hold of this news and had a good deal to say about it, not much of it complimentary to either Lloyd George or Bonar Law.

'I'd like to have five shillin's to *spend*, never mind *lend*,' said one.

'Maybe if the Gov'ment paid us what they owed us we might *hev* five shillin's,' said another.

'If my Frank hadn't bin gassed so 'e can't work, 'e might hev bin able to *earn* five shillin's,' said a third.

On 6 April, President Woodrow Wilson signed the declaration of war with Germany that had, not without a certain amount of opposition, been passed by Congress and at the end of June the first United States troops landed on the French coast. They were greeted by cheering crowds as they disembarked from the troop-ships and marched blithely on their way to the hell of the muddy battlefields.

Meantime, shortages were beginning to bite in England and even the king joined in to exhort people to eat less bread, as he and his family had pledged to do – an announcement that was received with some cynicism at the soup club, although of course nobody dared to utter a word of criticism towards the king.

In September the reality of war hit Meadowlands yet again.

It was a warm, sunny day early in the month when Violet Hadley rushed over to Pippin Farm, through the open door and along the passage to the kitchen, where she plonked herself down at the table, threw her apron up over her head and began to cry, huge wracking sobs.

Susan was at the sink, peeling vegetables for the never-ending soup. She turned at the commotion.

'Violet! What in the name of heaven's the matter? Are you ill?' Her voice sharp with concern, she dried her hands on her apron and went over and put her arm round Violet's heaving shoulders. 'Now, calm yourself, Vi, and tell me what it's all about,' she said more gently. 'I can't do anything if I don't know what the trouble is, now can I? Has Isaac been . . .?' She stopped. She couldn't see any marks of violence on Violet's tearstained face.

Violet shook her head impatiently. 'No, no, it's not Isaac. It's our boy. It's Tom,' she managed to hiccup.

'Oh, Vi, that's awful.' Susan cradled Violet's head on her ample bosom. 'To lose your youngest . . .'

'He's not dead,' Violet wailed. 'He's injured.'

'Thank God for that. Injured's bad enough but at least he's still alive.'

'Badly injured, they said. But what does that mean? How badly? They don't tell you, do they? All they said was he's being re . . . repat . . .'

'Repatriated. Brought back to England,' Susan explained.

'Oh, is that what it means? Isaac read me the letter but I don't think he was quite sure.'

'So you don't know what his injuries are?'

Violet shook her head. 'They just said *badly* injured. Could mean anything, I s'pose.' Her sobs had diminished and she managed a watery smile. 'You always think the worst, don't you?' she said apologetically.

'It's only natural, I reckon. I'll make us a cup of tea and we can talk a bit, if you want to.' Susan busied herself with the kettle and had just poured the tea when Will walked in.

She poured another cup and began to tell him the news but he held up his hand to stop her.

'I know. I've just seen Isaac. He's working like a demented navvy chopping down those trees in the copse that we've earmarked for pit props. Good thing. He needs to keep himself busy, I can understand that. He told me he wants to go and see Tom as soon as they get him back to England. I said he can take as much time as he needs, I'll look after the animals while he's gone.'

'That's very kind of you, Mr Catchpole,' Violet said with an attempt at a smile. 'Isaac won't like leaving his pigs but he'll be happier if he knows you're seein' after them.'

'It's the least I can do, Violet,' Will said. 'I hope the lad's injuries won't be as bad as you fear.'

'Tell you the truth, I don't know what to think, Mr Catchpole,' said Violet, calmer and more rational now. 'What does badly injured mean? Has he lost a leg? An arm? An eye?'

'Best not to speculate,' Will said, draining the last of his tea. 'You'll know soon enough. We all will.'

A week later, Isaac went down to the hospital in Eastbourne where Tom had been taken. He had never been that far from home before and never travelled much by train and Violet could tell he was nervous although he never said so. She packed his shaving gear, soap, face flannel and towel, together with a clean shirt and nightshirt in the little cardboard suitcase that had belonged to some relative or other and made sandwiches for the journey for him to put in his pocket. Then she waved him goodbye and went back inside and polished all the furniture.

It was the noise that got to him. Crossing London, he found himself bewildered by the crowds of people milling about. The soldiers, both the able-bodied – singing the latest songs, on their way to France – and the wounded, quieter, bandaged or stretchered, just returned. The WVS in their uniforms, greeting the troops with a smile and endless cups of tea and cigarettes. After the peace and quiet of Meadowlands the shouting and noise of the people and the rattling and screaming of the railway engines were scarier than rounding up a herd of mad cows, he admitted later. But he was determined to see his son so he gritted his teeth and went on, a solitary, weather-beaten, stocky figure in the ill-fitting suit he was married in, now only rarely taken out of the mothballs that both preserved and scented it, brown gaiters and boots and a bowler hat that had belonged to his father, now turning green with age.

Four days later he was back, tight-lipped. All he would say

when questioned was, 'I'm hevin' him home. He ain't spendin' the rest of his life down there.'

As to the extent of Tom's injuries, he wouldn't be drawn.

Even to Violet, all he would say was, 'We shall manage, you and me. We can look after him. We don't want no strangers fussin' round our boy.'

Fifteen

When, at the end of October, Tom was eventually brought home, the full extent of his injuries was not immediately apparent. He was in a wheelchair, pale-faced, with his ginger hair cropped short because of the ugly, not properly healed scar that dented his head and ran diagonally from his forehead to the back of his ear. His legs were covered by a blanket and his hands were resting in his lap, the only movement a restless twitching of his fingers.

But Tom could neither walk nor talk. And a look into his eyes confirmed that although Isaac had been assured that his eyesight was unimpaired, there was an emptiness behind them, a lack of expression, which proved that he had little awareness of what was going on around him.

'We shall manage, Violet and me. I look after my animals whether they're sick or well. Why wouldn't I do the same for my son?' Isaac said stubbornly if anyone dared to suggest Tom might be better looked after in a home for the war wounded. Not that anyone did, apart from some of his brothers and sisters who came to visit. But they only came once, never again. Charitably, Violet maintained that it was because they couldn't bear to see their brother brought so low, but privately she suspected they were afraid they might be called on to help if they came too often. Not that this was likely; Isaac refused to let anyone, apart from Violet, do anything at all for Tom. It was his burden and he would bear it.

Despite everyone's misgivings Isaac and Violet did manage, although she became thin and gaunt with worry and Isaac grew even more bad-tempered and hostile towards the outside world. But Tom was cared for like a baby; washed and dressed by his father each day and fed laboriously with a spoon by his mother, who prepared the meals he used to enjoy and mashed them to a pulp so that he could swallow them. Isaac carried him from his bed to his wheelchair each morning and back to his bed, now downstairs in the otherwise unused front parlour, at night. He even slept on a makeshift bed at his side in case there was any change in his condition, which there never was. As they mopped the dribble from his chin they talked to him all the time, deluding themselves that he understood what they were saying. Perhaps he did. Nobody could tell what, if anything at all, was going on inside Tom's scarred head.

Polly went to see him. Violet let her in because Isaac was at work, but insisted that she shouldn't stay long in case he came back.

As soon as she saw him Polly, hiding her shock, knew there would be no point in staying long. But she sat down beside him and took his hand, talking to him all the time about their childhood, how they used to play in the woods with Jamie.

'You'd never have known he was the son of Sir George Barsham, would you?' she reminisced. 'He was just like us, running about the woods, yelling blood-curdling war cries.'

She looked for a reaction from Tom but there was nothing, no change in his expression. No expression.

She ploughed on. 'Remember how you fell out of the tree, that day?' She smiled at him as she spoke. 'We said it served you right because you were always showing off. You were a dreadful old show-off when we were kids, weren't you? But strong! Goodness, you were strong.'

She thought she detected a faint smile as she said this but afterwards she realized she'd been deluding herself and it was only a trick of the light.

Because the old Tom had gone, blown up on the Somme, to somewhere nobody could reach him, leaving behind an empty shell of a man with Tom's features.

Violet suggested that it might be best if she didn't come again in case it upset him although Polly could see he was beyond being upset.

As she went about her work, at Meadowlands and even at the soup club, Polly couldn't get the memory of Tom's blank face out of her mind. The fact that he looked much the same, except that his fingernails were clean whereas they'd always been dirt encrusted as a boy. Except that his hair, growing back now (apart from the scar, which would always leave a white puckered line across his head where the hair would never again grow), was fading from its old bright ginger to a nondescript dull orange colour. Except that he sat quite still, except for fingers that constantly twitched, instead of being always on the move, either working for his father or bouncing around thinking up some new game to demonstrate his strength and prowess. Except for all these things, he looked like the same Tom. But he wasn't the same Tom; he was heartbreakingly different and Polly couldn't bear to see him like that.

It was not just Polly who was affected by Tom's return; a pall of sadness seemed to have settled over the whole estate. This was the ugliness of war, brought home to the peaceful English country-side. This was what war could do to young, healthy, virile young men. It was a message brought shockingly home to everyone, because everyone remembered Tom Hadley, the cheerful lad who in the past had been so harshly treated by his father.

But not any more. It was as if Isaac was seeking redemption for his past cruelty to his son, lavishing on him the care and attention he had previously shown only to his animals.

Some even began to wonder if Isaac was becoming unhinged, but since he carried out his normal work on the estate with the same attention he had always done, head down, speaking to nobody, there was nothing to suggest his behaviour was anything other than a jealous determination to guard his son. Unless it was lack of alcohol, some said with a touch of sarcasm, because since Tom's return Isaac was never seen the worse for drink, never in fact seen again at the Horse and Groom down in the village.

Every offer of help was refused. Even Max Rodwell was rebuffed. When he called, ostensibly on a friendly visit but with an offer of his professional services if required, he was not even allowed to set foot inside the door, but cursed and turned away by Isaac whilst Violet stood behind him wringing her hands. Whether Tom was suffering nobody could tell, but it was clear that Isaac was going through hell and dragging his wife with him.

Not long after Tom was brought home, James managed to get a few days' leave.

'They've made me a Major now, so I managed to pull rank,'

he told Gina, carefully omitting to add that with so many officers being killed in battle promotion was swift and usually, for all but the very lucky ones, short-lived. 'I felt I must come and see Tom. We've been through a lot together and if it hadn't been for the fact that I'd gone up to HQ for a briefing I'd have been where he was when the shell landed. There, but for the Grace of God . . .'

'Oh, James, don't! I can't bear it.' She turned her head so he shouldn't see the tears that started.

He shrugged. 'Well, anyway, I want to see him and thank him for everything.'

'You'll find him changed. Or so Polly says.'

'She's seen him, then?'

Gina nodded.

'I guess war changes us all.'

'Some more than others, though. But do go, James. Maybe you'll be able to talk to Isaac. Find out if there's anything Tom needs.'

James stayed ten minutes with Tom. Apart from the fact that Isaac wouldn't allow him to stay any longer, and refused all suggestions of help, it was as long as James himself could bear to stay. When he left the Hadleys' house he went straight down to the river bank and walked for miles, his shoulders hunched, his hands in his pockets and his head down. Finally, coming to a gap where the tide had breached the bank, he stopped, realized where he was and how far he'd come, then turned and walked back.

He was stunned. The sight of Tom sitting helpless in that wheelchair, oblivious to what was going on around him, that angry scar splitting his head, seemingly unaware that James was even there, had shocked him more than anything in his whole life. Oh, he was used to the sights of battle: men got wounded and killed in war, it was inevitable. He'd seen what happened; bits of bodies hanging in trees; men blinded, groping the empty air for a friendly hand; men coughing their gas-filled lungs up; dead bodies strewn in the mud as rats feasted; the stink of trench foot, of gas, of latrines; men screaming, hands over their ears, driven mad by the constant pounding of shells; men with horrible, gaping, bloody wounds. He'd seen so much horror he thought he'd become immune to it all.

But as soon as he saw Tom he realized he hadn't become

immune at all. This awful thing shouldn't have happened. Not to Tom, good old Tom, often the butt of good-humoured jokes, but strong and dependable Tom. Tom who was always ready with a laugh.

It wasn't bloody fair. He picked up a stone and savagely hurled it into the river. Then another and another, hurling them with all his pent-up fury until his arm ached. Then he squatted on his haunches and wept, remembering all they'd been through together in this bloody, sodding war; the way Tom had always been there for him, the times they'd laughed, sworn, even cried together. He couldn't remember a time when Tom hadn't been part of his life – not a big part, perhaps, but he'd always been there. It was Tom who had shown him how to make a whistle out of a reed; Tom who had shown him how to make bows and arrows; Tom with whom he had played cowboys and Indians. Tom and Polly.

At the thought of Polly he lifted his head and gazed across the river. How must she be feeling at the sight of poor wrecked Tom?

He got to his feet and took a few steps down the river bank, bent down and dashed some salt water over his face, dried it with his handkerchief and set off back to the house.

Polly finished ironing and hung the last of Lady Adelaide's petticoats on the airing rack. Then she pulled the rack up to the ceiling, cleated it off and went back to the kitchen. Mrs Bellman was dozing by the fire.

'Well, that's Her Ladyship's ironing out of the way. But where is everybody?' Polly asked.

Mrs Bellman looked at her over the top of her gold-rimmed spectacles, which had slid halfway down her nose. 'It's late; gone ten o'clock. Didn't you realize? Hetty's gone to bed. She has to make an early start in the morning. And Albert has taken Ruby to the music hall.' She gave a knowing wink. 'He asked me last week if they could have the time off to go.'

'I'm not surprised,' Polly said, sitting down at the kitchen table and stifling a yawn. 'He's always making sheep's eyes at her. Good luck to them, I say.'

'Yes. I've given Albert the back-door key so they can let themselves in because they'll be late back, I reckon.'

'You're a star, Mrs Bellman.' Polly got to her feet. 'I just hope Ruby appreciates it and makes sure she's up in time to do the breakfasts.' She yawned. 'I'm for bed now, too.'

'Ah, I nearly forgot. Mr Walford said would you see that the front door's bolted and the lights are all out in the house before you go up to bed? He usually does it when he makes his last rounds but his feet are bad tonight. He's gone to his room to soak them in nice hot water. I said you wouldn't mind. Quite an honour, really. He doesn't usually trust anyone else to do it.'

'I'll have to make sure I do it right, then.' She grinned, then yawned again, not bothering to stifle it this time. 'Goodnight, Mrs Bellman.'

'Goodnight.'

Polly went along the corridor and through the baize door into the main house, turning off lights as she went and thinking what a wonderful thing this electricity was – you flicked a switch on the wall and a lamp in the ceiling lit up the room. It was like magic. She opened the dining-room door a crack and turned off the light then crossed the hall to the drawing room and did the same.

'Hey! Who's switched the light off! Walford? Is that you?' From the depths of his armchair, James sounded annoyed.

'I'm terribly sorry, sir, I didn't realize there was anyone there. Will you make sure it's turned off when you leave the room, please?' Polly flicked on the light again and started to pull the door closed.

'Oh, it's you, Poll. No, no, please don't go. Come in and talk to me, I could do with a bit of company,' he said in quite a different voice.

She went in, nervously smoothing her apron, and saw that he was sprawled in his armchair in his shirtsleeves, a glass of whisky at his elbow.

'Close the door and come and sit down by the fire, or what's left of it.' He looked up at her and grinned as she stood, looking doubtful. 'It's an order.'

She smiled slightly and came forward to perch on the edge of the settee opposite to him. 'It's late, Mr James.'

'I know it is. Too late at night for you to be all formal and calling me Mr James, Poll, since everybody else has gone to bed.' He took a gulp of whisky from the glass beside him and she wondered if he was a little drunk. 'No, I'm not drunk,' he said, reading her thoughts. He rolled the glass between his hands, staring into the fire. 'I went to see Tom today.'

'Ah.'

He looked up. 'You've seen him?'

She nodded. 'Not that he knew. It's awful, isn't it? Poor Tom . . .'

'Makes you realize there are worse things than dying.' He returned his gaze to the dying embers of the fire.

'Oh, don't, Jamie.'

'It's true. Tom was always so full of life, always ready with a joke, however bad things were, and God, there were times when it was bloody awful. Gallows humour; good name for it. Now look at him.' He shook his head. 'I've seen some pretty horrible sights in this war, Poll, but this . . . Well, when it's a bloke you practically grew up with . . .' He looked up at her again and his voice changed. 'He was always talking about you, not that I minded that, of course.' He paused. 'You know he planned to marry you, after this lot's over?'

'Really?' She shot a glance at him to see if he was serious. 'Well, I don't know what put that idea into his head because I certainly didn't.' She paused thoughtfully. 'I've always regarded him more like a big brother to me than anything else. I suppose it's because we grew up together, more or less, went to school together, played in the woods – well, you know all that, you were there, too. Oh, no, I could never have married him; I don't love him. Not in that way.' She flushed slightly as she spoke, wondering if she'd said too much, hoping James wouldn't ask her what she meant by 'that way'. She stole a glance at him and saw he was watching her intently. She shrugged, embarrassed. 'I can't help it, but that's the way I feel,' she added.

'No, we can't help the way we feel.' He drained his glass and set it down. Then he sat up in his chair and ran his hands through his hair.

'Do you regard me as something of a big brother, Poll?'

She looked at him in surprise. 'Good heavens, no.'

'Then what?'

She bit her lip, not knowing what to say because she could never admit the truth. 'Why are you asking me that?' she prevaricated.

'Because I have to go back tomorrow, Poll, back to France,

maybe to Ypres, I don't know yet, but wherever it is it's not going to be any picnic. You know as well as I do that something awful could happen . . .'

'Don't, Jamie. Please, I can't bear it, I don't want to hear.' She put her hands over her ears, tears running down her cheeks, her actions speaking more loudly than any words.

He got up from his chair and came and sat beside her and took her hands in his. 'Hear me out, Poll. I could never say this to you before because of Tom. But now I know how you feel about him, and now I've seen how Tom is, poor devil, I can speak.' He let go of one hand and tilted her chin up so she had to look at him. Gently, he brushed a tear away with his thumb. 'I love you, Polly Catchpole. I think I've always loved you, ever since we were children and played in the woods together. I thought I would "get over it" as they say when I grew up, but I haven't; my love for you has got stronger and stronger as I've seen you grow into such a beautiful, caring, just simply wonderful young woman. I just want you to know this, in case . . . well, in case I don't come back.'

'Don't talk like that. You must come back. I couldn't bear it if you didn't, Jamie.' She put a finger to his lips. 'I simply couldn't. I love you so much; I always have, although I've always tried to hide it because I never, ever thought you might love me. I knew I could never marry anyone else and I used to dream of becoming nursemaid to your children so that I would always be near you. I knew it was the best I could ever hope for, because I'm only a servant in your father's house so you would never look twice at me. But it's just wonderful to hear you say the words, even though nothing can ever—'

He stopped her words with a long, lingering kiss. Finally, he lifted his head. 'That's where you're quite wrong, my darling. When – if – I come back from this war I shall marry you, I promise you that, and you will care for my children, our children, but as their mother, not their nursemaid.'

'But . . .'

'No buts.' He looked down at her uncertainly. 'Unless . . . Polly, you will marry me, won't you?'

'Oh, yes. Please.' She reached up and stroked a strand of hair away from his forehead as he bent his head and began to kiss her again.

A long time later she drew away from him. 'It's very late, Jamie, we should go to bed. I have to be up early in the morning.'

He nuzzled her neck. 'Yes, thoughtless of me. But I can't seem to let you go.' He began to kiss her again. 'Oh, Poll, I love you so much. And it's such a relief to be able to tell you.'

'I know. I love you, too, Jamie, but we can't stay here all night.'

'No, I suppose not.' He stood up and pulled her to her feet. 'I want you to know that whatever happens in the future, I've never been so happy as I am tonight, Poll.'

She stood on tiptoe and kissed him. 'Neither have I, Jamie.'

Hand in hand, they left the room.

'I'm not supposed to use these stairs,' she whispered as they started up the main staircase in pitch blackness.

'Well, you'll have to get used to it when we're married,' he whispered back and they both giggled.

'I'll have to say goodbye to you here, Poll; it'll be all formal in the morning,' he whispered as they reached his bedroom door.

She opened it and stepped inside. 'Just for a minute, in case someone comes out of their room. We don't want to get caught,' she said softly.

She didn't reach her own little room up under the eaves until dawn was breaking.

Sixteen

It was another quiet Christmas at Meadowlands. With half the family at the front there was little cause for celebration. Max Rodwell joined them again; he was like one of the family now and Lady Adelaide still cherished fond hopes that he and Gina would one day marry. Understandably, Max refused to make public his attachment to Millie until she could come home and share the announcement, although he talked about her all the time.

A few days after Christmas a message from Ned cheered them all. He wrote to say that he had managed to meet up with James and Millie for a drink and that they were all well, but weary. Almost identical messages came from both James and Millie in the following weeks. Post from the front was unreliable to say the least.

Polly heard nothing from James although she longed for a letter from him. But he'd never been in the habit of corresponding with her and they'd both agreed that it would look odd if he suddenly started writing to her.

She sent him postcards – pretty ones, funny ones, anything to keep his spirits up – but she never knew whether or not they arrived as he kept being moved around. So she prayed for him and for an end to the war and looked forward to the day she would feel his arms round her again.

It came as something of a distraction from the war when it was announced in the newspaper that married women over thirty would receive the vote.

'A bad day for English politics,' Sir George said as he read it in *The Times* at the breakfast table. 'I don't know what the country's coming to, letting women have a say in what goes on. Pass the marmalade, please, Gina.'

'Why shouldn't we have the vote?' Gina said, her temper getting the better of her. 'After all, women are doing men's work in factories, on buses, at the Front, on the land and hundreds of other places – why shouldn't they have a say in how things are run?'

'Don't exaggerate, dear,' Lady Adelaide said, concentrating on ladling butter on to her toast. 'Personally, I really don't know what all the fuss is about. I can't see why on earth women would want to vote. What do they know about government?' She shrugged. 'If I was asked to vote I wouldn't have the least idea who to vote for.'

'If you took a little more interest in what was going on instead of burying your head in fashion catalogues you might be better informed, Mother,' Gina answered tartly. 'Remember, you'll qualify, being married and over thirty, so you will be asked to vote.'

'Then I shall do what any sensible woman would do; I shall vote as your father tells me.' Lady Adelaide took a bite of toast and butter dribbled down her chin. As she wiped it away Gina remarked, with a touch of acidity, 'When butter is rationed you'll have to stop spreading it on your toast with a trowel.'

'Don't be unkind, dear – buttered toast is one of the few

pleasures I have left in this life,' Lady Adelaide said, putting on her plaintive voice. 'Anyway, who says it will be rationed? I'm sure you're mistaken.'

'If you were to read the newspapers, you'd know what was going on,' Gina replied, raising her eyebrows in despair towards Polly, who had just come in with fresh coffee.

'I'll have mine in my study, Polly.' Sir George got up from the table, the newspaper in his hand. He had no wish to join in the dispute between his wife and daughter. The fact that for once he agreed with his wife would only antagonize Gina further, so he wisely kept his own counsel. As far as he was concerned, to let women into politics was asking for trouble; they'd be wanting to run the country next, then where would we be?

'Soup run today, Polly, so I won't have more coffee, thank you,' Gina said, holding up her hand as Polly went to pour it into her cup. 'I've got one or two things to sort out before we leave. I forgot an important paper last time, so I want to make sure I don't leave anything behind.'

'Then I'll just have time to dust the drawing room before we go, Miss Gina,' Polly said. 'It'll help Ruby. She has more to do now Mrs Hadley can't come any more.'

'Ah, yes, of course. Her time is taken up with her poor son.'

'Shouldn't he be in some kind of home for wounded soldiers, Gina?' Lady Adelaide asked. 'If it was a matter of cost I'm sure your father would be happy to pay.'

'Begging your pardon, Lady Adelaide, but Tom's father would never allow him to be taken away,' Polly said. 'He's determined to care for him at home.'

'Oh, well, in that case . . .' Lady Adelaide shrugged, the subject closed as far as she was concerned.

As Polly quickly dusted the drawing room (no time for polishing today) she mused on the conversation she had just heard in the dining room. Nobody had been much excited about the votes-for-women business below stairs when Mr Walford, who'd garnered all the news as he ironed Sir George's *Times*, had spoken about it at breakfast, since no one there was eligible. *Mrs* Bellman was a courtesy title: Ada Bellman had never been married although she was well over thirty. But there was much more interest at the prospect of rationing.

'Can't see how they'll do it. People will just go from shop to shop and get their rations. And who's to know?' Mrs Bellman said. She gave a complacent shrug. '*We* shan't go short. I'll see to that.'

'There'll be ration cards,' Mr Walford said. He relished being the one who imparted the news. 'It says in the *Times*, everyone will have a ration card and they'll have to register with a butcher and a grocer and that's where they'll get their supplies. *And nowhere else.*' This last remark was aimed directly at Mrs Bellman.

She shot him a venomous glance and turned away. 'Oh, well. More tea anybody?'

Polly smiled to herself. Mr Walford and Mrs Bellman really didn't like each other very much. She looked at the marble clock on the mantelpiece. Time to go. Mustn't keep Miss Gina waiting.

The soup club was as busy as ever, although now the grievances were becoming more about husbands being sent home wounded, unable to work but with no pension forthcoming. Gina listened to endless stories of hardship and wrote countless letters, but children still went hungry and babies continued to be born into undernourished families. Women came from farther and farther afield as they heard that 'the soup lady' might be able to help them. But all Gina could do was to write to the Soldiers' and Sailors' Families Association, the Pensions committee and any other body she could think of that might be pressed to help. But her letters were either ignored or passed around to other bodies. Occasionally there was an answer and promises were made, but often they were not kept or else revoked before any money was paid to the families concerned.

'I sometimes feel I'm wasting my time and writing paper,' Gina said to Polly as they piled the empty soup saucepans back into the car. 'It gives these poor women hope when I tell them I've written letters on their behalf, but when nothing comes of it I feel they're worse off than before.'

'You mustn't think like that, Miss Gina. Think of all the good things. Think of the poor children who would have starved without our soup. Think of that woman whose husband came home, invalided out of the army, and they wouldn't pay his pension. You managed to get that put right, didn't you?'

'Yes, but don't you remember what happened? After a few months they stopped it, saying he was fit enough to work. So he got a job and after three weeks he collapsed and hasn't been able to work since, but his pension wasn't reinstated because they said he was no longer in the army so didn't qualify for an army disability pension. Oh, it's like knocking your head against a brick wall, trying to get some kind of justice for these poor people. It's just not fair.'

'I wonder if the Hadleys get a pension for poor Tom.'

'I don't suppose so,' Gina said with a sigh. 'They'll say there's no need because his father is working. But that's not the way things should be.' She banged her hand on the steering wheel. 'Tom sustained his injuries fighting for his country and it's Tom who should be compensated, regardless of whether or not his father can support him.'

'I guess the authorities will wriggle out of paying out for men who've been injured or killed because it's costing them so much to manufacture the guns and shells to kill and injure even more men, Germans though they may be. I think the world's gone mad.'

'Yes. It seems the only people making a profit out of this war are the arms manufacturers.'

'Blood money,' Polly said gloomily.

'You're right. Blood money.' Gina pulled up outside the house and turned to look at Polly. 'Well, we've had a right old rant all the way home.' She burst out laughing. 'I hope you feel better for it. I certainly do.' She put her head on one side. 'You're looking tired, Polly. Is it all getting too much for you? All this soup dispensing and child care? You do a great job, you know.'

Polly pushed a strand of hair back under her hat. 'No, I enjoy it, Miss Gina. I'm just sad and cross that it's so necessary.' She shuddered. 'The way some of those people have to live makes my hair stand on end.'

But it wasn't only that, as Polly admitted to herself as she washed and changed her dress before going downstairs to the kitchen. It was something that Nellie Jenkins had said to her as they were clearing things away.

'I can tell you what to do, if you want,' she'd said, with a glance at Polly's trim waist.

Polly had frowned. 'I don't know what you mean.'

'Oh, come on. How to get rid of it. I've helped a lot of these, here.' She'd sniffed and jerked her head in the direction of the women in the room. 'Doesn't always work, o'course, but mostly it does.' She'd tapped the side of her nose. 'Two shilluns to you, dear, and nobody any the wiser. How far gone are you?' She eyed her up and down. 'Near on three months, I'd say.'

'I don't know what you're talking about,' Polly had said and turned away.

But she did. She knew very well what Nellie Jenkins was saying. And she'd been right, even as to how far her pregnancy was advanced.

It was her own fault, of course. She'd known very well what could be the outcome of the wonderful night she had spent in James' arms. But she was not worried because she had no doubt he would stand by her. He loved her and he'd promised to marry her. There was not a shadow of doubt in her mind that he wouldn't keep his promise. She just wished he would come home before anyone else needed to know – or, indeed, before her condition became obvious. And so far she'd been lucky. Apart from missing her monthly curse, which nobody else needed to be aware of, she'd felt well and full of energy. Her appetite was good – at times she had to curb it because she was often ravenous – and she had had none of the fainting or sickness she had witnessed so often in the women at the soup club.

But it would soon be obvious to other people, and not just those women who were so used to continual pregnancy that they knew all the signs, because the buttons on her blouse were beginning to strain and her skirt was getting tight. Twice her mother had looked her up and down and said, 'You're looking bonny, dear. I believe you're putting on a little weight, too.'

She'd brushed her remarks off, saying, 'I expect it's a combination of your rock cakes and Mrs Bellman's apple dumplings, Mum. I'll have to stop eating so many. But I'll just have one more, they're delicious straight out of the oven.'

She managed to hide her condition until one day in the middle of March. It was a cold, blustery, typical March day although the sun was shining and snowdrops and crocuses were blooming in the borders. As she hurried across to Pippin Farm for a quick cup of tea with her mother, as she often did, her hat blew off twice in the wind and she had to chase it, annoyed because she'd forgotten to put her hatpins in.

'Goodness, you're out of puff, my girl,' her mother greeted her when she arrived.

'Yes, my hat kept blowing off.' She turned to hang up her hat and coat when suddenly the room began to spin and then everything went black. 'Oh, I think I'd better sit down.' She heard her own voice but it seemed to be coming from a long way off. Then nothing.

She came to with the sharp tang of smelling salts under her nose. 'Oh, I don't know what happened there,' she said weakly, leaning her elbow on the table and resting her head on her hand.

'You fainted, my girl, that's what. And I reckon I know why.' Her mother was standing over her, tight-lipped. 'So? When's it due? I've been waiting for you to tell me. And don't say you don't know what I'm talking about because you're not that stupid.'

'I'm not sure. July? August?' There was no point in trying to deny it.

'And are you going to tell me who the father is? Or are you going to try and keep that to yourself, too?'

Polly looked up at her mother, her eyes full of tears. 'Oh, Mum, don't be like that. He loves me. We're going to be married.'

'When?'

'When he comes home from the war.'

'Oh, Polly, don't tell me you've been going with one of the soldiers down on lower meadow.' Susan closed her eyes, shocked to the core.

'No, Mum, of course I haven't. You ought to know me better than that.'

'I thought I did. I also thought you'd got more sense than to let yourself get into this pickle. But evidently I was wrong.'

Polly bit her lip. 'Mum, if I tell you who the father is, you're not to say anything to anybody else. Promise?'

'Why? Do I know him?'

'Oh, yes, you know him.'

Susan regarded her for a minute, then nodded. 'All right.'

'It's Jamie. Jamie Barsham. I'm expecting his baby.' She smiled, unable to hide her pride.

Susan sat down at the kitchen table. It was possible, of course. They'd always been friends and she guessed that Polly's feelings had grown to be much more than friendship for James. But James? What of his feelings? Did he really love Polly or had he taken advantage of her by making promises he had no intention of keeping? A few years ago she would have discounted that idea completely, but who knew how his time in the army had affected him?

Polly leaned over and laid her hand on her mother's arm. 'It's true, Mum. He loves me and wants to marry me.' Her expression was so earnest that Susan was in no doubt that she believed it.

She sighed. 'Well, whether it's true or not he's not here at the moment so we'll have to make plans without him.' She pinched her lip. 'One thing's certain. You'll have to go away somewhere till it's born. Maybe you could go and stay with my sister Alice in Ipswich for a while, then we'll have so see about getting it adopted.'

'No. I couldn't bear to part with Jamie's baby. He'd never forgive me if I did,' Polly said in alarm, placing her hand protectively on her stomach.

'You'll have no choice, my girl,' Susan said sternly. 'We can't have shame brought on the family.' She shook her head sadly. 'God in his mercy knows what your father'll have to say, as it is.'

'Do we need to tell him?'

'Reckon he'll have to know in the end. But first things first. I'll write to Alice and ask if she'll look after you for a few months. I'll have to tell her why, of course, so she'll understand why you need to get away. And we'll tell everyone here that you've gone to look after her because she's not very well, which won't be too far from the truth – Alice has always got something or other wrong with her, or thinks she has.'

'What if she says no?'

'Then we'll have to think of something else. But she won't refuse. Heaven knows I've done enough for her in the past. And anyway, she's always had a soft spot for you.'

As Susan had predicted, a week later a letter from Alice arrived saying she was willing to 'help out' as she put it, under the circumstances, although Susan was not to think she was happy about Polly's shameful behaviour. She went on to say that her back had been bad lately and she was having trouble with her legs so she couldn't get about much now, so it would be quite useful to have another pair of hands about the place.

Susan waited until the letter arrived before she told Will, making sure he had a good meal inside him and was relaxing in front of the fire with his pipe.

His reaction was exactly what she had expected. He shot up

in his chair, dropping his pipe and spilling tobacco and ash all over the hearth, his eyes black with rage.

'The little slut! She's been rolling in the hay with the soldiers down on lower meadow, hasn't she? I warned her to keep away from them, the fornicating brutes. And as for her, she's no better than a whore!' He banged his fist on the arm of his chair to give weight to his words.

'Will! Calm down. Don't start saying things you'll regret. We need to talk about this sensibly,' Susan intervened sharply. 'It's no good you going off on a rant about the soldiers. Polly's already told me she's had nothing to do with them and I believe her. Now, listen to me and I'll tell you what we're going to do.'

'She'll have to be put away, that's what's to be done with her. You don't think I'm going to have my family's name dragged in the mud by her shameless behaviour, do you? I'm an Elder at my church, don't forget. What would people there think of me? They'd want to know why I couldn't control my own daughter. I'd never be able to hold up my head there again. How can I preach morality and clean living when there's a viper in my nest?'

'Oh, for goodness' sake, Will, don't start your preaching here,' Susan said irritably. 'But if you must preach, maybe the milk of human kindness might come into it, or a bit of compassion. Or even forgiveness.' Even as she spoke Susan realized that last was asking too much of her husband. He was not a man to forgive a wrong.

'Never mind all that. What about my good name?' He jabbed his finger at his chest. 'Just you remember, I have some standing in the village as well as my church. Am I going to let that little slut drag me down with her?'

'If you'll stop shouting for a minute I'll tell you what's going to happen. It's all worked out. Nobody will ever need to know there was a baby.'

Wincing at the mere mention of the word, Will sat back in his chair. 'Well? I'm listening,' he said, although it was plain he didn't want to hear. 'What cock and bull yarn have you cooked up between you?'

'I've arranged for Polly to go to stay with my sister Alice and then, when the child's born, it will be adopted and Polly can come back here and nobody any the wiser.'

'Hm. What does your sister have to say about that?'

'She's expecting her on the four o'clock train on Thursday. All you have to do is take her to the train.' She looked at him, her lip twisting bitterly. 'Then you can forget you've even got a daughter for a few months, if that's what you want.'

'Hm,' he said again, his mouth turned down in a disagreeable arc.

'I take it you won't object to taking her to the train?' Susan's voice was icy. At that moment she was hard put to it not to smash his head in with the frying pan for being so selfish and unfeeling

He sniffed. 'I s'pose not.'

In spite of his reluctance, he had the pony harnessed and the trap ready when Polly came to say her tearful goodbyes to her mother, her valise in her hand.

'I'll write to you, Mum. And you will keep making your soup, won't you? Miss Gina says she wants to keep the soup club going, even while I'm not there.'

''Course I will, dearie. Now, you look after yourself. And write soon.'

'I will. I'll drop you a line as soon as I get there.'

Susan waved till Polly was out of sight, then went back into the house and tried not to weep for her wayward daughter, consoling herself with the knowledge that Alice would look after her.

Seventeen

Susan looked for the postman every day, anxious for news that Polly had arrived safely, but to her surprise no letter came. Even more surprisingly there was no word from Alice either.

'I can't understand it,' she said as she ladled stew on to Will's plate when there had been no word for over a week. 'You did make sure she got the right train, didn't you?'

'What do you think I am, woman? Stupid?' he growled.

'Well, I can't understand why we haven't heard from her. I haven't heard from Alice, either, which is most unusual; she always keeps in touch. I keep writing . . .'

He threw down his knife and fork. 'Oh, for goodness' sake! I don't know what you're worrying about. If the little trollop can't be bothered to drop you a line, you should stop wasting good money on stamps.'

'Whatever's got into you, Will Catchpole?' she said with a frown. 'You've been like a bear with a sore head ever since Polly went. Don't you realize I miss her, too?'

He pushed his plate away and went and sat in his chair and lit his pipe.

'You haven't finished your dinner,' she said.

'I'm not hungry. I'm tired of hearing you forever going on about the little slut. Every time I sit down to a meal you keep on about her. It's taken my appetite away.'

Susan glanced over at him. He looked a bit peaky and she realized he was missing his daughter more than he cared to admit. She decided not to trouble him with her worries any more.

But she continued to look for a letter from either Polly or Alice. She simply couldn't understand why neither of them had written; it was not like Alice, with whom she had always corresponded regularly, nor like Polly; especially as her last words had been a promise to write. She'd already written three times asking why she hadn't heard. Surely, one or other of them could have dropped a line to say what the trouble was. It was all very worrying. In the end she could neither sleep nor eat for imagining all the bad things that might have happened.

'Are you ill, Susan? Or just missing Polly?' Gina asked one day when she came to return the empty soup pans. 'You don't look at all well and I'm sure you're losing weight. Or is it getting too much for you, making soup every week?'

'No, no, I'm perfectly all right,' Susan said quickly. 'Making the soup takes my mind off things.' She glanced at Gina as she spoke, and tried to smile, but the concern in the younger woman's face was just too much and she sank down at the table and burst into tears.

'Oh, Susan!' Gina pulled up a chair beside her and put her arm round her shoulders. 'It's all right, I know exactly what's troubling you and I'm really sorry.'

Susan looked up at her, trying to contain her tears. 'You do?'

Gina nodded. 'Polly's pregnant, isn't she? That's why she's gone to stay with your sister. I really don't want to pry, my dear, but you can talk to me if it will help.'

'How do you know? Did she tell you?' Susan said sharply. She couldn't prevent a stab of jealousy at the thought that her daughter might have confided in Gina first.

But Gina shook her head. 'No, Polly never said a word to me. It was the women at the soup club. They guessed and put two and two together. They know the signs of pregnancy only too well, as you can imagine; they don't need telling.'

'They're right. She is in the family way.' Her face crumpled again. 'But it's not only that, Miss Gina. She's gone to stay with my sister, Will took her and put her on the train to Ipswich, but I haven't heard a single word from her since the day she left. Nor from my sister, either. I can't understand it. I've written several times to ask what's wrong but I still don't get any answer. I don't know what to do. I'm afraid something dreadful must have happened. But I can't think what.' She began to cry again.

'What does your husband have to say?'

She sniffed and wiped her nose with her handkerchief. 'He won't even talk about it but I know he's as worried as I am because he's gone off his food. That's always a bad sign with Will.'

Gina looked at her watch. As Susan said, it was all very strange and the sooner they could find out what was wrong the better. She hadn't got anything particular planned for the rest of the day and if something bad had happened then Susan would need support. She got to her feet.

'Get yourself ready, Susan,' she said firmly. 'I'll take you to your sister's house in my car so you can find out for yourself why you haven't heard from them.'

Susan's jaw dropped. 'What, all the way to Ipswich?'

'It's not that far,' Gina said with a smile. 'We can be there in under an hour. Now, I'm sure there's a simple explanation, but we need to find out what it is and put your mind at rest. All this worry is making you ill, I can see that.' She glanced at her watch again. 'Just give me twenty minutes to go home and change my dress – I always smell a bit after I've been at the soup club – then I'll be back.' She patted Susan's shoulder, clearly pleased to be able to help. 'All right?'

'Oh, Miss Gina, I'd be ever so grateful.' Susan dried her eyes, relieved. 'If I can just find out what's happening it'll put my mind at rest.'

'Good. I'll be back in twenty minutes.' Gina left and Susan went upstairs and put on her Sunday best dress and coat, thankful to know she was at last going to find out what was wrong. At the same time she was excited at the thought of going all the way to Ipswich by car, since she rarely had the opportunity to travel anywhere, let alone in a motor car. She put on her best shoes, although they weren't very comfortable because she hadn't worn them enough to 'break them in', and she fixed her hat with the silver hat pin Will had bought her. Then she went downstairs to wait for Gina to return.

She was just licking her pencil to begin writing a note to Will to tell him where she had gone when he walked in.

'Where do you think you're off to, all dressed up in your Sunday best?' he asked, frowning at her.

She looked up. 'Oh, good. I'm glad you've come home, so I can tell you instead of writing it down. I'm going to Ipswich,' she said excitedly. 'With Miss Gina. In her motor car. What do you think of that?'

'What for?' His expression was wooden.

'What for? Why, to find out why we haven't heard from Polly or Alice, of course. You're as worried as I am, only you won't admit it.'

'I'm not worried at all,' he said, turning his back on her to reach his tobacco jar down from the mantelpiece. 'I know very well where Polly is.'

She stared at him. 'Then why haven't you said, instead of letting me stew for all this time?' She went over and shook his arm. 'Well, where is she?'

He turned and looked at her. 'She's where I said she deserved to be in the first place. I didn't put her on the train; I put her in the asylum.' He sat down and began to fill his pipe.

'You *what*?' Susan screamed. She sat down on her chair with a thump and stared at him, open-mouthed.

'I put her in the asylum, where she belongs,' he repeated truculently, putting a match to his pipe and puffing till it drew to his satisfaction. His voice softened as he saw his wife's horrified expression. 'Don't you understand, Susan, dear, if she's done it once she'll do it again, so I thought it best to put her out of harm's way. It's for her own good.'

'It's not for *her* good to be shut up with a lot of lunatics. It's yourself you're thinking of, you selfish brute. And don't "Susan, dear" me to try and justify what you've done to my daughter.' Her face was white with rage. She stood up and shook her fist at him. 'You're a wicked, wicked man, William Catchpole, to do such a terrible thing to our only girl.' She turned away from him, tears running down her cheeks.

'But girls who get themselves into trouble . . .'

She turned back and glared at him. 'Oh, she's done it on her own, now, has she? She's the one to blame. Hasn't anyone ever told you it takes two?'

'Well then, girls who go with soldiers—'

'Who says she's been with soldiers?'

'I don't know who else it could have been. And if she's done it once—'

'You said that before. But you don't know how it happened because you never stopped to find out. And you never gave me time to find out, either.'

'I thought the sooner it was done the better.' Will was getting angry. He slapped his hand on the table. 'Now, you listen to me—'

'I'll listen to you, Will Catchpole, when you fetch my Polly out of that place and bring her home,' said Susan, equally angry.

'I'm not fetching her home and that's that. How can I hold my head up in the community if everyone knows what a slut of a daughter I've got? Have you forgotten I'm an Elder of my church?'

'Oh, no. You make sure I never forget that.' She looked him up and down, her expression scathing. 'But tell me this, how will you hold your head up *anywhere* when people find out you've put your only daughter in the asylum?'

'People never need to know. Everybody thinks she's gone to your sister and that's what we'll let them believe.'

'Oh, so now you're prepared to add lies to your sins.' Her voice was full of contempt. 'You're an evil man, William Catchpole, but you're not going to drag me down to Hell with you. I won't lie for you and I won't cover up your sins. When people ask where Polly is I shall tell them what you've done with her. And I shall do everything in my power to get my girl out of that place.'

'You don't have any power. It was me that signed the paper that put her there and it's me that would have to sign to get her out.' He accompanied every word with a jab at his chest. Satisfied he'd made his point he sat back in his chair. 'And that I shall never do,' he finished.

She put her head in her hands, defeated. 'Oh, my poor girl,' she moaned. She looked up at him. 'And to think that all this time you've known why she hasn't written yet you let me eat my heart out with worry and never said a word,' she said, shaking her head uncomprehendingly. 'How could you do that to me, William?'

He shifted uncomfortably in his chair. 'I was waiting for the right time.'

She frowned, not listening. 'I can't understand why Alice didn't write to ask why she hadn't arrived. She was expecting her off that train.'

'She did write,' he mumbled. 'I took the letters off the postman. They're in the estate office.'

'Oh, God, is there no limit to your wickedness, William Catchpole?' Susan turned away from him and closed her eyes. After a long time she opened them and said quietly, her voice icily calm, 'May God forgive you for what you've done to Polly, William Catchpole, for I swear I never shall. And those are my last words to you. I shall never speak to you again until my daughter is out of that place.'

Shocked at her words, he stood up and tried to put his hand on her shoulder but she shrugged him off.

'Oh, come now, Susan,' he pleaded.

She gave him a look of pure contempt and went out, closing the door behind her, to meet Gina and tell her exactly why there was no need for the trip to Ipswich.

Shocked almost beyond words and knowing Susan was beyond consolation, Gina could do little but put her arms round her and hold her while she wept. When she was calmer Gina left her, after promising to try and think of some way to help, although privately she realized her comforting words were hollow while Will Catchpole refused to relent.

Susan went back into the house and found Will still sitting there. She ignored him and went upstairs to change her clothes, still numb with shock and misery at what her husband had done with Polly. But at least she knew she had an ally. Miss Gina would think of some way to rescue her. That was the only shred of hope she had to cling to.

That night when he went to bed Will discovered that Susan had moved all her things out of their room and into Polly's old bedroom. He didn't like it but he was too proud to demand that she return to the marital bed. But the bed felt cold without his wife beside him and he couldn't sleep. He couldn't stop thinking of how he'd left Polly at the asylum. How he'd nearly turned back when he saw the forbidding iron gates and the stark, grey buildings. It had been a long walk to the matron's office, dragging Polly with him, screaming and protesting, up echoing stone staircases and along cold corridors with chipped and flaking brown paint. The matron, seated behind a large desk, had iron-grey hair and a thin, pale face, with an expression that would have turned milk sour. When she stood up, a tall woman, dressed all in black, with a great bunch of keys hanging from her belt, she looked more like a jailer than a matron. She had said little, but sniffed as she looked the still screaming and protesting Polly up and down.

'Obviously insane,' she remarked, then pushed a form over for him to sign and took the money. Then she'd signalled that he should leave. He'd hesitated, in two minds whether or not to kiss the little slut before he left, knowing it was unlikely he would ever see her again, but he thought it would look better if he did. But she'd just stood there, quiet now, but as white as a sheet with terrified shock, tears still running down her cheeks, and then she'd stepped back and turned her head away when he tried to approach her. But not before he'd seen the look of helpless beseeching on her face.

That look haunted him. Every time he closed his eyes it was there. But he'd done the right thing, he convinced himself, over and over again. He'd done what any right-minded, God-fearing man would have done to prevent shame from falling on his house.

He still couldn't sleep.

Polly couldn't believe her beloved father could have gone away and left her in this dreadful place. Soon he would come back and fetch her, saying it was all a mistake, she was sure of it. Especially when that dreadful woman had said she was 'obviously insane'. Dad knew she wasn't insane, he knew she'd been screaming in terror at the thought of being left in this place, so why hadn't he said so? She couldn't understand him.

But he was gone now so it was up to her to prove to these people that she was perfectly sane and that there was no reason to keep her here. So she allowed herself to be taken without protest into another room, where she was made to strip off her own clothes and subjected to a most undignified examination by a cold-eyed doctor. Then she was given scratchy grey underclothes that might have been white a long time ago, black stockings and a grey, shapeless dress that felt as if it was made of mattress ticking. The shoes she was given were down-at-heel and a size too big. She had managed to remain calm and dignified throughout the whole procedure but when, finally, a rough mob cap covered up her beautiful hair she couldn't prevent a sob escaping. She never saw her own clothes again; she assumed they were sold.

For the first week she continued to keep her spirits up by expecting her father to come and fetch her home, saying it had all been a dreadful mistake. In that way she managed to survive all the indignities that she was made to suffer. Mealtimes were difficult; some of the girls and women, who were all attired like her, slobbered over their food or threw it about, for which they received a sharp slap; some made strange noises and shouted all the time. Everybody had to eat with spoons off tin plates. Some were quieter, keeping their heads down and shovelling in the unappetizing food as if they were afraid it would be taken away, and one girl sat alone in a corner with her plate on her lap, cringing if anyone got near her. Polly went and sat a little distance from her and tried to smile at her but the girl wouldn't meet her eyes.

But if mealtimes were difficult the nights were worse. In long dormitories, the iron bedsteads separated by wooden lockers, twenty-four girls and women either slept or paced endlessly up and down, shouted and screamed in nightmares, or moaned and made odd noises. Polly pulled the rough sheet up over her ears and tried to shut out the noise, but it went on and on until at last she fell asleep through sheer exhaustion.

She was soon put to work. She was taken to the laundry, along with some of the more capable inmates. There she was given a wash board and set to scrubbing some of the more filthy and disgusting garments. She kept her head down and made no complaint, noticing how some of the girls cringed when the overseer came near. Even so she often received a sharp slap for slacking, however hard she worked. Once, she lifted her head and met the woman's eyes. They were filled with malicious pleasure at her predicament. Polly cast her eyes down again, frowning. She had never seen this woman before, why should she take such pleasure in another's misfortune? It was several more days before she understood that 'Mrs Brown', as she was called, found her enjoyment in watching other people's suffering. The realization sent shivers down her spine.

The patients at the hospital were all classed as 'mentally defective'. Although this phrase was neither kind nor in most cases true, it was a better description than what was carved over the entrance when the place was built, early in the nineteenth century, which was HOSPITAL FOR THE INSANE. Most of the girls and women there were far from insane, but nobody had bothered to remove the words. Quite early on Polly discovered that she was not the only girl banished there because she was pregnant; she learned that it was quite a common practice to hide a daughter's 'shame' by incarcerating her in an asylum and there were at least two other girls in the same condition. With the shapeless dresses they were made to wear she realized there could well be more. Now she understood why the father she had always thought loved her had brought her here.

All the pregnant girls were put to work in the laundry, Polly found. Whether this was punishment for their 'sin' or in the hope that the heavy lifting would bring on a miscarriage she never discovered. They had to work hard and if they stopped to wipe the sweat from their faces or to rub their aching backs they received a slap or a punch from Mrs Brown. One girl fainted and had to be dragged outside till she revived and could be put back to work. She got no dinner that day.

Some of the patients who helped them in the laundry had been there for years, ever since their families had realized that, in the jargon of the day, they were 'not all there'. Most of them had never known any other life and for the most part they were sweet girls and very affectionate and willing as long as they were told exactly what to do. Polly was at a loss to know why their families had incarcerated them in such a place, although one or two of them had to be watched because their tempers were uncertain and violent and were ready to pick a fight at the slightest provocation. It wasn't long before Polly had scratches down the side of her face from an unprovoked attack.

She didn't much care. After all, there was nobody she cared about to see what she looked like. And in her bleaker moments she faced the fact that there never would be.

The weeks dragged on.

Eighteen

Gina worried endlessly about Polly. Because of what he had done to his daughter, she had difficulty in being civil to Will Catchpole when she had dealings with him over estate matters and she was disgusted to think he was keeping up the pretence that Polly had gone to look after her sick aunt.

At the soup club the women constantly asked about Polly; they missed her and wanted her back. After all, in their eyes anybody could get 'knocked up' – it was often a nuisance but there was no shame in it and the child would be absorbed into the family, no questions asked. They couldn't see why there should be such a fuss made and thought it ridiculous that her father had sent her away to stay with her aunt. Gina daren't divulge where Polly actually was, afraid of what some of the rough and ready members of the soup club might take it into their heads to do.

Sick with concern and confident of his discretion, Gina told her doctor friend, Max Rodwell, the truth one day when he was helping her load the car after the mothers had gone. He was amazingly adept with his crutches now, although he was counting the days until he would be fitted with an artificial foot, which wouldn't be long now.

'In the *asylum*?' he repeated, shocked. 'My God, who on earth put her there, poor child?'

'Her father.'

'Good God! The ba—' He covered his mouth briefly. 'Sorry, Gina, I'll start again.' He took a deep breath and went on, savagely: 'The man deserves to be shot. Has he any idea what it's like in there? And did he try and find out who the father was before incarcerating her there? The man might be willing to marry her.' He shut the car boot with unnecessary force.

'I don't think he even bothered to try. He simply assumed she'd been playing fast and loose with the soldiers on lower meadow.'

He shook his head. 'No, no. That doesn't sound a bit like Polly. I would have said she's quite strait-laced.' He got into the car beside her and stowed his crutches.

'I agree. That's exactly what I've been thinking.'

'Then assuming she wasn't raped, it must have been someone she's fond of. But who?'

Gina frowned. 'I can't believe it was rape. I think I'm close enough to Polly to have realized something was wrong if that had been the case. Even if she was afraid to speak of it at first, I think she would have told me in the end.' She gave a deep sigh as she started up the car. 'I really don't know who it could be, Max. I wish I did.'

That night, in bed, Gina went over in her mind for the umpteenth time all the men that, to her knowledge, Polly had dealings with. There weren't many. Elderly Mr Walford? That was ridiculous; in any case, a more upright and moral man would be hard to find. Other than him, Albert, the footman and hand-yman, was the only man left of the indoor staff and he had eyes for nobody but Ruby, that was plain to see. The men that worked about the estate? Most of them were elderly, or with families; in any case they had very little contact with the house servants. No, she could think of nobody that could be the father.

She tossed and turned for a long time, unable to sleep, her mind too active to let her body rest. In the end she tried to calm herself by going over in her mind the last walk she had taken with James before he returned to the Front. They'd walked down to the river, then across the meadow to the lake, where they'd sat on the bench talking about everything under the sun, savouring every precious moment. Then, just before they went back to the house he'd said urgently, 'Look after yourself, Gee. And make sure you look after Polly for me.' She'd thought at the time that was an odd thing to say, but then reasoned that James had always had something of a soft spot for Polly, since he and Tom and Polly had played together as children and he'd often ended up at

Pippin Farm for some of Susan's home-made cakes. Now, suddenly, she saw his words in a different light.

Could it be? Or was she doing James a terrible injustice, thinking he was the kind of man to take advantage of a servant girl? No, her brother was not like that, she was sure of it. She dismissed the idea. But who else was there? She tossed in her bed, unable to sleep, unable to think straight. She got up the next morning feeling drained and ill, glad it was not a soup club day, yet at the same time wishing it was because at least on those days she had no time to think.

It was a warm late-spring day so she went for a long walk down by the river, thinking all the time about Polly, incarcerated in that awful place, unable to enjoy the fresh air and sunshine. She brushed the tears from her face impatiently. Why was she weeping? Polly was only a servant. Yet she knew this wasn't true; Polly was much more than a servant, she was a very good friend. She always knew she could rely on Polly, no matter what. But now Polly was in trouble and she felt helpless.

Her steps led her past Pippin Farm and on impulse she turned in at the gate. Susan must be feeling even worse than she was so she might be glad of a little company.

She was in the back yard pegging sheets on the line and, seeing her silhouette, Gina could see just how much weight she had lost recently. She turned at the sound of Gina's footsteps and forced a smile.

'Oh, Miss Gina. How lovely. Have you got time for a cup of tea?'

'I was hoping you'd say that,' Gina answered, smiling back at her. 'I'm always in such a hurry on soup club days there's never time to talk.' She followed Susan into the house. Her voice softened. 'How are you managing, Susan?'

Susan shrugged. 'I keep myself busy.' She pulled the kettle forward and got cups and saucers down from the dresser and Gina could see she was biting her lip against tears. 'I try to think of her being dead, which would be bad enough. But she isn't. It's almost worse, knowing she's shut up in that place. I don't know how that man can live with himself, treating his daughter in such a shameful way.' She sniffed and wiped her eyes on her apron.

'What does Catchpole say now?' Gina didn't bother to grace him with his title.

Susan clamped her lips together, then said tersely, 'I don't know. I don't ask. I haven't spoken to him since the day he took her away. I wash his clothes and I cook his food, but that's as far as it goes. I sleep in Polly's old room, partly because it helps me feel close to her but mainly because I can't bear to be near the man. I can't even bear to eat at the same table. I never knew I was capable of such hatred. There! Now I've said it. You'll think I'm as wicked as he is.'

Gina laid an arm round her shoulders. 'I don't think anything of the kind, Susan. I think I'd feel the same if I was in your place. So, let's have that cup of tea and we can talk properly.' She poured the milk into the cups and waited while Susan poured the tea. Then they both sat down on either side of the table.

'Now,' Gina said as they drank their tea, 'I've been trying to think of some way we could get Polly out of that place.'

'He'll never agree to it,' Susan said flatly. 'He might regret what he's done; he might know in his heart he shouldn't have done it; but William Catchpole is not a man to go back on a decision, right or wrong.'

'What if we could find the father of the child?'

Susan shot her an uneasy glance. 'What good would that do?'

'Surely, if he agreed to marry her they would release her.' Gina leaned forward and put her hand over Susan's. 'Have you any idea at all whom it might be? Did she give you any clue?'

Susan looked out of the window. 'She made me promise never to tell a soul.' She shifted uncomfortably in her chair.

'She didn't know what was going to happen to her then and neither did you,' Gina reminded her.

Susan chewed her lip. After a minute she looked up. 'I don't know if I should say. Almost the last thing I did for her was to promise not to tell.' She picked up her cup, then put it down again. 'Do you really think it would get her out of that place?'

'Anything's worth a try, Susan.' Gina looked at her intently. 'Now, so that you don't break your promise, let me tell you something. All you need to do is tell me if I'm wrong, nothing more.' She took a deep breath. 'Before he went back to France my brother James made a point of asking me to look after Polly. He's never mentioned anything like that before, so what reason could he have had to say it then? Do you think he might have been afraid she would need looking after because she might be pregnant?'

Susan said nothing for a long time. Then she nodded dumbly and said in a low voice, 'She told me Jamie loved her and that they were to be married when he came home. She was quite certain about that, and although she knew she was in trouble she was very happy to be having his baby. Of course I've known she's been in love with him ever since she was a child, but I never thought anything could ever come of it and neither, I think, did she.' She looked up at Gina. 'I'm quite sure she was telling me the truth, Miss Gina. And knowing how she's always felt about Jamie, I can't believe my Polly would ever have looked at another man.'

Gina drained her tea and stared into the tea leaves thoughtfully. It was ironic that Polly should be pregnant and in such trouble, whereas she herself would have been delighted to have found herself pregnant with Archie's child after his death, scandal though it might have caused. She gave herself a mental shake at the direction her thoughts were taking and smiled up at Susan.

'Thank you, Susan. Now, I think the best thing is for me to write to James and tell him what's happened to Polly. If I don't miss my mark he'll have her out of that place before many more days.'

'He might say it's nothing to do with him,' Susan said anxiously, fearful of being too optimistic.

'Well, let's assume for the moment that he won't say anything of the kind and that he'll be as anxious to rescue Polly as we are.' Gina gave Susan's arm a squeeze. 'It'll be all right, Susan. I know my brother.'

She sounded more confident than she felt; at that moment she was wondering if she knew her brother at all. Had the army changed him to the extent that he would take advantage of Polly and treat her as nothing more than a 'dolly-mop' and then go off and leave her to face the consequences? No, that couldn't be right. He would never have considered that Polly might need 'looking after' if that was the case.

But soon she would find out his feelings. She hurried home to write to James and tell him what had happened. But it would be a good deal longer than she expected before she had any word back from him.

*　　*　　*

The days and weeks went by. The only way Polly knew a week had passed was when she was allowed a tepid bath in the cold, concrete bath house and clean clothes afterwards. That was on Saturdays. On Sundays they all filed into the chapel – a bleak room with rows of benches and a table at the end with a wooden cross. There they were forced to sit and listen to the vicar telling them at great length what happened to sinners and urging them to repent while there was still time. Polly felt no sense of urgency. She had the rest of her life to think about repentance; for the time being hatred for her father was the emotion uppermost in her mind.

During the rest of the week she did as she was told, worked hard even when the things she had to do sickened her, and tried to keep out of trouble, because a number of the so-called nurses were short-tempered and handy with their blows. She ate the unappetising and often unidentifiable messes she was given at mealtimes because she knew her baby needed nourishment, not because she was hungry. In the end, after trying to keep account of the number of Saturdays and Sundays, she lost track of time and had no idea how long she had been there. Only her baby, growing and beginning to move inside her, gave her any idea of time passing. At night, ignoring the shouts and calls around her, she would think about Jamie and how much she loved him and in her mind she would relive that wonderful night they had spent in each other's arms. In spite of everything that had happened since she didn't regret that night and she hoped and prayed that the memory of it sustained Jamie as it was sustaining her. Some nights she would circle the baby growing within her – she was sure it was a boy – with her arm and whisper to him about his father and promise him that one day they would all be together, out there, where the world was free. She would tell him about Meadowlands, the woods, the parkland and the lake, and in her mind she would retrace the steps she had taken with James and with poor Tom when they were all carefree children, never imagining all the dreadful things that would befall them in the future.

But in the cold light of day she realized that there was no hope of escape. She had heard no word, no letter, nothing from anybody since she was imprisoned here. She was not even sure that anybody, other than her father, knew where she was.

And if they did, it was plain they didn't care. On that thought the tears would fall into the laundry tub, where nobody could see them in the steam.

On sunny days the girls were allowed to sit outside in the fresh air for five minutes at eleven o'clock to drink the watered milk they were given. Inevitably the pregnant girls grouped together. They were all from respectable homes, having been put there to avoid shame on their families, and they shared their stories.

'Harry was in the army,' said Barbara, a pale girl, slender except for the growing bulge under her pinafore. 'We were to have been married at Christmas. I'd got my wedding dress and everything. When he knew he was being sent back to France we . . . well, we loved each other so it didn't seem to matter, since he'd soon be home and we'd be wed . . . But he was killed. Blown up in his tank.' She shrugged and looked at Polly with huge blue eyes. 'Now Harry's gone I might as well be here as anywhere else. I really don't care any more.'

'But what about your baby?' Polly asked, surprised.

'I hope I shan't survive its birth. I don't want to live now Harry's gone. And they won't let me keep my baby if I do live; they'll either give him away or put him in an orphanage.' Her eyes filled with tears. 'And I'm never going to get out of here to rescue him. My parents will see to that. So I'll be better off dead.'

A cold finger of fear clutched at Polly's heart. Was that to be her fate, too? She turned to the other girl sitting on the bench in the sun. She had been a pretty girl once, but now she looked ill and her face wore a bitter look.

'I've got one more month to go and I'll be rid of this thing,' she said viciously, pulling her dress tight to show how far her pregnancy had progressed. 'I hate it. I hate what it's done to me and I hate the man who put it there. If ever I get out of this place I shall kill him and I don't care if I swing for it.' She glared at Polly. 'Yes, you might well look shocked, but maybe you'd feel the same if your uncle had raped you and then denounced you as a trollop and encouraged your parents to have you put away in this place, miles from where we live so nobody will know.' She shuddered. 'He's an animal. Yet he's a rich man, a respected pillar of the community . . . looks after his workers . . . gives to the poor . . . everybody thinks he's wonderful. If only they knew what he's capable of they'd soon change their tune.' She thumped the bench beside her. 'And, by God, if ever I get out of this place I'll make sure they do know, too. I'll shout it from the rooftops.'

'Back to work.' The strident tones of Mrs Brown had them all scurrying back into the steamy heat of the laundry.

Polly was glad. She didn't want to tell anyone her story. She had a superstitious fear, which she clung to, that if she revealed what had happened to her she would never be rescued from the asylum, but if she kept her secret there was a chance that one day she might be. It was a stupid hope and cold common sense told her that it was an impossible idea. But she still clung to it.

Nineteen

Gina found it more difficult to write to James than she had expected. Although she had corresponded with him regularly all the time he had been in the army – telling him about family matters, incidents on the estate, even the most trivial things, just to give him the feeling that he was still a part of Meadowlands – she had never before had to write about anything of quite such a delicate and personal nature. She made several false starts, screwing the paper up and throwing it into the waste-paper basket, disgusted at her inability to string the words together coherently. In the end she decided to write as if she was reporting any other family gossip and leave it to him to act on it as he saw fit.

> *Sadly, we have lost Polly. She became pregnant, and was sent, as we thought, to stay with an aunt at Ipswich until after the birth. Unfortunately, her father took matters into his own hands, assuming (I'm sure incorrectly) she had been with soldiers on lower meadow, and instead incarcerated her in the asylum as punishment. A punishment that is likely to last for the rest of her life, if he has his way, which doesn't bear thinking about. I miss her terribly, as you can imagine, and so do all the women at the soup club. I feel so desperately sorry for her and wish I could find some way to rescue her from that place.*

She wasn't particularly happy with what she'd written – it didn't begin to tell how frustrated and helpless she felt, nor her fury with Will Catchpole at what he had done to his daughter – but she'd thought it best to simply lay out the facts and wait to see how James would react. Obviously, this would depend on his feelings for Polly and whether or not he had played any part in her predicament. After many nights spent sleepless with anxiety, Gina was long past trying to work out the answer to that. She posted the letter to the latest address she had for James and waited impatiently for his reply.

Three weeks later she was still waiting to hear from him when Millie got leave and came home for a few days' much-needed rest. She was very pale and looked deathly tired; even her frizzy hair had lost its bounce.

'Well, we don't exactly live at the Ritz, Gee,' she said with a laugh when Gina commented on the fact that she had lost weight. 'I'll make up for it while I'm home. Yes, please, Ruby, I'd love another helping of Mrs Bellman's treacle pudding. I've dreamt of her cooking.'

After Ruby had left the room she asked with a frown, 'Why is Ruby serving? Where's Polly? I haven't seen her since I got home.'

'Hardly surprising, since you've only just arrived,' Gina said, giving her a glance that warned her that something was not quite right.

'She's not here any more,' Lady Adelaide said peevishly, picking at her pudding. She laid down her spoon and fork with a clatter. 'I think it was most inconsiderate of her parents to insist that she left us to go and look after some elderly relative or other who's not well. What about me? I often feel unwell and need her attention, but nobody bothers about that.'

'Ruby looks after you very well, Mother,' Gina soothed.

'Indeed she does not,' Lady Adelaide said, her voice sharp. 'She pulls my hair when she brushes it and have you seen what she's done to the ruffles on my negligee? No, I thought not. She scorched a hole in them. It's sheer carelessness. Polly would never have done a thing like that.' She gave a discontented shrug as Ruby came in to clear the dishes.

'Shall I take the coffee into the drawing room, m'lady?' she asked. It was clear from her expression that she was no happier than Lady Adelaide with her role as her personal maid.

'That would be lovely, Ruby. Thank you very much,' Gina said, smiling at her and helping her to stack the dishes.

Lady Adelaide gave a heavy sigh. 'I didn't bring you up to do the work of a servant, Georgina,' she remarked when Ruby had left the room. 'Have you no respect for your position?'

Gina always knew her mother was displeased when she used her full name, so rather than antagonize her further she smiled brightly and said, 'Let's go into the drawing room. The coffee will be waiting.'

'Will you pour it, Gina?' Lady Adelaide said, reclining gracefully in her chair. 'I feel singularly weak tonight.'

'Of course, Mother.' Gina caught Millie's eye and they both had difficulty in suppressing their giggles at their mother's theatricals. 'Max will be here later, when he's finished his rounds,' she told her sister.

'He would finish them a good deal earlier if he didn't visit the poor,' Lady Adelaide remarked. 'It isn't as if they can pay him.'

Once again Gina and Millie exchanged glances, this time of exasperation. They both heaved a sigh of relief when their mother finished her coffee and decided to go to her room.

'God, Gina, she gets worse!' Millie said, stretching out full-length on the settee. 'I don't know how you put up with her.'

'I don't really have much choice. I can't leave the poor old thing here on her own and Father doesn't make an appearance all that often.'

'Still got his little floozy in London?'

'I guess so. Not that I blame him.'

'Indeed no.' Millie reached over and helped herself to a cigarette. When she'd lit it she frowned. 'What's this about Polly?'

Gina copied Millie and lit a cigarette before she answered. 'You heard what Ma said.'

'Yes, but it didn't ring true, somehow. Polly would never take herself off to go and look after a sick aunt we'd never heard of.'

Gina grinned at her through the cigarette smoke. 'You're very perceptive.'

'I'm very curious to know what the truth is. Is she pregnant or something?'

Gina nodded. ''Fraid so. But it's more complicated than that.'

'How so?'

Millie listened intently as Gina told her Polly's story, leaving nothing out, relieved to be able to share every last detail with her sister, whom she knew she could trust.

'Bloody hell! The bastard!' Millie said, shocked. 'Pardon my French, but locking his only daughter up in that place to save his own face is enough to make anyone swear. He ought to be shot.'

'And you're not the first one to say that,' Gina replied.

Millie stubbed her cigarette out and lit another one. 'Do you think it's possible our brother might be the father of Polly's child?' she asked thoughtfully.

'I do wonder,' Gina answered. 'He specifically asked me to "look after" Polly, before he went back after his last leave. And Polly confided to her mother that it was James.' She took a last drag on her cigarette. 'I felt sorry for Susan. Poor woman, she was in a dreadful dilemma. I could see she was desperate to confide in me but Polly had sworn her to secrecy so she refused to tell me at first. But when I told her I thought I'd guessed who it was, she opened up and told me exactly what Polly had said.'

'Which was? Tell me again. Exactly.'

'That they loved each other and planned to marry.'

'A good many rich young men have said that to servant girls in order to have their way with them,' Millie said cynically.

Gina's head shot up. 'Do you think James is like that?'

Millie shrugged. 'I wouldn't have said so. But he's a man. Look at our sainted father!' She leaned over and tapped ash off her cigarette into the ashtray. 'But speculating about our brother's morals doesn't help Polly. What do you propose to do about her, poor girl?'

Gina spread her hands. 'What can I do?' She stubbed out her cigarette in the same ashtray. 'The only thing I could think of was to write to James and simply tell him what's happened to Polly in amongst all the other local gossip and wait for his reaction.'

'That was clever. And what was his response?'

'He hasn't replied yet, which worries me a little. I sent it to the last address he gave me.'

Millie lit another cigarette and picked a shred of tobacco off the tip of her tongue. 'I'm not surprised. Now the Americans have arrived and with this "big push", as they call it, troops are being moved around at a minute's notice,' she said. 'He could have been sent anywhere, in which case goodness knows when he'd get his mail.'

'So how can we find out where he is?' Gina's voice dropped. 'I try not to be pessimistic, but I find myself searching the lists of men killed in battle every day.'

Millie didn't reply. She couldn't see how the lists could possibly be accurate with so many lying dead in the field as each side fought for a few yards of territory.

They sat in silence for several minutes, then Gina said, 'Do you think Ned might know where James is?'

'He might, if we knew where Ned was so we could ask him,' Millie replied dryly.

'Oh, this bloody war!' Gina said savagely.

Millie raised her eyebrows. 'I thought it was only me that swore,' she said with a smile. 'But I couldn't agree more.' She stretched luxuriously. 'We'll see what Max says when he gets here. You did say he was coming?' When Gina nodded she went on: 'He might know someone he could contact.' A faint flush spread over her face. 'Has he told you? About us, I mean?'

Gina smiled. 'Yes. And I can't tell you how pleased I am, Mill.'

'It's not official, of course. We thought we'd wait . . .'

'What for?'

'I'm not sure. The war to end, I suppose. Silly, really.'

'Yes, it is. Quite ridiculous.' Gina's smile widened. 'You could cheer us all up by announcing your engagement while you're home. Not, of course, that I'm trying to push you into anything,' she added wickedly.

The door opened and Max walked in on his crutches.

Gina immediately got to her feet. 'I think I'll go to bed.'

Millie burst out laughing. 'There's no need to be quite so obvious, Gina,' she said as she stood up and went to greet him. 'But I'll remember what you said.'

'Good. And I'm being tactful, leaving you together, so you should be grateful. In any case I'm sure you've got lots to talk about without me chiming in all the time. Goodnight to you both.'

As she left the room she stole a glance at them. They were locked in each other's arms and she was sure they hadn't heard a word she'd said.

The next day they announced their engagement and by the

time Millie went back to France she was wearing a pretty diamond and turquoise ring on her finger, even though they both knew that once she got back into uniform it would spend most of its time on the chain round her neck that Max had also bought her.

Life seemed very flat after Millie had gone back. Gina missed her, but she missed Polly more and she realized how she had taken for granted Polly's cheerful demeanour and encouragement. Especially on soup club days, although the women were used to looking after the big teapot and washing the cups and soup mugs. But some of them were inclined to be slatterns, which Polly hadn't tolerated. Gina knew she used to send them back to wash again the things that weren't clean, always with a smile and encouraging word so they couldn't take offence.

'We'll have to get you some spectacles, Gladys, if you can't see this isn't clean,' she'd say with a grin. Or, 'Are you saving what's left in the bottom of this mug for next time, Ethel?' This always raised a chuckle.

Oh, how she missed her and wished she was back, not only to organize the children into some kind of order, but because she was a friend with whom she could talk things over.

She was sitting behind her screen making notes on what Ada Morland had just told her so that she didn't miss any details when she wrote to the relevant authority, when a shadow fell across her notebook. She looked up and saw Max standing in front of her, grinning.

'What . . .?' A delighted smile spread over her face. 'Max! Your crutches!'

'Yes, I'm at last able to stand on my own two feet.' He looked down. 'Well, two feet, anyway. I've got a way to go before the new one feels like mine.' He reached behind him. 'They've given me a walking stick, just to give me confidence, because it still feels a little strange. But at least it'll make me look a bit more like a doctor than a patient.'

'Oh, what a pity Millie didn't see.'

'Ah, but she did,' he said with a grin. 'She was there when I first tried it and she helped me practise walking. She let me lean on her like a good nurse should.'

'Which, of course, was no problem to either of you,' Gina said, laughing. 'But she didn't tell me.'

'No, I swore her to secrecy. I wanted to surprise you.'

'Well, you have! And I'm delighted.' She saw him wince. 'Is it painful?'

'Rubs a little. But I'll get used to it. By the time I walk down the aisle with Millie nobody will know I haven't got two good feet.' With a cheerful smile he left her to go and sort out the problems he was there to deal with, leaving Gina with hers.

They hadn't changed much in the years she'd been running the soup club; in nearly all cases it was a continual fight to get money for people who desperately needed it from faceless authorities who found endless excuses not to pay it. Sometimes it nearly broke her heart to hear of the desperate plight of starving families where the breadwinner had returned from fighting for his country a broken man, too ill to work but with no pension or compensation.

A few days later Gina was cheered by a letter from Millie saying she'd seen Ned, quite by chance, as he was passing through, having been posted to another sector. She reported that he, like everyone else, looked worn out and filthy. But he was cheerful, mainly because he had seen James. He saw him at a field hospital near Ypres, just as he was about to be moved away from the battle zone so that his badly wounded arm could be treated properly.

'From what Ned said it looks as if that's the end of James' war,' Millie wrote, 'but I can't find out where he's been taken so I don't know quite how bad his arm is. I'll keep trying, and if I manage to see him I'll discover what he's got to say about Polly and let you know.'

Polly knew nothing of any of this. Her days blurred into a pattern of washing boards and mangles, damp concrete floors and walls running with water, backache and misery. She was becoming resigned to the fact that she would never see green fields again, so in the few moments respite in the drudgery of each day she tended a scrappy little geranium growing in a corner that nobody else seemed to have noticed. Sometimes she wondered why she bothered, but the little geranium flourished and flowered with her care, proving that with a bit of love and care anything could survive, even in such bleak surroundings. She took it as an omen and resolved never to give up hope.

But it was difficult and there was no consideration given to her in her advancing pregnancy. She was still expected to haul heavy sheets in and out of the boiler, still expected to turn the handle on the heavy old iron mangle and still expected to peg them out on the washing line. She didn't mind this last task; it meant she saw a bit of blue sky and an occasional glimpse of the sun. She would turn her face up to it to feel the warmth, but a sharp slap from Mrs Brown soon had her hurrying back to the dank laundry.

The nights were the worst. She would curl her arm round her swelling belly and whisper to her baby, telling him how much she loved and wanted him and promising him that she wouldn't let him be parted from her.

But in her heart she knew this was a forlorn hope, especially when Barbara, the girl whose young man, Harry, had been killed in the war, went into labour and gave birth. Three days later she was back, looking washed out and weak. But she was still expected to work.

'What was it?' one of the other girls asked.

Barbara shook her head. 'Dunno. They wouldn't tell me. They just took it. Said it was best that way.' She burst into tears. 'I don't even know if it's alive or dead. They just took it away,' she sobbed. 'My Harry's baby and they wouldn't even let me hold it. Oh, I wish I was dead.' Suddenly, she doubled over, clutching her stomach. Polly ran to help her and saw the darkening pool of blood between her feet. They carried her back to the infirmary and by the next morning Barbara had got her wish.

'That's not going to happen to me,' said the girl who had been raped by her uncle, when she heard. 'When I get rid of this,' she pointed to the bulge under her pinafore, 'I'm going to get out of this place, somehow.'

'I can't imagine how. We might as well be in prison,' Polly said, feeling more than usually pessimistic as she took a few more sips of her watered milk and gazed up at the blue sky, her only contact with the outside world.

'I've got plans.' The girl, whose name was Moira, tapped the side of her nose mysteriously.

'Oh, yes? What plans?' Polly couldn't see how she could possibly get out through those tall iron gates, nor over the high brick wall that circled the asylum. Even the garden, which some of the girls looked after, could only be reached through a locked gate in the wall. They grew the vegetables for use in the asylum, watched over by vigilant nurses, or warders, as Polly came to think of them.

'You don't think I'm going to tell you, do you? You might try to copy me.' Moira finished the last of her drink and jerked her head towards Polly's belly. 'When's yours due?'

Polly pushed a strand of hair back under her mob cap. 'In another couple of months, I think. I've sort of lost track of time so I'm not really sure.'

'Oh, I'll be gone by then.'

'I wish you luck,' Polly said without enthusiasm.

'Back to work.' Mrs Brown banged the tea tray that had held the watered milk. 'Put your mugs here as you go past. Eileen, you can take them back to the kitchen and wash them up.'

Eileen, a big fat girl of twenty or so, with bulbous eyes and the mental capacity of a four-year-old, frowned and shook her head. 'No, don't want to,' she said.

'You'll do as I say, my girl.' Mrs Brown put the tray down on the seat and grabbed the girl by the hair.

Polly leaped forward. 'Leave her alone. You know she doesn't understand,' she said, trying to prise the woman's fingers from Eileen's hair. She was fed up with Mrs Brown's bullying.

Letting go of Eileen so suddenly that the poor girl fell over, Mrs Brown turned on Polly and gave her a stinging blow across the face that caught her off-balance and brought her to her knees. 'And you can mind your own business and get yourself back to work. There's two soiled blankets that need washing.' She laughed grimly. 'That'll keep you out of mischief for a few hours, my lady.'

My lady. Polly was reminded of another life where she was at the beck and call of another My Lady – Lady Adelaide. But that life had gone and would never return.

Gingerly, testing her jaw to make sure it wasn't broken, she hauled herself to her feet and went back into the steamy darkness of the laundry, where the bright sunshine never penetrated.

Twenty

Gina made a point of visiting Susan Catchpole as often as she could, not just because of the soup and cakes she made for the soup club, but at other times to stay and have a cup of tea with her. She knew the poor woman had few other people she could confide in, and she liked Susan, who was a kind, caring woman who didn't deserve the burden she carried.

It was a warm, sunny afternoon in June as Gina made her way across to Pippin Farm. Opening the wicket gate she could see Susan in the kitchen garden gathering raspberries. She looked thin and ill – defeated was the word that came into Gina's mind at the sight of her. How could Will Catchpole not see what was happening to his wife? Worse, how could he be so inhuman as to leave his only daughter to rot in the asylum? Blind fury welled up inside her at the thought of the way he was destroying his family and she paused and took several deep breaths before carrying on down the garden path. Her feelings of anger and frustration would be of no help to Susan; support and hope were what she needed.

Susan looked up as she heard Gina approach and her expression immediately brightened and a smile spread across her tired features. 'Oh, Miss Gina. How nice of you to call.' She picked up her basket of raspberries. 'You've time for a cup of tea?'

'That's why I've come, Susan. And for a slice of your delicious fruit cake,' Gina said, smiling back.

'I'm sure I can find that. Do come inside. The kettle's on the hob so it won't take me a minute.'

'Why don't we stay out here in the sunshine? We can sit on that seat in the corner over there.'

Susan frowned. 'It may be a bit dusty.' Her face cleared. 'Never mind, I'll bring a cushion for you to sit on.'

'Please don't fuss, Susan, I'll be perfectly fine,' Gina insisted. She took a raspberry out of Susan's basket and popped it in her mouth. 'Mm. These are lovely. Take them indoors quickly or I'll eat the lot.'

'I was going to make jam for you to take to the soup club,' Susan said. 'I don't reckon many of them there can afford to buy decent jam. Anyway, home-made's so much nicer.'

'That's really kind of you, Susan.'

Susan shrugged. 'It gives me something to do. Stops me thinking too much.' She went off to make the tea.

Gina sat down and turned her face to the sun, thinking of Polly and wondering if the sunshine penetrated the grounds of the asylum where she was incarcerated. Did they let the inmates walk in the gardens? Were there gardens? Were they treated well? These and a hundred and one other questions went round and round in her mind as they did every night before she went to sleep and every time she had a moment to herself during the day.

She had written to Polly several times but had never had a reply so she wondered if the letters had ever reached her. She suspected they hadn't. She'd even tried to visit her but had received such a peremptory and rude refusal that she had never tried again in case it might reflect badly on Polly.

Susan came back with tea and cake and sat down beside Gina.

'Polly used to come over for a cup of tea in the afternoon when she had a minute to spare,' she said, handing Gina a cup of tea. 'I used to look forward to that. Maybe she would only stay ten minutes or so, but she was like a breath of fresh air.' She took a sip of her own tea. 'I miss her.'

'So do I, Susan,' Gina said quietly. 'I just wish there was something I could do . . .'

'There isn't. Until *he* has a change of heart, my poor girl won't get out of that place. And he's not likely to do that. He's got a heart of flint, that man.'

Gina took a bite of Susan's delicious fruit cake, weighing up in her mind whether or not to tell Susan she was trying to contact James.

'If only there was some way . . .' Susan's voice trailed off. Then she added, 'I've thought and thought, but there isn't.' She wiped away a tear with the corner of her apron.

Gina laid her hand over Susan's. 'I'm trying to get in touch with James,' she said at last. 'Oh, it's all right, Susan,' she hurried on, seeing the look of consternation on the older woman's face. 'I didn't give away any confidences. I simply told him what's happened to Polly as if it was local gossip, which it no doubt is, however much your husband might choose to think otherwise. These things have a habit of getting out, however much you try to hide them. However, my thoughts are that if James feels in any way responsible he'll get in touch. Otherwise . . .' She spread her hands eloquently.

Susan sat quietly for a long time, thinking over Gina's words. She was in no doubt that Gina had acted with the best possible motives, but she was not convinced it had been the wisest thing to do. At last she said, 'And have you heard from Mr James?'

Gina shook her head. 'No. In fact I don't even know if he's received my letter. My sister Millie told me that with the Americans coming in and this Big Push they keep talking about, men are being moved up and down the line at a minute's notice so it's quite likely mail gets lost. My brother Ned saw him at a field hospital not long ago and said he was quite badly wounded in one arm and was annoyed because he hadn't received any mail for some time. But we've heard nothing since.' It was Gina's turn to fight back tears. 'We don't know where he is now. We don't even know whether he's alive or dead.'

'I'm sorry, Miss Gina. It's a terrible worry for you.' It was Susan's turn to take Gina's hand. 'But either way I don't see it could help my Polly much.'

'No, you're probably right.' The two women stared at the flowers in the garden without really seeing them as a cloud covered the sun.

A little later, as Susan was pouring a second cup of tea for them both, Gina said, 'How is Violet? Do you see her often?'

Susan shook her head. 'Not often. Most of her time is taken up with poor Tom. And that's a tragedy, if ever there was one. A big, strong lad like that cut down in his prime.' She caught her breath and went on: 'Violet and Isaac keep him looking spotless, but it means she has her hands in the wash tub most of the time.'

'Poor woman. There's no improvement in him, then?'

'No. Nor ever will be. They know that.' She sipped her tea. 'It's killing them, looking after him, but they wouldn't have it any different. He's their boy and they're determined to care for him.' Her eyes filled with tears as she added bitterly, 'It's a pity Will Catchpole doesn't feel the same about his child.'

'Oh, Susan.' Gina put her arms round Susan and let her cry, while she tried to understand the mentality of a man who could wilfully bring such pain and suffering to his wife and only daughter. She found it totally beyond her comprehension.

After a long time, Susan lifted her head and dabbed at her eyes.

'I'm sorry, Miss Gina. I don't usually let myself go like that,' she said with a hiccup. 'I'm afraid that once I start I shan't be able to stop.' She gave Gina a watery smile. 'Oh, dear, I'm afraid I've made the front of your dress all wet with my tears.'

'That doesn't matter a bit,' Gina said gently. 'Sometimes you need to just let go instead of bottling it all up inside.'

'Funny, that's exactly what I tell Violet. She's very brave, though.'

'And so are you.' Gina got to her feet. 'And unlike Violet, at least you've got hope, Susan. Eventually, we'll get Polly out of that place, I'm sure of it.'

'Not if *that man* has his way,' Susan said, hardening her jaw. 'You don't know him like I do.'

It was several days later at the soup club that Ivy Clench slipped behind the screen to talk to Gina. Ivy had eight children and a husband crippled in the war; she'd been coming to the soup club ever since it started.

Gina looked up with a sigh. 'Oh, Ivy, has your extra money still not come through? I've written to everyone I can think of. They really should increase your allowance. They've been told your husband is incapacitated enough times.'

Ivy smiled brightly. 'We manage, miss. At least we get a bit, so we don't starve. And my brother's a coalman so he gives us a bag of coal dust now and then.' Her voice dropped. 'And there's usually a few nuggets of coal mixed in with the dust so we're luckier than a lot of folks.'

'I'm glad to hear it.' Gina smiled back at her. She was so often amazed at the resilience of these women. 'So what's your trouble, Ivy? Sit down and tell me and I'll see what I can do.'

'Oh, it's not my trouble I've come about.' Ivy sat down, twisting a corner of her apron in her hands and began uncomfortably, 'I don't want to speak out of turn, Miss Gina, and if I hevn't got it right I hope you won't take it amiss.'

Gina frowned. 'I don't quite understand . . .'

'It's about Polly, miss.' Ivy took a deep breath and her words came out in a rush. 'The story that was put about that she'd gone to Ipswich to look after a sick aunt. Well, all of us here knew that wasn't true. We knew very well what her trouble was, God knows we've all been there enough times to know the signs; but we didn't know what had really happened to her and we was quite worried, 'cause we all like Polly. But now we've found out.' She sat back in her chair and shook her head sadly.

'Where do you think she is?'

'I know where she is. Somebody's put her in the asylum, poor little mawther. My brother's seen her there.'

'Ah.' Something like relief flooded through Gina although she wasn't sure why.

Ivy went on: 'Y'see, he delivers coal to that place and he reckernized Polly. He used to see her sometimes when he delivered the coal up to your house; he remembered her because she'd always give him a smile and the time o' day, whereas most of the other servants ignored him. He said she's . . .' She made a curving motion with her hand over her belly. 'Well, o'course we knew that. But he's right, ain't he? That is where she is? In the asylum?'

Gina nodded. 'Yes, I'm afraid that's just where she is. Her father had her committed there when he found out she was pregnant.' She saw no reason to hide Will Catchpole's callous treatment of his daughter.

'The rotten bugger! Well, Fred told me she's bin put to work in the laundry and it don't look like they knock her about too much like they do some of 'em. I jest thought you'd like to know, miss.' Her voice trailed off, thinking from Gina's preoccupied expression that she wasn't paying attention.

This was far from the case. Gina's mind was working frantically. 'How often does your brother deliver coal there?' she asked quickly.

Ivy shrugged. 'Dunno. Every week, I reckon.'

Gina leaned forward. 'Ivy, if I was to give you a note for Polly, do you think your brother could smuggle it to her?'

'Yes, I reckon he could do that, if he was careful.'

'You see, if I could get a note to her then at least she'd realize that we know where she is and haven't abandoned her.' Already, Gina was busy scribbling. When she'd finished she sealed the note in an envelope and gave it to Ivy. 'Tell your brother he mustn't do anything that might risk him losing his job. I wouldn't want that.'

'He'll be careful, Miss.' Ivy took the letter, feeling important.

'And thank you, Ivy. It means more than I can tell you to be able to get in touch with Polly.' Gina leaned over and squeezed her arm gratefully.

It was a week later that Ivy's brother managed to smuggle an envelope, grubby with coal dust, into Polly's hands under pretext of needing a bit of rag to bind round his sore thumb. As soon as she could she escaped to the privy to read it. It was brief and to the point. *Dear Polly. We know where you are and we are trying to find a way to get you out. Your friend, G. Barsham.*

On reading the words she cried with relief. Her fear had always been that her father hadn't told anyone where he'd taken her, but now, knowing that Miss Gina knew where she was, she was confident that somehow she would be able to help her. Suddenly there was a glimmer of hope on the horizon. Taking from her pocket the stub of pencil she used for checking the laundry list – this was her responsibility since she was the only one who could read and write – she wrote on the back of the letter just two words: *Thank you.* Then she put it back in the envelope and hid it behind a brick at the back of the privy to wait until the coalman came again.

After that she went back to the laundry, where her tears of relief could mingle with the sweat that ran down her face as she scrubbed the dirty linen while Mrs Brown hit her about the shoulders for being a long time in the privy. Now, although nothing had actually changed, the world suddenly didn't seem quite so grim and the sun seemed to shine more brightly because she knew that somebody who cared about her knew where she was.

Gina was getting more and more worried because there was still no news from James. After Ned's contact with him at the field hospital there had been nothing. Clearly he had been moved on, but neither Millie nor Ned could discover where he had been moved on to.

'*It's organized chaos all down the line, as far as I can gather. And there's been a bit of a flu epidemic which has added to the confusion, but that seems to be over now. I'll keep trying to get news of him.*' Millie wrote this to Gina and it was followed by a letter from Ned in much the same vein.

Gina read the letters again and again and the question rolled round and round in her brain – where was James? Was he still alive? Did he get this flu that they spoke about? And had he received her letter and read of Polly's plight? If he had, why hadn't he answered? Didn't he care what happened to her? On the other hand, if it was nothing to do with him why should he care? She leaned her elbows on the desk in her room and rubbed her temples with her fingers to ease the tension as the thoughts went on, getting ever more complicated and outlandish.

At last she put on her hat and went for a walk in the summer sunshine. As she walked she faced the fact that she was pinning all her hopes – and fears – on James, when in fact Polly's situation might have nothing at all to do with him. And even if it had, what could he do about it? Her father had put her in that place and it was her father alone who could sanction her release. And since that was something Will Catchpole was unlikely ever to do, some other solution would have to be found. Because it was unthinkable that Polly should have to spend the rest of her life incarcerated in the asylum.

She walked down to the river, where the calming sound of the ripples relaxed her and soothed her aching head. But she found no answer to the problem.

Three days later a letter arrived from James.

Twenty-One

The letter had an English postmark. That was the first thing Gina noticed. She tore it open and found a single sheet inside, written in large, childish, ill-formed letters. It read:

> *Dear Gina,*
>
> *Sorry about writing, learning to use left hand since lost other one. Repatriated after complications with arm plus nasty attack of flu to above address. V. smart hotel, taken over as army convalescent home. Had no mail for ages. Please write soon. Or better still, come and visit and bring me some decent clothes.*
>
> *Love Jamie*

The printed address at the top of the page was The Imperial Hotel, and it was situated on the outskirts of Bournemouth.

She sat back in her chair, weeping with relief. So Jamie was alive! Thank God for that. And he was safely back in England, thank God for that, too! She dried her eyes and immediately began to make plans to leave for Bournemouth, excitedly dithering between looking up train times, or going to his room and packing a suitcase with his clothes.

But first she hurried to tell her mother the wonderful news and give her the letter to read, and together they wept with relief to know that James was back in England and safe. Then, with Lady Adelaide's blessing, Gina continued to make plans, her head spinning with excitement. Even the fact that her brother had lost an arm couldn't dampen her spirits; the important thing was that he was alive!

Then sanity prevailed. Tomorrow was soup club day; Susan would have the soup ready and the children in particular would be waiting for it so she couldn't let them down by simply not turning up. But once she had done that she would be free for a day or two.

The next morning, after a night spent sleepless with excitement, she went to collect the soup from Susan and told her the wonderful news.

'Oh, thank God for that, Miss Gina. Maybe he'll be able to do something about getting my girl out of that awful place,' were Susan's first words when she heard.

'I'm sure he'll try.' Guiltily, Gina realized she'd hardly given Polly a thought; she'd been far too excited over his letter and the plans she'd been making to visit him. 'I intend to go and see him today. There's a train to London this afternoon that will connect up with one to Bournemouth without too much of a wait. I don't know how long I'll be there so I've arranged for one of the estate workers to collect the next batch of soup from you with the pony and trap if I'm not back in time.'

'My goodness, it seems you've thought of just about everything, Miss Gina,' Susan said with a smile.

'I've tried to. I can't let the people down by saying there won't be a soup club just because I'm not there, can I? The women will manage to run it perfectly well by themselves as long as the soup's there.' She put her arm round Susan and gave her a peck on the cheek. 'You're the important one, Susan. You're the one who provides the soup and I can't tell you how grateful I am for what you do.'

'Just get my Polly out of that asylum, Miss Gina. That's all the thanks I want,' Susan said.

'I promise I'll do whatever I can.'

But although she didn't mention this to Susan, she realized that having lost an arm in battle and then being laid low by influenza, just now might not be the best time to worry her brother with the plight of Polly Catchpole.

When Max Rodwell called in to the soup club to do his usual medical check Gina, still bubbling over with excitement, told him the good news and her planned trip to see James.

'Bournemouth? And you're going by train? Why don't you drive down?' he asked, looking puzzled.

'I thought about it, but . . .' She didn't like to admit she felt apprehensive about driving to unfamiliar places, especially as she had no map and no idea how to get there.

'I'll drive you, if you like.' He grinned at her surprise. 'As you know, I've had my car adapted and now I've got my wooden foot I'm perfectly capable. I've been buzzing around visiting my patients like a demented bee. Saves me an enormous amount of time.' He looked at his watch. 'When can you be finished here? One o'clock?'

'Yes, if I leave one of the women to lock up, which I often do.'

'Good. Then I'll pick you up at your house at two. And pack a bag because we'll have to stay somewhere overnight.' He grinned as he saw a look of alarm pass fleetingly across her face and leaned over to whisper, 'You needn't worry, I'll be booking two rooms. I'd never cheat on my Millie.'

She relaxed and smiled back at him. 'Good, because neither would I.'

They found the convalescent home, a large hotel set in beautiful grounds, and drove straight up to the door. The receptionist directed them to a sheltered corner of the garden where they could see a man sitting in a wheelchair with one arm in a sling and his face turned to the late afternoon sun. In repose he looked pale and gaunt, his face lined beyond his years and dark circles under his eyes. He turned his head as he saw them approach and a wide grin spread across his face, immediately making him look ten years younger.

'Gina! Max! Oh, it's so good to see you.' He held out his good arm and pulled Gina into a bear hug, then shook hands with Max. 'Sit down, sit down.' He indicated a nearby garden seat. 'Max, would you do the honours and push me a bit nearer? I'm perfectly capable of walking but they still insist on pushing me around in this thing. Thanks, that's better. Now, tell me all the news.'

'Not a lot to tell,' Gina said, shooting a covert warning glance at Max. 'Meadowlands goes on much the same as ever. But what about you? What's happened to your arm? And how did you manage to get back to England?'

James shrugged. 'My hand got crushed in a shell attack, didn't get treated quickly enough and went a bit bad so they had to cut it off halfway up the arm,' he said briefly. 'It ended up as a "blighty".'

'An injury, like mine, that gets you invalided out,' Max said, for Gina's benefit.

'That's right. Only before they could get me on to a boat I got a dose of rather unpleasant flu, which laid me low for a week or two, not sure how long, I wasn't very compos mentis at the time. As soon as I was deemed fit to travel they shipped me home and I landed here. End of story. Except, and the most annoying thing, being shoved around so much I haven't been getting any mail, so I feel completely out of touch. I don't know whether it's all gone astray or whether it's following me around like a stray dog, keeping its distance. All I know is I haven't had any letters for the past . . . I dunno, six weeks? Two months? Seems like ages. So I'm completely out of touch and relying on you to fill me in with what's been going on.'

A young nurse came by. 'Are you ready to come inside, Major Barsham? It's getting a little chilly out here.'

'No, I'm fine at the moment. I'll ask my friend to wheel me in presently.' He smiled at her.

'Pretty girl,' Max said with a grin.

'Yes, I think it's part of the treatment to have pretty nurses around,' James agreed. 'And talking of pretty girls, how's Polly?'

Gina licked her lips. 'Why do you ask?'

He frowned. 'Because I want to know, of course.' He looked from Gina to Max and back again. 'What? What is it? Is something wrong?'

'I'm afraid she's been a bit of a naughty girl,' Gina said lightly. 'She's pregnant.'

'Oh, Christ.' James put his hand over his face. 'Oh, my poor little love. She should have told me. Why didn't she write and tell me?'

'Ah, it's true, then,' Gina said with a sigh.

'What, that the child is mine? Yes, of course it is,' he said impatiently. 'Why didn't *you* write and tell me? I asked you to look after her.'

'I know you did, but I'd no idea you were concerned she might be pregnant. How could I?' She shook her head sadly. 'I thought you were above taking advantage of a servant, Jamie.'

He ground his teeth, barely in control of his temper. 'Don't be so bloody offensive, Gina. Polly may be a servant in my father's house now but we more or less grew up together and it's never seemed like that. It hasn't stopped me falling in love with her either.' His voice dropped. 'Polly Catchpole means all the world to me and I want her for my wife.'

'You intend to marry her?' Gina carefully kept the surprise out of her voice.

'Yes, of course I do. I know it'll cause a certain amount of consternation in the family but if this bloody war has taught me anything it's taught me that class doesn't matter; it's people that matter. I love Polly and she loves me and if she'll still have me I'm going to make her my wife as soon as I can arrange it.' He did rapid calculations on his one hand. 'I don't want my child to be born out of wedlock.'

Gina and Max exchanged glances and at an almost imperceptible nod from Max, Gina said, 'There's something else you should know, Jamie,' she said gently.

He looked up in alarm, sensing trouble from Gina's tone. 'What? What is it? Is Polly ill? She hasn't been married off to somebody else, has she? If she has I'll kill him. She's mine!'

She shook her head. 'No, it's nothing like that.' She licked her dry lips again. 'But she's in the asylum. When her father found out that she was pregnant that's where he put her.'

He banged his good hand on the arm of the wheelchair. 'He *what*? The bastard!' He turned to Gina. 'You didn't let her stay there, did you? You got her out, poor love.'

Gina shook her head. 'How could I, Jamie? It was a family matter. I couldn't interfere, much as I hated what he'd done. Of course I didn't know then that you . . .' She hesitated. Any doubts she'd had about her brother's feelings for Polly had gone, dispelled by his fury at her father's actions. 'Maybe you can . . .'

'Too bloody right, I can.' He shifted impatiently in his wheelchair. 'Did you bring me some decent clothes? I think they've burnt most of mine.'

'Yes, of course. They're in Max's car.'

'You've come in Max's car? Oh, excellent! That means we can leave and be home tonight.'

'But you're not fit to travel. They haven't discharged you, Jamie.'

'They soon will, as long as Doctor Rodwell assumes responsibility for me. You'll do that, Max?'

Max nodded. 'I suppose so. But if I do take responsibility as your doctor you'll have to obey my orders. And the first one will be straight to bed when you arrive home. There'll be no storming the asylum tonight. Is that understood, James?'

'Yes, yes,' James said impatiently. 'Now, wheel me inside so we can do the official stuff.' He looked up at Max. 'You see? I'm sensible enough to realize I must conserve my strength for the journey. Then if you'd be kind enough to help me into decent clothes we can get going.'

'I'm dying for a cup of tea, and so is Max, I think,' Gina said.

'We'll stop somewhere. The tea here is like dishwater. I haven't had a decent cup since I got here. It may have been a luxury hotel once, but it's gone downhill since the army commandeered it, I can tell you.' It was obvious James couldn't wait to be on the road.

By the time they arrived back at Meadowlands, after stopping for a meal and a brief rest on the way, James was absolutely exhausted. Max ordered him straight to bed and gave him something to ensure he had a good night's sleep.

When Max called at ten o'clock the next morning, James was sitting at the breakfast table, bathed and shaved and, watched by his doting mother and sister, making short work of kidneys and scrambled eggs despite having only one hand.

'Well, at least you're looking rested,' Max remarked, casting a professional eye over him.

'Yes. Whatever it was you gave me knocked me right out,' James said. 'But I'm feeling fine this morning.'

'You're still rather pale, darling,' his mother said anxiously. 'And very thin.'

'No doubt Mrs Bellman's cooking will soon change that,' he said, helping himself to toast, which Gina unobtrusively spread with butter and marmalade for him.

'Thanks,' he said. 'I'd normally want to do it myself, but we're in a bit of a hurry today.'

'Oh, are you going out?' Lady Adelaide asked, her mouth turning down in disappointment.

'Yes. I have a very important appointment this morning,' James said.

Lady Adelaide nodded knowingly. 'Ah. Of course. Army business.'

Nobody contradicted her.

An hour later James, leaning quite heavily on a stick, accompanied by Gina and Max, was ushered into the office of a very disgruntled matron at the asylum.

'This is very irregular,' she said coldly, getting to her feet. 'I'm not in the habit of allowing people to burst in on me in this manner. Didn't you know you should have made an appointment?'

'We didn't have time to make an appointment and we didn't burst in,' James said with a disarming smile that masked the fury inside him. 'Your secretary opened the door for us.'

'I shall have words with her. But now you're here please state your business and leave. I'm a very busy woman.'

'It's quite simple. We're here to collect Miss Polly Catchpole. It was all a mistake. She should never have been brought here in the first place,' he said. 'So if you'll send someone to fetch her we'll take her home and not waste any more of your time.'

'I'm afraid that won't be possible. Her father had her committed because she was insane. I must say she's been very quiet since she's been here, but I have no power to release her without his authority.' She lifted her chin triumphantly.

James turned to Max. 'Doctor Rodwell, could I trouble you to go and fetch Catchpole? He'll be somewhere around the estate. Tell him Mr James needs to see him as a matter of some urgency.'

'Of course, Major Barsham.' Max left, hiding a smile at the surprise on the matron's face.

James turned to Matron and said, his voice reasonable, 'I'm not leaving this office without Miss Catchpole, madam, so perhaps you'd be kind enough to provide chairs for my sister and me while we wait.'

Henrietta Sadler was flustered, although years of self-control meant she hid it quite successfully. She had no idea that these people had come from Meadowlands until the doctor mentioned the name Barsham. Then, of course, she knew, because Sir George and Lady Barsham were well known in the town. She wondered if she'd made a mistake in insisting that she needed the authority of the girl's father, since the signature of a Barsham would carry as much, if not more weight. However, the deed was done now and all she could do was wait and see what happened when the Catchpole man arrived. She ordered two comfortable chairs to be brought in from her private sitting room and they settled in silence to wait.

The day had not started well for Polly. Somebody had stolen her clean stockings so she had to put on an old pair with a hole in the heel. Then a new girl had thrown her porridge on the floor, screaming, and it had been Polly who had to clean it up, which made her late at the laundry. Mrs Brown did not deal kindly with latecomers and had given her a sharp slap across the face and shouted at her for being lazy.

This was how life was always going to be, Polly thought dejectedly, plunging her hands into the bath of slightly too hot suds and beginning to scrub at the filthy bedding it was her lot to clean. The note she had received from Miss Gina she didn't know how many weeks ago, which had given her so much hope, had yielded nothing else. So although it was a comfort to know that Miss Gina was aware of her incarceration in this place, it was plain that she could do nothing about it. She brushed away the tears and sweat from her face and scrubbed on.

Suddenly there was a commotion behind her. She turned and saw two of the more violent inmates fighting. They were both large, fat girls and they hated each other. At the moment Elsie, the stronger one, was trying to turn the mangle on Tabby's fingers.

'Stop that!' Polly pulled the handle of the mangle out of Elsie's hands just as the tips of Tabby's fingers were about to disappear between the rollers.

Elsie punched her for spoiling the fun while Tabby clung to her, sucking her fingers and weeping loudly, although she wasn't really hurt.

'What's going on?' Mrs Brown came in and saw Elsie meekly folding dirty clothes, while Polly comforted Tabby. 'Oh, it's you again,' she said, pulling Polly away from the other girl. 'There's always trouble wherever you are. Now, get back to work.' With another slap she pushed Polly so that she overbalanced and slid across the wet floor, banging her shoulder on the table leg. When she got to her feet her dress was nearly as wet as the sacking apron she was wearing over her overall. 'Serves you right,' Mrs Brown said nastily.

Polly went back to work. For a moment she wished she was dead and her baby with her.

Later, when she was hanging the sheets out to dry, Mrs Brown came up and prodded her. 'Matron wants to see you,' she said with a twist of her lip that Polly could never decide was meant to be a smile or a sneer.

Polly knew what that meant. She was going to be blamed for the mangle incident. Mrs Brown always managed to turn things so that she was blamed, even if she'd been nowhere near the trouble. But she never complained. Mrs Brown was not going to break her spirit; it was the only thing she had left and without it she would crumble into nothing.

She went up the stairs to Matron's room, her too-big boots making a scraping sound on the concrete floor as she went. She hadn't bothered to take off the sacking apron and her dress had only partly dried, leaving dirty streaks where she had fallen. She tucked a strand of hair back under her mob cap but it didn't make much difference; she couldn't tuck it all back.

She reached the door and knocked. Then she took a deep breath and went in, ready for the onslaught.

Twenty-Two

Polly stood just inside the door, eyes cast down, looking at nothing, the way she'd found least likely to cause trouble when summoned to Matron's room. She was a gaunt, thin figure, apart from the growing bulge of her pregnancy, which could no longer be hidden under her overall and the long, damp sacking apron. Wearing a pair of lace-less scuffed boots that were clearly too big, her hands and arms were red and chapped from constant immersion in hot water and rat's tails of hair were escaping from under her cap.

Her face was parchment white, apart from the red weal across her cheek where Mrs Brown had struck her earlier, and the grey striped dress she was wearing was several sizes too big in order to accommodate her pregnancy. She waited with a kind of abject resignation to hear the list of misdemeanours she had been called to answer for.

'Oh, for the love of God, Catchpole! Just look what you've done to your beautiful daughter! Oh, Polly, my Polly.'

She looked up, blinking at the sound of such an anguished cry. It was just like James' voice. But how could it be?

Then he was holding her close, rocking her and telling her she was safe now. He was saying he'd come to take her home, which was what she'd dreamt of night after night. She knew it couldn't be true, so she must have died and gone to Heaven. Then she fainted.

Will Catchpole was indeed shocked at the sight of his daughter as she stood just inside the door, although it was not in his nature to admit it. He turned his face away, his jaw set, and looked out of the window to hide his shame, so he didn't see her crumple.

It was Max who stepped forward to catch her as she collapsed and he lowered her gently to the floor, with James still holding her and cradling her in his one good arm.

'I'm so sorry, my darling,' he was saying. 'It's all been my fault. I'm so, so sorry.'

Gina, with tears in her eyes, went over to where the matron sat, cold-faced, at her desk, leafing through a large ledger. When she found what she'd been looking for she smoothed the page.

'Is this where it has to be signed?' Gina asked, pointing.

The matron nodded and Gina indicated the place to Will Catchpole. He came forward and signed his name without a word.

'Thank you, Catchpole. That will be all. We'll take responsibility for Polly,' Gina said briefly, turning her back on him. To the matron she said, 'Where are Polly's own clothes?' The matron looked taken aback and Gina nodded knowingly. 'Ah, yes, of course, you'll have sold them. Never mind, we'll take her in what she's wearing.'

'It's asylum property,' the matron protested.

'And you'll get it all back as soon as I can find something decent for her to put on.' Gina turned to James and Max, who were now helping an ashen-faced Polly to her feet. 'Let's get her out of here and home to her mother as quickly as possible,' she said.

Will Catchpole saw the car carrying his daughter speed past as he walked the long road back to Meadowlands. He wasn't to blame, he told himself over and over again. It wasn't as if he'd *wanted* to put Polly away. He'd done what he thought was best. How could he have known it was James Barsham who had been playing fast and loose with her? She never said. Not that he'd have listened if she had. Or believed her. He'd been so sure she'd been with the soldiers, so sure he was right. He wasn't used to being proved wrong.

But now what? Would they keep him on as estate manager? Would he want to stay there, having been made such a fool of? Could he remain an Elder at his church? Oh, the humiliation Polly had brought on him; he would never forgive her for that. Because he would never be able to live down the shame, never forget it; her bastard child would always be there to remind him of the terrible mistake he'd made.

He walked doggedly on.

Polly still couldn't believe she was out of that awful place. It had all happened so quickly. It seemed to her bewildered mind that one minute she'd been scrubbing filthy sheets in the laundry and the next, here she was, sitting at her mother's kitchen table with Max and Gina, drinking tea out of the old familiar flowered china cups, with James close beside her, encircling her with his good arm and her mother beaming at her from the other side of the table through happy tears. Even Doctor Max and Miss Gina couldn't stop smiling.

But Polly wasn't smiling, as she looked from one to another and round the familiar kitchen. She couldn't yet take it in that her nightmare was really over and in spite of their reassurances she clung to James, fearful that her father would suddenly appear and take her back to that dreadful place.

But eventually Max insisted that James must go home. He was not yet properly recovered from the amputation of his forearm, let alone the unpleasant bout of flu he'd suffered, so it was not surprising that he was looking exhausted and ill. Even Gina was looking worn out with the strain of the past two days.

Obediently, but with reluctance, James got to his feet. 'I shall come back, darling, soon. I promise,' he said, kissing Polly again.

'But not until tomorrow. You both need to sleep,' Max said in his best bedside manner, ushering both Gina and James out of the door.

Susan was relieved to see them go. She couldn't wait to get her daughter out of the dreadful, oversize grey dress and horrible boots she was wearing and into a warm bath, where Polly couldn't stop crying with happiness at being safely home after her dreadful ordeal. She didn't realize that her mother's tears of relief were mingled with horror at the bruises she found on Polly's back and arms.

When she was again clean and sweet-smelling Susan tucked her into bed in her old, familiar room and watched over her until she fell asleep. Then she went downstairs with her own Sunday best dress and began to alter it to fit Polly's growing figure, all the while offering up silent prayers of thanks to a God she was beginning to think just might exist after all.

Over at Meadowlands, James sank gratefully into his own bed and, contrary to what he'd expected, slept soundly for several hours. He woke, refreshed and hungry and feeling much better, so he rang for Albert to help him dress for dinner. When he arrived downstairs he was surprised to find his father already there, a glass of whisky in his hand.

'Welcome home, my boy,' Sir George said, shaking him by his left hand. 'Gina telephoned me and told me you were back so I came as soon as I could. You're looking decidedly groggy, James, but I suppose that's not surprising, under the circumstances.' He nodded towards the sling covering James' arm. 'Is it still painful?'

'At times. Not as bad as it was, though.'

'But your right hand! My God, man, how on earth will you manage?'

James gave a twisted smile. 'With a certain amount of difficulty, I imagine. But I expect I'll get used to it. I'm lucky it's only my hand and half my arm. When I think of some of the other poor buggers . . .'

'Indeed.' Sir George gulped his whisky and got up for more, holding up his glass invitingly.

'No thanks, not for me,' James said, interpreting the signal.

'I'm not sure it would agree with all the pills Max is giving me. If you picked me up and shook me I'd rattle.'

'Ah, best not then.' He sat down again, thoughtfully rolling his glass between his hands. After a minute he looked up. 'How much longer do you think this bloody war will last, James?'

James shrugged and sat down opposite him. 'Who can say? Personally, I can't see it going on for too much longer. Both sides are worn out and sick to death of fighting and if this Spanish flu really takes hold everyone will be too ill to carry on, anyway.'

'Is that what you had? Spanish flu?'

'That's what they called it. It's not pleasant. And if it gets to the trenches it'll go through like wildfire because most of the troops are at a pretty low ebb anyway.'

'Well, let's hope it fizzles out before then.'

They both stood up as Lady Adelaide entered the room.

'Look at this,' she said by way of greeting and indicating the skirt of her long purple silk dress. 'Ruby is really very careless. She's left creases where they shouldn't be and hasn't ironed the pleats. It's most annoying. I shall be glad when Polly comes back from Ipswich, or wherever she's gone. I miss her.'

'Hullo, Mother,' James said, going over to her with a half smile on his face. His mother hadn't changed; her world was very small.

'James, you're up! How nice.' She held up her face for his kiss, then sat down.

Gina had entered the room in a pale green shantung dress that didn't quite reach her ankles. Her father thought it was quite attractive to see a girl's ankles but he was wise enough not to comment.

She poured two sherries.

'I heard what you said about missing Polly, Ma. No doubt you'll be glad to know she's home,' she said as she handed a glass to Lady Adelaide.

'Then why hasn't she come back to me?' Lady Adelaide sounded quite put out. Then she gave a smug smile. 'I'm glad she's back. Now I can be rid of that Ruby; she's useless as a lady's maid.'

'Polly won't be coming back as your maid, Mother,' James said. He glanced at Gina, who was looking at him with a half-smile on her face, waiting for him to drop his bombshell. He winked at her and went on: 'She'll be coming back as my wife. She's pregnant with my child.'

'Oh, James! No!' Lady Adelaide fell back in her chair, spilling her sherry, and reached for her smelling salts.

At the same time, Sir George harrumphed loudly and said, 'No need to go to those lengths, my boy. These things can be arranged, you know.'

'I don't want things "arranged", thank you, Father,' James said, annoyed. 'I'm in love with Polly and I intend to make her my wife as soon as I can. I want my son to be born in wedlock, even if he was conceived outside it.'

Sir George turned red and harrumphed again. 'Steady on, old chap, ladies present,' he warned, embarrassed.

'It's all right, I've said what I've got to say. Now you know what the score is, there's no more to be said so we can go in to dinner.' James got to his feet, completely at ease.

Lady Adelaide, fully recovered, banged her hand on the arm of her chair. 'Wait! There's a great deal more to be said, James,' she said, her voice shrill. 'For instance, do you imagine you can bring a servant here, to live as one of *us*? To sit at *our* dining table? To eat *our* food with *us*?'

'I don't see why not. I'm sure Polly's table manners are perfectly acceptable and equal if not superior to many I've seen in big houses. Some rich people eat like pigs at a trough.'

'What does Polly say about it?' Gina asked, a smile still playing round her mouth. Her parents had reacted in exactly the way she had anticipated.

'I don't know. I haven't asked her. But I'm sure she'll be happy to do the right thing.'

'Which is obviously to call the whole ridiculous idea off,' Lady Adelaide said firmly. 'You really can't expect us to welcome Polly Catchpole, daughter of our estate manager, into the bosom of our family. We'd make ourselves a laughing stock among our friends.'

'You don't have any friends, Ma,' Gina said, a trifle cruelly.

'Well, acquaintances, then.' She looked at her daughter. 'How would *you* feel, Georgina, sitting at table with a servant? Not very comfortable, I think.' She gave a righteous shrug.

'In the first place, I really don't think of Polly as a servant, I regard her more as a friend. She's a sweet girl and I'll be delighted to have her as my sister-in-law,' Gina said. 'On the other hand, I can see there could be difficulties. Polly might not want to sit at your table, Ma, and I wouldn't blame her for that. But we're splitting hairs. I'm sure James and Polly will sort things out between them. In the meantime . . .' She raised her glass. 'Congratulations, James. Polly is a delightful girl and the important thing is, I'm sure she'll make you an excellent wife.'

Lady Adelaide turned her head away disdainfully. Sir George raised his glass. 'If you're determined to do the right thing I wish you well, James,' he said gruffly.

'I am determined to do the right thing, Father,' James said. 'Because the right thing, as far as I'm concerned, is to marry the girl I've loved since we were both children. It took me a long time to realize it, but it's true. I've been in love with Polly Catchpole ever since we climbed trees together and fell in the lake. She's always been part of my life, and please God, she always will be.'

'Well said, James,' Gina said, patting him on the back. 'Now, let's go in to dinner.'

'I'm sure I won't be able to eat a thing,' Lady Adelaide said plaintively. She then proceeded to demolish a large helping of almost everything that was put on the table.

It was the middle of the next morning when James arrived at Pippin Farm. Polly was sitting in the garden under a sunshade, wearing the dress her mother had sat up half the night altering for her. Her hair was washed and shining and apart from a bruise under her eye where Mrs Brown's ring had caught her when she slapped her face, all traces of her stay at the asylum were gone.

James took her in his arms. 'Oh, my love, I'm so sorry you had to suffer so much because of . . .'

She put a finger to his lips so he couldn't finish what he was going to say.

'It was my fault, too, James,' she said softly. 'I wanted you to know how much I loved you. And still do, whatever happens. Remember that, my dearest dear.'

He frowned. 'Whatever happens? What do you mean? Has your father forbidden you to marry me? He can't do that. You're over twenty-one.'

'My father hasn't come home,' she said. 'I haven't seen him since you rescued me from that place. Mum reckons he's kept out of the way because he's ashamed of himself. Not that he'll ever admit it, of course.'

'So where does your mother think he is?'

'Probably gone to stay with one of his church cronies so they can pray for my sins.' She smiled at James. 'The trouble is I don't feel as if I've sinned at all, James. How can loving someone the way I love you be a sin?'

He kissed her. 'If it is then I'm heading straight for damnation,' he replied.

She pulled away from him a little and looked away. 'There's something else, Jamie.'

He took her chin and made her turn back and look at him. 'Yes?'

'I've thought and thought and I know it can't be. I can't marry you, Jamie. I can't come and live at the house and expect your family to accept me as one of them when I've waited on them hand and foot for all these years. They wouldn't feel comfortable and neither would I. I simply couldn't do it, Jamie.' Tears were running down her cheeks as she spoke. 'Please understand.'

He kissed her gently. 'I do understand, sweetheart. I've thought about it a lot, too, and I realize it would be an impossible position to put you in. But I've got a solution to the problem. Since you couldn't possibly move back into Meadowlands as my wife, I shall move out into one of the farm cottages as your husband.'

She looked at him in horror. 'But you couldn't do that, Jamie! Those cottages are tiny and they . . .'

He put his finger over her lips. 'Then we'll knock two together. Or I'll see if one of the disused farmhouses can be renovated. Yes, that's a better idea. The one on the other side of the wood. It hasn't been lived in for years, not since old Harry Bartlett died.' He laughed. 'Do you remember how he used to chase us when we went scrumping his apples?'

She leaned her head on his shoulder, smiling. 'Yes, I remember.' She looked up at him. 'You'd do that, Jamie? For me?'

'*With* you, Polly,' he corrected. 'I'd live in a hole in the ground, if it was necessary, as long as I could have you by my side. And now, having said all that . . .' He slipped off his seat and down on to one knee. 'Darling Polly Catchpole, will you do me the great honour of becoming my wife?'

She bent her head and kissed him. 'Yes, Jamie Barsham, I will. Please.'

He got to his feet and pulled her up too. 'Shall we go and

take a look at this farmhouse? See what needs to be done? Can you walk that far?'

'Yes, of course I can.' She didn't tell him the hardships she'd been suffering at the asylum. She didn't want to think about that ever again. It was over.

They spent a couple of happy hours at the farmhouse, deciding what needed to be done to make it habitable, with Polly making notes in the notebook James carried in his pocket.

'That's a habit I learned from going round the estate with your esteemed father,' he said with a grin. 'He used to say to me, "If you write everything down it won't get forgotten," which was pretty sensible advice. So that's two things I've got to thank him for.'

'What's the other?'

'Why, you, of course, Polly-wolly-doodle.' He hugged her. 'Whatever he's done, I'll always be grateful to him for having such a lovely daughter.' He held her away from him and looked her up and down. 'Now, I don't know too much about these things but how long have we got to get this place into shape if we want our son to have a home?'

She flushed as he laid his hand briefly on her belly. 'About two months, I think,' she said shyly.

'Well, I'd better get the men to start working on it, then, hadn't I? Now, let's go and tell my future mother-in-law the good news.'

They walked back through the wood hand-in-hand, blissfully unaware of the news that awaited them back at Pippin Farm.

Twenty-Three

Polly and James arrived back at Pippin Farm, flushed and happy, to find Susan sitting at the kitchen table staring into space. She looked up as they walked in, her eyes dull.

'They've found him,' she said in a flat voice, before they had a chance to speak. 'Face down, in the mud. Dead.'

'Dead! But what . . .? How could . . .?' Polly's face was a mask of horror.

'Threw himself in the river at high tide, that's what they reckon. Body was washed up in one of the creeks down river and got left there in the mud as the tide fell. That's what they reckon, anyway,' she repeated. She shrugged. 'Best thing that could have happened, if you ask me.' Still she spoke in a flat, emotionless voice.

'Oh, Mum. You don't mean that. It's a dreadful thing to say!' Polly went over and put her arm round her mother with an anxious glance towards James.

Susan put her hand up to cover Polly's. 'Yes, it is, isn't it? And I know I shouldn't say it. I know I ought to be crying. But I don't feel a bit like crying. It's more a feeling of relief that he's gone.' She glanced up, looking if not for approval, then at least for understanding.

But Polly was frowning uncomprehendingly. 'What could have made him do such a thing?'

'Oh, I know exactly what made him do it,' James said grimly. 'And if you could have seen yourself standing in the matron's office that day, Polly, you wouldn't need to ask that question.'

Susan nodded. 'You're quite right, Mr James. I reckon he couldn't live with himself once he realized the terrible thing he'd done to his daughter.' She paused. 'William was never a man to admit he was wrong and say he was sorry; he always thought it was a sign of weakness. Yet in the end he took the coward's way out.' Her mouth twisted. 'And he hadn't even seen the worst of her bruises,' she added bitterly. She wiped away a tear. 'Maybe I'm wicked, but I can't help thinking it's a good thing he's gone. I could never have lived with him again. Not after what he did to you, my girl.' She looked up at Polly, her face anguished.

'It's all over now, Mum. We can start again,' Polly said, sitting down beside her and taking her hand.

But Susan hadn't finished. She shook her head and went on, perplexed: 'I couldn't understand why he changed the way he did. He never used to be like that. He was such a lovely man when I married him; all he thought about was me and the children – well, me and Polly after we lost the boy through the diphtheria.' She screwed her face up in thought. 'I don't think that was what turned him to that funny church, though; I'm sure he didn't start to go there till several years later. But once those people got hold of him he went all sanctimonious and righteous and holier-than-thou and there was no living with him.' Her breath caught on a sob. 'How could that lovely man I married have changed so much?'

Nobody answered.

A week later William Catchpole was laid to rest in the un-consecrated corner of the churchyard reserved for people who had committed the cardinal sin of taking their own lives, the approbation he so desperately craved from a church that preached nothing about love and forgiveness and everything about hellfire and damnation lost to him forever.

Susan watched granite-faced as the coffin was lowered into the ground, still wondering how the fresh-faced, warm-hearted young man she'd been so in love with could have turned into such a hard, unforgiving man. Then she went home with Polly to dispense cups of tea and cake to the estate workers who had gathered to pay their last respects to the hard-working man they had always regarded as fair-minded and who were impressed and a little overawed by the fact that Mr James and Miss Gina were also there.

At the same church, and almost before the flowers on the grave had had time to wilt, Polly Catchpole and James Barsham were married, on the last day of June 1918. It was, of necessity, a quiet ceremony, carried out at eight o'clock in the morning. Nevertheless, Major James Barsham was immaculately dressed, wearing his freshly cleaned and pressed uniform for probably the last time, his right arm still in its sling. Dr Max Rodwell was by his side to act both as best man and medical officer, since despite his assertion to the contrary, James was still far from recovered and carried his discharge papers in his pocket to prove it. Polly, by contrast, looked the picture of health. At Gina's insistence she was wearing the beautiful blue dress and matching hat that Gina had bought for her own wedding and which had never been worn. Fortunately, the loosely fitting style meant it hadn't needed too much alteration and the colour suited Polly perfectly. With Susan and Gina as witnesses the ceremony was carried out by a faintly disapproving vicar – although it was not clear whether the disapproval was on account of the early hour or the fact that the bride was quite obviously pregnant, a fact that even the beautiful blue dress couldn't quite conceal. But as James slipped the ring on Polly's finger and kissed her nobody could be in any doubt that here was a true love match. At that point, even the vicar blew his nose and nearly smiled.

Behind a pillar, at the back of the church, Mrs Bellman and Ruby, determined not to miss it and wearing their best hats, dabbed their eyes with their handkerchiefs and then slipped back to the House to prepare breakfast for Lady Adelaide, who didn't even realize this was the day of her son's marriage.

Sir George knew and would have liked to attend but thought it diplomatic not to. Instead he went back to London, to be comforted by his long-standing and faithful paramour. But the day before he left he called James into his study.

'You're quite sure you want to go through with this, my boy?' Sir George asked, handing him a stiff whisky. 'There are other ways, you know.'

'You mean hide Polly discreetly in a little house somewhere that I can visit, while I marry some horsey-faced girl of my own class?' James asked, barely hiding his disgust. 'No, thank you, Father. Polly is the only woman I want; she'll be the mother of my child – or children, I hope – and I'll be proud to have her by my side for the rest of my life.'

Sir George nodded and patted him on the shoulder. 'Well said, James. I admire you for standing your ground. Maybe I should have done the same, years ago, instead of keeping Eileen . . .' He drew in a noisy breath. 'Too late now, of course.' He pulled out his cheque book and wrote a cheque, which he handed to James. 'A small wedding present. Should cover the cost of renovating and furnishing Beech Farm to your liking.' He allowed himself a small smile of satisfaction as he saw James' jaw drop at the magnitude of the cheque. He lifted his glass. 'To your health and happiness with the lovely Polly, my boy.'

'Thank you, Father. That's terrifically generous of you.' James pocketed the cheque and, still reeling from the size of it, swirled the amber liquid in his glass. 'There is one thing. But after such generosity on your part I'm not sure if this is the time . . .'

'Maybe it's the best time. Catch me while I'm in a good mood,' Sir George said with a chuckle. He hadn't enjoyed himself so much for years.

James took a gulp of whisky. 'Well, it's like this, sir. I don't know whether you intend to advertise the post of estate manager now Catchpole's dead . . .'

'Mm. Bad business, that. He was a good man. Dependable. Don't know what came over him. Won't be easy to find the right man to replace him.'

James let his father's first words pass without comment. He simply said, 'Well, if you don't object, Father, I'd like to have a crack at being the right man. I'm not entirely without experience; I used to ride around the estate with Catchpole quite a lot during the school holidays when I was growing up and he taught me a lot about the way things were run. In fact I always dreamed that one day I might do his job.' He paused. 'That doesn't mean to say I don't realize I've still got a lot to learn, of course.'

Sir George puffed out his cheeks. 'Well, if that's really what you want, I can't see any reason to object, James. In fact, it seems like an excellent idea to me. An excellent solution to the problem.'

'Well, you see, with a wife and family I'll need to earn some money,' James added, flushing with pride as he spoke the words. 'I wouldn't wish to be a burden on the estate. Obviously, I wouldn't expect any favours if I worked here,' he added quickly. 'Even with half an arm missing I can still ride a horse, so I won't have any trouble getting round. And I'm learning to write with my left hand.'

'Enough said.' His father took his left hand and shook it. 'I'm sure you'll do extremely well, my boy.' He stroked his chin. 'Gina's been helping out with the accounting side, hasn't she?'

'I believe so.'

'Well, you and she get on well together so I don't see any difficulties there, do you?'

'None at all, sir.'

'Good. That's settled, then.' He sat down in his favourite chair and lit a cigar. After a few minutes he said, 'Of course, you're aware that Ned will inherit the estate, when the time comes, being the older twin?' He raised his eyebrows questioningly.

'I don't see that as a problem. I've never known him take that much interest in estate matters. In any case, my children will be his heirs, so I'll have their interests at heart, too.'

'How can you be so sure of that? What about Ned's heirs? When he marries . . .'

'I'm pretty sure Ned will never marry,' James said quietly, looking out of the window.

Sir George frowned. 'How can you be so sure about that?'

Slowly, he turned his gaze and looked at his father. 'Ned's not the marrying kind.'

Suddenly Sir George understood and his face reddened. He barked, 'Good God, man! You're surely not trying to tell me . . .'

James held up his hand. 'I'm simply telling you he's not the marrying kind, Father. Make of it what you will.'

'Yes, but . . .'

'That's all I have to say on the matter.'

Sir George digested this. He'd often wondered about Ned, but his philosophy had always been that some things were best ignored. He shrugged. 'Well, it'll be between the two of you, it's not going to concern me, is it? By the time the wrangling over the estate starts I'll be six feet under.'

'There won't be any wrangling, Pa. Ned and I aren't likely to start fighting over the family pile, don't worry.'

'But Ned . . .' Sir George couldn't help coming back to the subject like a dog worrying a bone.

'Ned is a son you can be proud of, Father,' James said firmly. 'He may be a conchie but he's certainly done his bit for this bloody war. In fact, he's done things that many men would baulk at. Ned deserves a medal for the lives he's saved and the awful things he's had to do without complaint, and I wouldn't be surprised if he gets one. If there's any justice in this world he will.' He held up the cheque his father had given him, deliberately changing the subject. 'Thank you for this, Father, it's more than generous of you. I very much hope you'll come and visit my wife and me in our new home at Beech Farm.'

Sir George nodded. 'I very well might.' He looked up at James. 'I think you've handled a tricky situation admirably, my boy. It wouldn't have done, you know, to bring Polly into the house as your wife. Your mother . . .'

'I know. And Polly understood this. She wouldn't have been happy. In fact, she even said she couldn't marry me if that was expected of her.'

'Sensible girl.' Sir George smiled. 'You know, I always liked young Polly. I think you may have done very well for yourself there, James. I wish you luck.'

'Thank you, sir.' James left. For almost the first time he'd seen his father as a man and not simply as an absent father. He discovered to his surprise that he both understood and liked him.

Beech Farm was not yet ready for habitation so Polly and James began their married life at Pippin Farm. Susan was happy to have them there for a few weeks, and secretly, she hoped they would stay until after the baby's birth. Not that she missed Will; since she discovered he had incarcerated Polly in the asylum she had spoken not one word to him in spite of his efforts to justify his actions. In the end he'd given up trying, realizing but never admitting that he had no justification for treating his daughter so shamefully, and so they had continued to live under the same roof, leading quite separate, silent lives in an atmosphere of unspoken animosity and misery that was almost tangible.

But all that was over now. James and Polly were happily married and James spent most of his time riding round the estate on Banjo, his horse, visiting the estate workers, listening to their views on what could and couldn't be done and making notes of everything he saw and heard.

He went to see the Hadleys. They were looking old and bent with the impossible task they had set themselves of caring for Tom, at the same time keeping their smallholding in working order and looking after the animals. Since Tom had done the lion's share of the work when he was young and healthy, whilst Isaac drank away the profits, such as they were, it was little wonder that things were in a desperate situation now that Tom's care took up most of their time, even though Isaac had given up alcohol completely.

James saw little change in Tom, except that most of his hair had gone now, exposing even further the livid scar, like a great crater, across his head. He showed no sign of recognizing him, no sign that he heard or understood when James spoke to him. He sat in his chair holding a shabby, much-darned cloth monkey that James recognized from when they were very small children. It had been given to James and he'd passed it on to Tom, who called it Pongo and carried it with him until he was too old to be seen with a stuffed toy.

Just before he left him James said, 'I see you've still got old Pongo, Tom.' And Tom nodded almost imperceptibly and stroked Pongo with a finger.

'See? I think he's improving,' his mother whispered to James. 'He didn't do that a week ago. He seemed to brighten up when I gave him Pongo, and now he won't let go of him.'

James nodded, too full of emotion to speak. It was heartbreaking to see his old friend so helpless whilst Violet and Isaac worked themselves to death caring for him.

He turned to practical matters. He had already told them he was taking over as estate manager and after he had taken a good look round he suggested, tentatively, that they could do with a little help with the heavy work.

'We could,' Violet said firmly. 'It's all getting too much for Isaac.'

'That's what I was thinking,' James said. 'Because with Tom—'

'Oh, Tom's no trouble,' they both insisted, clearly afraid of him being taken away from them.

'Well, I'll see what I can do. A willing fourteen-year-old lad, that's what you need.'

'Yes,' they agreed. 'That's what we need.'

'A boy what loves animals, like Tom always did,' Isaac added, nodding.

James left feeling he'd already scored a small victory in his new job.

Later he discussed the matter with Gina, who was in the estate office busy with the accounts. She pinched her lip thoughtfully. Then she smiled.

'My soup club. I'm sure I can find a suitable lad there. Most of the children have been coming with their mothers ever since I started it so I know them all pretty well. There are several boys there who'll be looking to start work very soon, too,' she said with enthusiasm. 'One or two whose fathers were wounded so badly in the war they'll never work again, so they'll become the breadwinners. That's a great burden for a young lad to carry, isn't it?' Suddenly, her expression lightened and she smiled up at him. 'In fact, come to think of it, I know the very boy. He's willing – always ready to help and he's as honest as the day is long. And his father was gassed very badly in France so he can't work. Yes, I think young Peter will do very well, if his parents agree.' She made a note on the pad she always carried, then looked up. 'And how is Polly? I haven't had a chance to go and see her for several days.'

His face lit up at the mention of his wife. 'She's blooming. Her mother fusses over her all the time and won't let her do a thing.'

'She deserves that, after all she's been through,' Gina said. 'That asylum must have been a hellish place to be.'

He nodded. 'She doesn't talk about it much, although she has nightmares, imagining she's back there, poor love. But it doesn't happen so often now and she's getting really excited at the prospect of moving into Beech Farm. We take a walk down there every evening to see how the work's progressing. It's almost done now. With any luck it will be ready for the furniture to be delivered next week. Then we'll be able to move in.'

'So you'll need to engage some staff.'

'Oh, no, we don't want a vast retinue of people – there won't be room, for one thing.'

Gina laughed. 'I hadn't thought of a vast retinue, James. What I had in mind was one little housemaid, with a woman in once a week to do the heavy work.'

'That sounds about right.' James nodded. 'But you'd better discuss it with Polly; she's the lady of the house.'

'I'll do that. But, again, I'm sure my soup club will provide a suitable young girl.'

'Are you still providing people with soup every day?'

'No. We only do that when the weather's really cold – the little ones look for it. We open twice a week now. Soup's not needed so much in the summer, but the women still like to come for a cup of tea and a chat and to see Max about their children's problems, so it still serves a useful purpose.' She pinched her lip. 'One or two of the women have heard from their husbands that there's quite a lot of this Spanish flu in the trenches, James. I hope it's nothing serious.'

He nodded, his expression grave. 'Yes, Gina. So do I.'

Twenty-Four

Polly's baby was born in the early hours on the thirteenth of August, 1918. Both Susan and James were fearful that the punishing three months she had spent in the asylum had done her lasting harm and they had watched over her and nurtured her, unobtrusively making sure she was never left alone to brood over her suffering.

Although she rarely spoke of it during the day, James knew how those months had affected her; he alone knew how many nights she would wake terrified and crying from the nightmare of dreaming she was back there, with no hope of escape. Then he would hold her in his arms and comfort her, reminding her that her ordeal was over and she was safe with him and that he would always be there to look after her. Gradually her fears would subside and she would sleep again, safely nestled in his arm. As the weeks went on the nightmares grew less but they never entirely ceased.

But when the time came the birth was easy and uncomplicated and the trauma of her months in the asylum faded into the background as Polly held her beautiful, perfect son in her arms and held up her face for her husband's kiss.

A month later James took his wife and baby son to live at Beech Farm. Susan smiled when they left, careful not to let them see how bereft she would be, quite alone now at Pippin Farm, the home she had shared happily with Will Catchpole since the day they married over twenty-five years ago – happily, that was, until his personality changed and he became so obsessively puritanical. Now she must try to forget those last years and remember only the loving, caring man she had married. There would be plenty of time on her hands for that, she realized as she watched Polly and James walk away to their new life together, although they would be only a field and a walk through the wood away so she would see them often.

The work at Beech Farm was not quite finished but James and Polly were anxious to begin their life as a family, living in their own home, so they were prepared to put up with the sounds of hammering and sawing and the smell of paint as the workmen put the finishing touches to the old farmhouse, which was being tastefully enlarged and modernized so that the character of the house was not lost.

This was where the Meadowlands Estate first began, James told Polly excitedly as they explored their new home together, and as they went from room to room he told her the story.

'It started out as a small parcel of land given to Henry Barsham for his allegiance to Cromwell at the end of the Civil War. On this land Henry built a two-roomed cottage not far from the river and together with his wife, Alice, they kept chickens scratching round the back door, a cow and a few sheep. Henry tilled his land and they sold what they produced at the local market. They both worked hard and prospered so that Henry, an ambitious man, could soon buy more land and as the children were born could build more rooms on to his little house. Gradually the estate grew, until at the end of the eighteenth century, with rolling parkland and the addition of two more farms, Alfred Barsham – Gentleman, the equally ambitious great-great-great-great grandson of Henry – decided that Beech Farm, although already much extended, was not grand enough for a man of his standing. So he built himself an imposing mansion on the highest point of his land, and had the grounds landscaped and the lake dug, discreetly tucking the now rather ramshackle Beech Farm behind a little wood. He renamed his estate Meadowlands.'

Polly beamed as James finished the tale. 'Oh, what a lovely story,' she said. 'And I'm really glad this is the house we're to live in, the place where it all started. It seems right, somehow.'

'That's exactly what I think,' James said. He laughed. 'Although it all looks a bit different from the two-roomed cottage where it all began. For a start we've got five bedrooms and a bathroom, a drawing room, a sitting room and a dining room, as well as the kitchens and all that goes with them.'

'And we don't have to draw every drop of water from the well or rely on rush lights and candles when it gets dark, thank goodness,' Polly added. 'Yet we've still got the original oak beams and inglenook fireplace and some of the rooms are a bit of an odd shape, which I love.' She gave a contented sigh. 'We're so lucky, James. We've got everything we could possibly want, and it's all thanks to your father's generosity. I do hope he'll come and visit us so that we can thank him and show him what's been done.'

'I'm sure he will.'

As she stood beside her husband, gazing out of the window at the trees with their son, George Edward James, in her arms she said thoughtfully, 'I never, in all my wildest dreams, imagined this day, Jamie. I never thought that I would ever be actually married to you and standing here in our own home.' She smiled up at him. 'The best I could imagine was becoming nursemaid to your children.'

He put his arm round her and squeezed her. 'Oh, no, Polly-wolly-doodle. This is where you belong, as my wife and the mother of my children. That's a far better arrangement.'

She laughed at the old name he used and laid her head on his shoulder. 'I think that too, Jamie.'

They retraced their steps to the sunny sitting room and Polly laid the baby in his crib. Then she looked up. 'James, has your mother shown any curiosity about her grandson?' she asked. 'Gina often comes to see him, but . . .'

'Maybe she will now we're in our own home,' James replied briefly. He didn't tell Polly that when he had excitedly broken the news of his new son to his mother her reaction had been disappointing but no more than he'd expected.

'I really don't see why you had to ruin your life by marrying the girl, James,' she'd said, her tone petulant, ignoring the news of the baby. 'These things can happen even in the best circles. Something could quite easily have been arranged and nobody any the wiser.'

'I'll ignore that remark, Mother,' James had said, keeping his temper with difficulty. 'And tell you again, my wife' – he'd laid emphasis on the word – 'has given birth to a son, your grandson, and we are both absolutely delighted. She is staying at her mother's house until Beech Farm is ready for us but you will be more than welcome at Pippin Farm should you wish to visit them there.'

Lady Adelaide had pursed her lips. 'I don't think so, James,' she'd replied, as if he'd suggested visiting a pigsty.

Disgusted and disappointed, although not at all surprised, he'd left her and gone downstairs to telephone his father on the private number George had entrusted him with.

A woman with a pleasant, low voice had answered the telephone. 'Oh, what wonderful news,' she'd said warmly. 'I'm afraid Sir George isn't here at the moment but I know he'll be delighted when I tell him. What name are you giving him?'

'George Edward James.'

'Oh, George will like that! And is all well with mother and child?'

'Yes. Absolutely tip-top.'

'I'm so glad.'

Such a contrast to his mother's indifference. James couldn't decide whether sadness or fury was uppermost in his mind at her reaction to the birth of her first grandchild.

Gina came to tea often, anxious to watch her baby nephew's

progress and also to make sure that Midge, the fourteen-year-old girl she had recommended as a maid for Polly to train, was giving satisfaction. Midge was the eldest of eight so she was used to hard work and babies.

'Oh, yes. She's got a lot to learn but she's very willing, and she loves Georgie,' Polly said enthusiastically. 'She reminds me of myself, when I first started work at the house, so I know exactly what she's going through. And where did you find Mrs Webster? She's a wonderful cook.'

'She came to the soup club, of course,' Gina said with a smile. 'She'd been cook in – oh, I forget where, but of course she had to leave when she got married. Unfortunately, her husband, who was a soldier, was killed on the Somme soon afterwards. She had no pension because the authorities said he had a weak chest before he enlisted so it was that, not the gas attack that killed him, although it hadn't stopped them taking him into the army. All very sad. But she's settling in well?'

Polly nodded. Then she burst out laughing. 'My trouble is, I feel I should be down in the kitchen, helping out, instead of playing the lady up here in the drawing room.'

Gina laughed with her. 'I'm sure you'll get used to it before long.' Then she became serious and put her hand out to her friend. 'But don't change, Polly. Just think of my poor out-of-touch mother.'

The weeks passed in a flash for Polly, busy and happy in her new home. James, too, was busy, working to make sure the estate was running smoothly and looking to see where improvements could be made. There was no longer an army camp on lower meadow and he was in discussion with Gina as to the best use for the land there, but no decision had yet been taken.

The news from the Front was becoming more encouraging, too. A combined effort of British, American and Australian troops, together with the French, had broken through and pushed the enemy back to the old Hindenburg Line, without much opposition, it was said. On the other hand, it was clear that both sides were becoming exhausted; equally weary of war, equally weary of fighting back and forth over the same muddy battleground. And now cases of influenza had reached epidemic level in the trenches, attacking the tired and undernourished troops, regardless of where their allegiance lay. Even those in charge were beginning to realize that the carnage couldn't go on much longer.

They were right. It had to stop and on the eleventh hour of the eleventh day of the eleventh month of the year 1918 an Armistice was signed, ending four years of bloodshed that had cost millions of lives and in the end had achieved very little.

So, after four years of the 'War to End All Wars' peace reigned at last and Christmas could once again be a time of celebration. Troops who came back home to their loved ones sound in wind and limb brought joy, relief and, gradually, a sense of returning normality. In other less fortunate households, of which there were many, there was the grief of loss, the sadness of disability and the worry of unemployment. And over all the spectre of influenza lurked, waiting, striking indiscriminately, careless of rich or poor, young or old. Before long there was hardly a street without at least one house with a black ribbon tied to the door knocker and many streets had several.

Fortunately, there were no such worries at Meadowlands. Preparations for Christmas were in full swing, because for the first time in four years the whole family would gather at home. Stretcher bearers were no longer needed to retrieve the dead and dying from no-man's land so Ned had been able to relinquish the army uniform he'd hated so much and Millie had given up her VAD duties and returned home to marry Max. Gina, putting the finishing touches to the decorations on the Christmas tree, felt the familiar pang of sorrow that Archie wouldn't be there. But for the war, she mused, she and Archie would have been married with at least one and very likely two children by now, instead of which she was among the ranks of women destined to remain spinsters for the rest of their lives because so many eligible men had perished in the fighting. It was a depressing thought.

'I hope that tree isn't going to drop pine needles all over the carpet.' Lady Adelaide, sitting by the fire watching her and eating Turkish delight, licked her fingers as she spoke.

Gina sighed. She couldn't see that it mattered to her mother if it did; she was hardly likely to be the one to sweep them up. But she wisely didn't say so. 'James chose it for little George. It will be replanted after Christmas. The idea is for it to grow during the year and be brought in again each Christmas. Until it gets too big, of course. It will be little George's special tree. I think it's a lovely idea.'

Lady Adelaide frowned. 'Why hasn't he put it up in his own house, then, instead of cluttering up this one?'

'Because James and his family will be spending Christmas here, of course. It will be lovely to have a real family Christmas again.'

'I hardly think so. Your father will never countenance sitting at table with a servant and neither will I.' She helped herself to another piece of Turkish delight, putting an end to the conversation. Or so she thought.

Gina came and sat down opposite her, mentally counted to ten and then said calmly, but with an edge of ice, 'If you're alluding to Polly, Mother, she is now James' wife and the mother of his son. She has her own very happy household, her own servants, whom she treats with great kindness and respect, and a husband who idolizes her. You really should move with the times, Mother. The war has changed everything. The world is very different now.'

Lady Adelaide sighed dramatically. 'Yes, I fear all the old values are disappearing. But one tries to uphold them as far as one can.' She sat up straight in her chair. 'And to that end, I refuse to eat with a servant.'

'Then shall we have a tray brought up to your room, Mother? Because the rest of the family will be more than happy to welcome Polly – who, I repeat, is no longer a servant but your daughter-in-law – into our midst. Not to mention the fact that none of us would want to insult James by refusing to receive his wife.'

'We shall see what your father has to say about that.'

'We shall, indeed.'

Sir George arrived home on Christmas Eve. He was in an unusually good humour and was surprised when his wife spoke of the impropriety of allowing Polly to join the family celebrations on the following day. She had chosen her moment carefully, when everyone except James and Polly, who were not due to join them until Christmas luncheon, were present to support her.

Sir George looked at her benignly. 'I'm not quite sure I understand what you're saying, my dear. Are you suggesting that James' wife should wait on us at table? I really don't think that would be at all appropriate, do you?'

'Well, no, of course not.' Lady Adelaide moved uncomfortably in her chair. 'On the other hand, George, I don't feel it appropriate that she should eat with us. After all, she was a servant until . . . well, until what happened did happen.' She shrugged. 'And one suspects that she—'

'Mother!' Gina cut her off, outraged.

'That will do, Gina,' Sir George said quietly. He turned to his wife. 'I have never heard such bigoted snobbery in my whole life, Adelaide. Of course Polly will be welcome at our table; she is our daughter-in-law and in my view James couldn't have chosen a more delightful wife. I've always liked her.' His voice hardened. 'What you were about to insinuate just now does you no credit, Adelaide. Anyone with half an eye could have seen James was head over heels in love with the girl and had been for years. And I don't blame him, either.'

'Pa's right, Ma,' Millie said. 'You have to realize times have changed. We shall never go back to the way things were.'

'Indeed, no. War is a great leveller,' Ned joined in. He yawned. 'Quite frankly, I can't see what all the fuss is about. Polly's a nice girl and she's married my brother so she's one of the family. As far as I'm concerned that's all there is to it.'

'Well said, Ned.' Gina smiled warmly at him. 'I couldn't agree more.' She turned to her mother. 'So, what do you intend to do, Mother, have a tray brought to your room?'

Lady Adelaide shook her head almost imperceptibly.

'Certainly not,' Sir George said, a note of steel in his voice. 'Your mother will take her rightful place at the table and behave as impeccably as she always does. Won't you, my dear.' It was a command, not a question.

James and Polly joined the family at church for the Christmas morning service and then returned to Meadowlands with them for luncheon. Looking far more composed than she felt, Polly was wearing a sage-green dress trimmed with cream lace under a darker green coat with a fur collar and a matching fur hat in which James had assured her she looked 'absolutely stunning'.

Sir George obviously agreed, saying somewhat less effusively, 'You're looking quite charming today, my dear. Motherhood clearly suits you. But where is my grandson?'

'Midge will be bringing him over a little later.'

'Good. That's good. I want to see how much he's grown since I saw him last.'

In the event luncheon passed without incident. Sir George insisted that Polly should sit at his right hand with her husband beside her, an obvious ploy to make her feel safe and welcome. Not that this was necessary because everyone treated her with easy familiarity, Ned even joking, 'Oh, look, she's already got him eating out of her hand,' when she tried surreptitiously to cut up the turkey on James' plate so he could manage with his one hand.

Everyone laughed at this, even Lady Adelaide, who had been rigorously plied with enough sherry before the meal to ensure she was mellow enough not to make a scene.

Towards the end of the meal Max got to his feet and cleared his throat. 'Before the ladies leave the table I'd like to announce to you all that Millie and I are to be married tomorrow.'

Everyone expressed their congratulations and delight. 'On Boxing Day. How lovely,' they all agreed.

'Is it legal to marry on Boxing Day?' Lady Adelaide asked, her voice just a teeny bit slurred from several glasses of wine on top of the sherry.

'Yes, of course it is, Ma,' Millie said, beaming. 'It's all arranged. Just a quiet wedding, no fuss, which is what we both want. Oh, and we've invited the vicar back to have luncheon with us. We knew you wouldn't mind, there's always oodles of turkey and Christmas pudding left over.'

'That's capital!' Sir George said. He stood up. 'Let's raise a glass to the happy couple.' A moment later he said, 'And am I to be allowed the privilege of giving my daughter away?'

Millie planted a kiss on his cheek. 'Of course you are, Pa. It's what I want.'

'I'm sure I don't know what I shall wear,' Lady Adelaide complained. 'After the deprivations of the war I've hardly a rag to my back.'

Stifling a smile and not daring to catch her sister's eye, Gina said, 'Oh, I daresay we'll be able to find you something suitable, Mother.'

'Well, just don't upstage me, Ma,' Millie said. 'I haven't had time to go shopping so I'll just have to wear what I've got.'

'As far as I'm concerned, darling, you'd look lovely in a sack,' Max said gallantly.

She blew him a kiss. 'I love you too, Max.'

Twenty-Five

It was a beautiful crisp morning, with the sunlight glinting on a white hoar frost making everywhere look like fairyland the day Miss Millicent Barsham and Dr Max Rodwell were married.

With no time to shop for traditional bridal wear she wore a simple dove-grey dress and hat under a short fur cape. Instead of a bouquet she carried an ivory prayer book with a tiny spray of lily-of-the-valley that matched those in Max's buttonhole. Gina, as bridesmaid, was dressed equally simply and elegantly in her best coffee-coloured costume, which had a well-fitting jacket and a skirt just below calf length. The ruffles on her cream blouse softened an otherwise rather severe outfit, as did the cream and brown feathery concoction she wore on her head, which she had stayed up half the night to make.

Sir George got his wish and gave his daughter away, even though he was feeling slightly under the weather with a nasty headache he put down to rather too much Christmas whisky, whilst Lady Adelaide had driven Ruby almost to distraction trying to decide what to wear. She eventually decided on a rose-coloured silk dress more suitable for evening wear and a large hat generously festooned with flowers. Happily overdressed and wearing her mink cape to keep out the cold she sallied forth, just in time to make her entrance at church before the bride arrived, leaving Ruby to spend the rest of the morning clearing up the wreckage she'd left behind.

Polly, sitting alone since James was Max's best man, had time to study Gina as she stood just behind her sister and she noticed how hard she bit her lip as Millie made her vows and received her first kiss from Max as her husband. Life was so unfair, Polly mused. But for the war Gina would have been married by now to her beloved Archie and the mother of his children. Instead, she was like thousands of other single women who were destined to remain alone for the rest of their lives because the men they might have married had had their lives brutally cut short on the battlefield. These were women who would be forced to make their way in life as best they could with no husbands to support them and no prospect of children to comfort their old age. She glanced at the straight back of her own husband, the right sleeve of his jacket neatly pinned up, and sent up a prayer of thankfulness that he had come back safely. The loss of his hand and part of his arm was inconvenient, to say the least, but he was learning to live with it whereas poor Tom Hadley . . . Her eyes filled with tears at the thought of their old friend, once as strong as an ox but now as helpless as a baby. She gave herself a mental shake as the strains of Mendelssohn's wedding march filled the church and smiled as a radiant Millie appeared on the arm of her new husband. Gina, walking behind with James, had recovered herself and was also smiling broadly, although Polly realized the effort it was costing her. She felt a sudden rush of affection for her sister-in-law, who had always been such a good friend and support to her, and she made a mental promise to make sure that Gina was never left out but always included in her own precious family at Beech Farm.

After showering the bride and groom with rice and rose petals outside the church they all went back to Meadowlands to the feast that Mrs Bellman had somehow managed to create out of the remains of the previous day's Christmas luncheon.

'So, where's the honeymoon to be, then?' Ned asked as they raised their glasses for yet another toast. 'Or is it a secret?'

'I'm afraid the honeymoon will have to wait, Ned,' Max said, shaking his head. 'We're going straight back to my house. I've got patients I must visit.'

'We'll have a holiday when this wretched flu business is over,' Millie said, reaching for her husband's hand. 'At the moment poor Max is rushed off his feet trying to get round to all the new cases, so he can't spare the time. I thought it was confined to the trenches but I suppose it was inevitable that it would spread once the troops started to return home.'

'Actually, it's not just here in England; thousands are dying all over the world,' Max added. 'They're calling it a pandemic now and there doesn't seem to be any end to it. It's very worrying.'

The vicar nodded in agreement. 'I've never taken so many

funerals in all my life,' he said. 'I'm having to recruit grave diggers from wherever I can get them and with the ground so frosty . . .' He spread his hands eloquently.

'This is hardly the subject for a wedding celebration,' Lady Adelaide said, a distasteful expression on her face. 'Surely we should just be thankful that we are not affected here at Meadowlands.'

'I don't know what you mean by "not affected", Mother,' Ned said. 'Several of the estate workers are ill and Isaac Hadley has just lost the young lad who was giving him a hand with his animals. He was at work one day and the next Isaac got a message to say he was ill with flu. Two days later he died.'

'Oh, I didn't know that.' She began to look slightly worried.

'No, I don't suppose you did.' Ned's tone was slightly acid. After what he had been through in the war he was finding his mother's unworldliness more than a little irritating.

'It's very odd,' Max said thoughtfully. 'Time and time again it's the young and healthy that are struck down, although you would expect the elderly to be more vulnerable. The trouble is, nobody has yet found out what causes it, nor how it spreads, only that it is very infectious. Yet three people in a house might get it, while everybody else stays well. Or all but one in another household might be affected. So why does that one escape?' He shook his head. 'So many questions but so few answers.'

'And some people who get it are better in a few days whilst others don't survive at all. It's all very puzzling,' Millie added. She glanced adoringly at her new husband. 'At least now you've got me to help you battle against it all, Max.' She held up her hand as he opened his mouth to speak. 'No, don't argue. Of course I shall be there with you.'

'I hope our friend Max realizes what a forceful woman he's married,' James chuckled as Polly helped him off with his coat on their return to Beech Farm.

'No doubt he does. Don't forget he met her at a hospital in France, so he knows just what she's made of.'

'Ah, yes, of course.' He sat down in his favourite armchair and waited while she tamped tobacco into his pipe. Then she lit a spill and gave it to him. 'Useless, aren't I?' he said through a haze of smoke when he'd got it going.

She put her head on one side. 'Oh, I don't know. Without

you I'd only have two hands. Now I've got three, so I reckon I'm lucky.' She grinned at him.

'Not as lucky as I am, Polly-wolly-doodle,' he said, reaching for her. 'You're the best thing that's ever happened to me, did I ever tell you?'

'Once or twice. Maybe more.' She sat on the stool at his feet and rested her head on his knee.

They were quiet for some time, then he said thoughtfully, 'I think it would be wise for Midge to stay with us and not go home at all till this flu business is over, don't you? We don't want to risk you or young Georgie catching it. Remember, I've already had it. It's not pleasant.'

'She won't like not seeing her family, but I'm sure you're right, although Gina still carries on with the soup run.' She looked up. 'Did you know my mother helps her there now? She's even taught some of the women how to make soup for themselves. And how to shop for bones and cheap vegetables.'

'Oh, that's good. Life must be rather lonely for her at times.'

'She keeps busy. And she spends time with Violet Hadley. By the way, did you know your brother Ned goes to see Tom quite often?'

'Yes. He was telling me the other day that he's very interested in men with injuries like Tom's, and men with shell-shock, which has never been properly recognized as a real illness.' He shook his head. 'It's criminal. Men have been shot for cowardice, or sent back to the line, when they should have been sent home and properly cared for. Anyway, Ned's thinking of training to specialize in that area.'

'He'd be good. He's very caring and thoughtful.'

'Yes.' His mind went back to the conversation he'd had with Ned that day in the trenches and the secret his twin had shared with him; a secret that could land him in prison if it ever became known. 'Yes, he is. One of the best.'

The following morning Ned came to Beech Farm looking slightly worried.

'Pater's not so good today, James,' he said. Pater was the name they'd privately used for their father since they'd learned the rudiments of Latin at school.

'What? Still hungover?' James' tone was scathing. 'He had difficulty walking a straight line up the aisle with Millie yesterday, which I thought was a bit bad. He could have laid off the drink long enough to give his daughter away, I would have thought.'

'No, it wasn't that at all. Didn't you notice, he ate hardly anything at the reception? He felt really ill, although he didn't want to spoil Millie's day by saying so. I'm sure he's got this damned flu, although I haven't told Mother that. I was up with him most of the night and so was Albert. He's no better this morning so I've telephoned Max. I think perhaps you should come, James. He's pretty bad.'

But by the time they reached the house they were too late. Sir George was dead.

The whole household was stunned. Even Lady Adelaide was silenced as she sat with her daughters in the morning room drinking tea, too shocked even to weep. Tears would come later: tears of sorrow for the man of whom they had seen so little from the girls; tears of grief, liberally mixed with self-pity, from the wife he had largely neglected.

The funeral took place a week later, despite the coffins already lined up in the undertaker's parlour awaiting burial. But Sir George was an important man and took priority in death just as he had in life. And people flocked to watch the cortege, followed by the Great and the Good, go by, and they doffed their caps and bowed their heads, whilst their own dead relatives, victims of the same indiscriminate scourge, quietly rotted in their coffins as they awaited their turn to be laid to rest.

The little church was packed so few even noticed the small woman, all in black, her face covered by a veil, sitting at the back. As the family gathered round the grave for the interment Gina saw her standing, half-hidden by a large memorial stone, and realized she must be Eileen, her father's long-term mistress. But when she went to speak to her afterwards she was nowhere to be seen. The next day, Gina and Millie went together to take a closer look at the carpet of wreaths and saw, tucked almost out of sight near the head of the grave a single red rose, with the simple inscription: To My Love.

'I wish we'd known her,' Millie said.

'Yes, so do I. I think we'd have liked her,' Gina agreed.

Although Sir George had been so rarely seen at Meadowlands, paradoxically, his death left a huge gap. Even in his absence Sir

George had been head of the house and had made all the important decisions. Now suddenly it was Ned, as heir, who was pitchforked into his place as Master at Meadowlands, with all the privileges and responsibilities this entailed. It went without saying – although it was in fact carefully spelled out in the Will – Lady Adelaide would continue to live in the house for as long as she wished. Gina and Millie would each receive a substantial legacy; James received nothing. He was more than happy about this, glad to know his father had seen where the money that would have been his inheritance had been spent.

When James told Polly the news he could tell she was only listening with half an ear because she was distracted by the baby, who was being fractious and difficult.

'I'm telling you important news, darling, and you're not listening. Can't you let Midge look after Georgie? After all, that's what we pay her for.'

'She's not very well. I told her to stay in bed. She's very hot and flushed so I've given her a powder. Now, what were you saying, Jamie?' She brushed a strand of hair away with one hand, rocking the baby to quieten him at the same time.

He shook his head impatiently. 'Oh, never mind, I'll tell you later. But what's this about Midge, Polly? Are you sure she hasn't got this bloody flu? It sounds as if it could be, although I don't see where she could have got it from, do you? It isn't as if she's been home to her parents.'

'No, she hasn't, but from what she said I think she'd been seeing quite a bit of young Peter Roper – you know, the lad who was helping out at the Hadleys' place.'

'Oh, God.' James closed his eyes briefly. 'He died from it.'

She nodded. 'I know.'

He got to his feet. 'You must go to your mother, Polly. Take Georgie and go. Now. This minute. I won't have you exposed to this. I know what it's like and if you were to . . .' He shook the thought away. 'Come on, darling, get a bag packed and I'll take you, right away.'

'Don't be silly, James. In any case, what's the point? I've been tending Midge and if I go who'll look after her?'

'Mrs Webster.'

'Lydia Webster's our cook, not a nurse. She told me she'd be happy to take on Midge's duties but she'd be no use in a sickroom. She went pale at the thought, so I quite believe her.'

'Then I'll do it.'

'Now that really is silly, James. In any case, I couldn't allow it. You ran off with a maid once before, remember.' She grinned at him.

'That was different. Please, Polly, don't joke. You know I couldn't bear it if . . .'

She put her finger over his lips. 'It'll be all right, darling. Midge is not that ill, it's probably only a cold. But if it'll make you feel better I'll get my mother to fetch Georgie. She'll love to have him all to herself and it'll keep him out of danger.'

'So you agree there is danger?'

She shot him a look. 'Here, take your son while I go up and see if Midge needs anything.'

Three days later, as Midge recovered from what had proved to be only a mild case of infection, Polly fell ill. James, frantic with worry, tended her himself and as her temperature soared he hardly left her side. For him, almost the worst thing was when she became delirious and thought she was back in the asylum. He had difficulty in holding her as she tried to climb out of bed, whimpering that she must go down to the laundry because Mrs Brown would beat her if she didn't work. He had never cursed his injury so much as when he tried to ease her back into bed with one hand.

Max visited her but said there was little he could do but give her something to ease the aches and pains. Other than that the illness would take its course.

He put his hand on James' shoulder. 'Please don't think I'm not concerned about Polly, James. God knows, I'd do anything to have a cure for this bloody flu. But you seem to be doing all the right things and you've had it yourself, so you probably know more about it than I do.'

James looked up at him, his face haggard with fatigue and worry. 'Thanks for that, Max.' He shook his head as if to clear it. 'You and Millie, you're in the thick of it all the time. How do you stay clear?'

'By God's good grace, I'd say,' he replied sombrely. 'We both wear masks when we come into contact with it, but whether that helps or whether we're just lucky, we don't know.'

'And Gina?'

'She's fine. She often helps Susan with young Georgie. She'd visit Polly if you'd let her.'

'When Polly's up to it she'll be the first, tell her.' He went back to his vigil, not even daring to think about what life would be like without his beloved wife.

As Max had said, Gina visited Susan as often as she could. She loved to help with Georgie and to play with him whilst they both worried over Polly.

'I've resigned myself to not seeing her, although I worry about her all the time,' Susan said, pouring the tea. 'But we couldn't risk Georgie . . .' She couldn't even finish the sentence.

Gina nodded. 'I know. I don't think she's well enough to see anyone at the moment, to tell you the truth.'

'How is the soup club?' Deliberately, Susan changed the subject and pushed the plate of cakes in Gina's direction. 'Have you managed to find anyone else to help you run it?'

'No, but there's no need. The women really run it themselves. It's more of a place where they congregate for a cup of tea and listen to each other's troubles, of which there's no shortage, as you can imagine,' she added with a smile.

'Your work there is done, then.'

'Let's say I've done all I can.' Gina pushed her cup over as Susan picked up the teapot again. 'The trouble is, now the war is over the authorities aren't interested. They don't want to be reminded about men who've had their lives ruined fighting for their country, have no jobs and not enough money; they're too busy congratulating each other on the fact that we've won, although I must say that sometimes I wonder just what it is we've won. As far as I can make out the Treaty that was signed was not very satisfactory.'

'I don't know about that,' Susan said. 'I'm just glad and thankful the fighting's stopped.'

'Yes, Susan, you're right. That's the important thing.' She finished her tea and stood up. 'I must go. I don't know what you put in that young man's milk today but he's slept the whole time I've been here so we haven't been able to have our little game.'

'I'll make sure he's awake when you come tomorrow,' Susan promised, smiling.

'You'll miss him when he goes back to his mummy,' Gina said, regarding her thoughtfully.

'Of course I shall. But I'll be glad to see him go because then I'll know my Polly's recovered,' Susan said.

'Amen to that,' Gina said.

In the kitchen at Beech Farm, Lydia Webster also worried. She cooked tempting little dishes for Polly, which she couldn't eat, and berated Midge, who went about the house weeping because it was all her fault her lovely mistress was ill.

'Oh, for goodness' sake,' Mrs Webster said sharply. 'Stop snivelling and put your feelings to some use. Go and polish the furniture in the drawing room ready for when the missus comes back downstairs. Then you can come and do the ironing.' Her voice softened. 'Oh, here you are, girl, here's a jam tart, straight out of the oven. That'll cheer you up.'

Midge dragged the back of her hand across her nose. 'Oh, thank you, Mrs Webster, you're ever so kind.' She took a bite. 'Do you think the missus will get better?' she asked timidly, almost afraid to say the words.

'That's in the hands of the Almighty,' Mrs Webster said. 'But I hope and pray she will.'

Gradually, it seemed that Lydia Webster's prayers were being answered. Polly's fever abated and she began to recognize her surroundings and to realize that she was in her own home and that the visions of the asylum had been nothing more than a recurring nightmare.

She held out her hand to James. 'You need a shave, darling,' she whispered.

It was then that he knew she would live.

Twenty-Six

Polly's recovery was slow but by the spring she was more like her old self and glad to have care of her baby again.

'He's grown so much, James,' she said as she sat playing with him on the floor. 'What has my mother been feeding him on?'

'Of course he's grown, my darling,' James said, smiling at them both. 'Don't you realize how long you were ill?'

She gazed out of the window at the daffodils and primroses in the garden. 'No, but I can see now it must have been several weeks. I thought it was strange the daffodils were flowering so early this year.'

'When in fact they're quite late. They've been waiting for you, sweetheart.' He kissed the tip of her nose, thankful to have his beloved wife safely recovered and well again.

Reluctantly, he left her and went over to the estate office, savouring the fresh spring sunshine. He realized with a stab of guilt that in spite of paying brief visits he had been too concerned with Polly to pay much attention to what was going on in the business, and had become quite out of touch at a time when Ned might well have been glad of his input. He was not in the least troubled by the fact that his twin had taken their father's place as owner of the estate, he'd always known this would happen, just as he'd always known Ned wouldn't do anything without consulting him or asking his advice. In fact, while he'd been caring for Polly he'd used odd moments to consider ways of making things more profitable – schemes he had not yet had a chance to discuss with his brother.

Gina and Ned were both in the office when he arrived.

'Good to see you, James,' Ned got to his feet and shook James' hand. 'And I'm so glad Polly's on the mend.'

'Yes, she was looking much better when I saw her yesterday,' Gina said as he kissed her. 'It's lovely to have you back with us, James.'

'And you've come at exactly the right time.' Ned said, rubbing his hands together.

'Oh, dear. That sounds ominous.' James looked from one to the other as he took his seat. 'What's been going on that I've missed? You haven't put the old pile up for sale, have you?' He grinned at his own joke.

'No, nothing quite that extreme.' Ned straightened the sheaf of papers in front of him on the table. He cleared his throat. 'OK. Well, it's like this. While you've been caring for Poll, James, Gina and I have been through all the account books. We've found the place is solvent although we're not making huge profits. You probably know that, though.'

James nodded. 'Yes. I've been thinking of ways to run the

farms more profitably, and for a start, there's no reason why we shouldn't sell the venison when we cull the herd every year.'

'Yes, that's a good idea. And I'm sure there are other things we can do. But of course, the main drain on finances is the house. Beautiful and elegant though it is, it swallows up money like nobody's business.'

James frowned. 'But you said you weren't thinking of selling it.'

'No, of course it won't be sold, no need for that,' Ned said with a laugh. 'In fact, there's no shortage of money in the coffers: Pater was actually a very rich man, with investments all over the place. However, and Gina agrees with me, I don't feel we should just sit on our arses and watch the house erode it all to no purpose.'

'So what do you propose?' James leaned forward, interested.

'I'm wondering if we could turn it into some kind of home for shell-shocked soldiers. What I mean is men who've come back from the war with their nerves all shot to pieces, or have head injuries like Tom; men who have incurable problems nobody seems to know quite how to handle so they shut them up in a hospital ward or asylum and try to forget about them. Well, my idea is to give them somewhere pleasant to live that isn't too much like a hospital. We might even be able to help them to recover a little. I've been spending quite a lot of time with Tom, and whilst he'll never be much better I believe the quality of his life could perhaps be improved a little. As you know, I've been interested in this sort of thing for some time.'

'Yes. Weren't you hoping to train as a doctor, specializing in that area?' James said.

Ned shrugged. 'I was. But under the circumstances I'll have to shelve that, at least for the time being. I believe there's a lot to be learned just by talking to these men and by letting them talk. Simply listening is quite an art, you know. Most people don't listen. They're too intent on offering a solution, telling people what they should do, when all that's really needed is a sympathetic ear. That's my theory, anyway – that's what I'm prepared to offer and if it does no good at least it should do no harm. Incidentally, Max and Millie both think it's a good idea and want to help where they can.'

'How do you propose to finance it?

Ned shrugged. 'Those who can afford it can pay a bit; for the rest, we'll have to try and make the estate even more profitable, which I'm sure we can. I just feel we owe it to these men to do what we can for them,' he added half-apologetically. 'We three are so lucky to live in these lovely surroundings, I think we should share them a bit.'

'Well said, Neddy,' James said, using the name Ned hadn't heard since nursery days. 'I think it's a wonderful idea. What about you, Gee?'

'Oh, like you, I'm all for it,' Gina said enthusiastically.

'Then there's only one fly in the ointment: Mother. What does she say about it?'

'I don't see why she should object. We'll make sure she has her own quite separate quarters. In any case, I don't envisage the whole house being taken over, not at first, anyway, so I don't see a problem there,' Ned said quickly.

'Well, in that case, I think we should go ahead. And the more able-bodied could be encouraged to help on the farm, out in the fresh air, which can only be good for them. But you still haven't answered my question. What does the mater have to say about it all?'

Ned grinned. 'Ah. Well, she doesn't actually know yet. We were waiting till you were here before we put it to her.'

'Hm. I might have guessed. You're obviously expecting opposition.'

They got it.

Lady Adelaide was horrified at being expected to share her beautiful house with strange men. She and Gina could be murdered in their beds, the house could be vandalized, and the fact that there might be common men in various states of undress in the corridors and on landings did not bear thinking about, especially if they made funny noises and did strange things. She fanned herself and called for her smelling salts, feeling faint at the mere idea.

Gina caught James' eye and had to look away quickly before they burst into giggles at the thought of Lady Adelaide's reaction at being confronted by the kind of gibbering naked man she was envisaging.

But Ned wasn't laughing. He was annoyed with his mother, as he frequently found himself these days. 'Very well, Mother,' he said. 'If you don't want to stay here in the house you can move into the gatehouse.'

After a first look of shocked surprise she put on a long-suffering air. 'Oh, I see, Edward,' she said, her annoyance manifesting itself in her use of his full name. 'Now you're master here you think you can push me out of the way into a hovel.'

'The gatehouse is by no means a hovel and naturally we would make sure it was turned into suitable habitation for a lady of your standing,' he replied, his sarcasm quite lost on her. 'And it will be entirely your choice. You can stay here in the house if you prefer it.'

'I'm too shocked to even think about making such a decision at the moment,' she said, mopping her brow in a theatrical gesture that once again caused Gina and James to stifle their giggles. 'I must go and lie down. Gina, please ring for Ruby to bring some camomile tea to my room.'

'Poor old thing,' Gina said, still smiling, when she'd gone. 'She lives a very cloistered existence.'

'Then it's time she woke up to the real world,' Ned said, unsympathetically.

'We'll have to think of a way of mollifying her,' James said, scratching his chin. 'Something to prevent her going around with a hard-done-by air.'

'Oh, yes. And our mother can do persecuted like nobody's business.' Ned raised his eyes to the ceiling.

'I've got it!' Gina made them both start as she suddenly banged her hand on the table. 'Her friend Lady Amersham is planning a cruise to America on the *Mauretania*. It's all I've been hearing about for weeks, Lady Amersham and her damned cruise. Ma's obviously green with envy, although she pretends she isn't. So why don't we send her as well? From what Ned says we can afford it and it won't be until next spring, so it'll give her something to talk about while you get on with what you're planning.'

'You're brilliant, Gina,' the twins enthused. 'That's a capital idea. And we'll have the gatehouse modernized just as she'd like it so it's all ready for her to move into by the time she gets back.'

Suddenly, Ned frowned. 'But what do you mean, what *we're* planning? You're as much a part of this as we are. We need you to do all the administrative bits. After all, you know more about running things here than anyone; you've been doing it single-handed for the past four years.'

'I know,' Gina said quietly. 'And I don't want to let you down, Ned, but I really feel it's time I made a fresh start and did something with my life, instead of remaining here, cocooned in the family. I'd hate to end up as the perennial, wizened, dried-up stick of a maiden aunt.'

'But we need you, Gee,' Ned repeated, a hint of desperation in his voice.

'What do you intend to do?' James, ever practical, asked.

She took a deep breath. 'I'm going to move to London and enrol in a very good secretarial college so that I can become a first-class secretary, hopefully to someone interesting and important, perhaps even a government minister. There are thousands of women, like me, who are never going to find a husband, since most of the eligible young men lie dead on the battlefield, so good qualifications are essential in the fight for jobs.'

'But you've got a job, readymade, right here, under your nose,' Ned insisted stubbornly.

'But I need something new; something different. Don't you understand? I need to widen my horizons.'

James nodded. 'Yes. I hate the idea but I do understand, Gee.'

'I've been in touch with Eileen Marshall. If you remember she was dad's . . .'

'Paramour,' James finished for her. 'A very pleasant woman.'

'Yes. We get on really well together. She recommends the college where she trained, she says it's excellent. She even suggests that I stay with her till I find myself a flat.'

Ned blew out his cheeks. 'Well, you seem to have it all worked out. And I don't blame you, Gee, really I don't. It's just that I don't see how we can get my scheme off the ground without you.'

James was twiddling a pencil between his fingers. 'I may have an idea.'

'Yes?' Four eyes turned to him.

'We've agreed how important Ned's scheme is, but he's going to need all the help we can give him to get it started. So, Gina, would you be prepared to put your plans on ice for, say, twelve months? In that time we can all pull together to get everything up and running and you'll have time to train someone to take your place when you leave.'

She made a face. Then she smiled. 'When you put it like that I can hardly refuse, can I? OK. Twelve months and then I'm off. But you must promise you won't try to stop me.'

'We promise. Scouts honour,' they said together, making the appropriate gesture.

Even though the cruise was months ahead Lady Adelaide was so busy making and discarding lists to prepare for her adventure that she hardly noticed the changes going on in the house. She was having great difficulty in deciding what kind of clothes to buy, torn between courting sympathy as a grieving widow, in which case she would have to wear unrelieved black which didn't really suit her, or buying trunk loads of the pretty things she loved and foregoing the sympathetic attention. The pretty clothes won. She would find some other way to court the attention she craved.

After she had gone Gina made a bonfire of the library of catalogues that had been an essential part of choosing her mother's wardrobe, and also the mountain of cardboard boxes in which it had all been delivered. Then, with her brothers, she got on with more important and interesting work.

By the time Lady Adelaide returned, full of the sights she'd seen and the people she'd met, dropping names like confetti into every conversation, the gatehouse was ready for occupation. Gina had made sure that all her favourite furniture and pictures were there and Ruby was safely ensconced and ready to attend to her every need. Lady Adelaide loved it. She no longer had grounds to complain that it was a hovel, since everything had been done to the highest standard; even the tips of the iron railings were gilded, which delighted her.

'I'm sorry, Gina, but I hope you're not expecting to come and live in my house,' she announced. 'I shall need so much space for my possessions there really won't be room for you. But you must come and see the things I bought in Bloomingdales – that's the big department store in New York, you know – when you have time.'

'Oh, indeed I will, Mother,' Gina said, heaving a sigh of relief as she escaped.

Twenty-Seven

At first, only a small part of the big house was converted for use as a convalescent home. Ned contacted the military hospital at the nearby garrison, advertising what Meadowlands had to offer and although at first response was slow, as it became more widely known, wives or parents of badly mentally scarred men were relieved to find a haven for their loved ones.

Naturally, Tom Hadley was the first occupant. Isaac and Violet, his parents, were relieved to see him settled there, where they could see him every day, and guiltily glad that they no longer had responsibility for his care. To be near him and to fill in the time no longer needed to care for him, Violet offered her help on the domestic side and Isaac was able to concentrate once more on the care of his animals.

In the late summer of 1920, as Polly wheeled her new baby daughter in the grounds of the park, and Georgie played with his ball on the grass, she looked up at the wheelchairs on the terrace. It was nearly a year since the house had been turned into a haven for these men, and so much good had come out of it. Several of them were able to tend the gardens or help with the animals, finding solace and peace in the weeding and planting, feeding and milking, work that helped them overcome the traumas and nightmares that had blighted their young lives. One had even become well enough to return to his family, which was a real success for Ned, who had spent hours simply listening as he talked, over and over, about the things that troubled him.

But today Polly's thoughts were of Gina. In a few weeks her sister-in-law and best friend, with whom she had been through so much, would be gone, to start her new life in London. She would miss her terribly, yet she knew it was the right course for Gina to take, because although most of the time she seemed happy and looking forward to the new future she had planned, in unguarded moments Polly sometimes detected a note of sadness in her sister-in-law as she played with Georgie or nursed her new niece. Polly's great regret was that Gina would never experience the profound happiness she herself knew as a wife and mother. She sat down on a nearby bench, watching Georgie and savouring the sunshine with a feeling of deep peace and gratitude for all the blessings in her own life, and the hope that Gina would find happiness and fulfilment in her chosen future.

'Excuse me, madam. Can you help me?'

She looked up, startled. She had been so busy with her thoughts she hadn't noticed the tall army officer with a slight limp approaching.

'May I?' He indicated the space beside her.

'Of course.' She smiled at him as he sat down beside her and a feeling that she had seen him somewhere before tugged at her brain although she couldn't think where it might have been. 'What is it you want to know?'

'Well, it's like this. I'm looking for somewhere comfortable for my ex-batman. Binks was a marvellous bloke; we went through hell together in the war. Whatever happened he was always there; he looked after me, whatever I needed he found it – God knows how. He made me laugh; in fact, he kept me sane at times when I was ready to crack.' He glanced at her. 'No doubt you get the picture?'

She nodded.

He went on: 'In the end, he saved my life when a shell exploded in our trench. But it did for him, poor sod – oh, I beg your pardon . . .' She waved away his apology so he went on. 'He didn't die, but he's in pretty poor shape. The trouble is he has no family of his own so I feel I owe it to him to do what I can for him. When I saw Meadowlands advertised at the garrison hospital I realized this could well be what I'm looking for. You see, I know it quite well because I was encamped down there at one point during the war . . .' He gestured towards lower meadow.

Suddenly, Polly burst out, 'Of course! I remember you. You came up to the house to apologise when your men shot and ate one of the deer in the park.' She held out her hand, smiling at him. 'Major Palgrave, isn't it?'

He shook it. 'Colonel, actually, but yes, it was major, then.' He frowned. 'How do you know all that?'

'I was a maid there at the time. It's different now, of course . . .'

His face lit up. 'Ah, so you would have known Miss Barsham, Miss Gina Barsham?'

'Oh, yes . . .'

'Obviously, she's married now and probably with a string of children . . .' His voice tailed off.

'Gina's my sister-in-law and godmother to both my children, Colonel Palgrave. But tragically her fiancé went down with his ship at the battle of Jutland so she's never married.'

She watched for his reaction and was gratified to note that he was not quite able to conceal the expression of – was it hope? – that flitted across his face before he could hide it.

She went on: 'In fact, if you want to know more about what happens here at Meadowlands it's Gina you'll need to talk to.' She looked at her watch. 'She'll still be in her office.' She got to her feet. 'It's at the top of the steps, just inside the front door. Would you like me to show you where . . .?'

But he had gone, hurrying as fast as his limp would allow.

Polly watched him go, then, seeing a familiar figure coming towards her, called to Georgie and started towards her husband, pushing baby Olivia in her pram.

'You look like the cat that's stolen the cream. Who was that you were talking to?' James asked, giving her a kiss before swinging Georgie up into the crook of his injured arm.

'Oh, just someone looking for Gina,' she said, smiling contentedly as they walked home together.

Andrew Palgrave reached the office slightly out of breath. He waited a moment, straightening his already immaculate tie, then took off his cap and knocked on the door.

Gina, pinning up yet another list for the benefit of the young woman who would, in a few short weeks, take her place in the office, glanced towards the door and, pushing a strand of hair back behind her ear, spoke the words that were about to change her life.

'Do come in.'

CPSIA information can be obtained at www.ICGtesting.com
Printed in the USA
BVOW02*0635100615

403158BV00002B/4/P